The Printer of Malgudi

The Printer

of

Malgudi

By

R. K. NARAYAN

MICHIGAN STATE UNIVERSITY PRESS

1957

Library of Congress Catalog Card Number: 57-5845

First published in the United States of America

1957

The Printer of Malgudi

C.1

Chapter One

UNLESS YOU had an expert knowledge of the locality you would not reach the offices of *The Banner*. The Market Road was the life-line of Malgudi, but it had a tendency to take abrupt turns and disrupt itself into side-streets, which wove a network of crazy lanes behind the façade of buildings on the main road.

Kabir Lane was one such; if you took an inadvertent turn off the Market Road you entered it, though you might not if you intended to reach it. And then it split itself further into a first lane, a second lane, and so on; if you kept turning left and right you were suddenly assailed by the groans of the treadle in the Truth Printing Works; and from its top floor a stove-enameled blue board shot out over the street bearing the sign "The Banner."

It was the home of truth and vision, though you might take time to accept the claim. You climbed a flight of wooden stairs (more a ladder), and its last rung was the threshold of *The Banner*. It was a good deal better than most garrets: you wouldn't knock your head on roof-tiles unless you hoisted yourself on a table; you could still see something of the sky through the northern window and hear the far-off rustle of the river, although the other three windows opened on the courtyards of tenement houses below. The owners of the tenements had obtained a permanent legal injunction that the three windows should not be opened in order that the dwellers below might have their privacy. There was a reference to this in the very

3

first issue of *The Banner*. The editor said: "We don't think that the persons concerned need have gone to the trouble of going to a court for it, since no one would open these windows and volunteer to behold the spectacle below."

This stimulated a regular feature entitled "Open Window," which stood for the abolition of slums and congestion. It described the tenements, the pigsties constructed for human dwellings in the four corners of the town by rapacious landlords. It became an enemy of landlords. In fact, it constituted itself an enemy of a great many institutions and conditions. Within twelve pages of foolscap it attempted to set the world right.

From the garret of *The Banner* the world did not appear to be a common place. There always seemed to be something drastic to be done about it. It had all the appearance of a structure, half raised—and the other half might either go up or not at all. "Some day," *The Banner* felt, "it must either go down or go up. It can't be left standing as it is indefinitely." There was a considerable amount of demolition to be done, and a new way to be indicated. The possibilities of perfection seemed infinite, though mysterious, and yet there was a terrible kind of pig-headedness in people that prevented their going the right way. *The Banner* thus had twin work to do: on the one hand, attacking ruthlessly pig-headedness wherever found, and on the other prodding humanity into pursuing an ever-receding perfection. It was an immense task for anyone, with every conceivable equipment and support. It would be a tall order to give an editor. But in this case it worked because the editor had to take orders from only himself. And he felt that, after all, he had not made such a fool of himself as his well-wishers had feared, although the enterprise meant almost nothing to him financially.

In 1938, when the papers were full of anticipation of a world war, he wrote: "*The Banner* has nothing special to note about any war, past or future. It is only concerned with the war that is always going on—between man's inside and outside. Till the forces are equalized the struggle will always go on."

Reading it over a couple of weeks later, Srinivas smiled to himself. There was a touch of comicality in that bombast. It struck him as an odd mixture of the sublime and the ridiculous. "There is a curse hanging over an editorial table, vitiating everything a man wishes to say. I can't say 'I want a cup of coffee' without appearing to be a slightly pompous donkey," he told himself. "I wish I could write all that stuff here," he reflected, lying on his mat at home. Going to an office, sitting up in a chair at the table—there was something wrong with the entire procedure. "I wish I could do all my writing here," he said to himself again and looked forlornly about him. The house was very quiet now because it was eleven at night and all the nerve-racked neighbors and their children were asleep.

There were four other families living in the same house. The owner of the house himself lived in a small room in Anderson Lane—an old widower who tried to earn the maximum money and spend less than ten rupees a month on himself. He had several sons and daughters, all of them in various prosperous activities all over the country, from the Himalayas down to the South. He had a daughter in Malgudi, with whom he was not on speaking terms. He had led a happy family life in this house till the death of his wife, when the family scattered and disrupted. There-

5

after the old man, with the help of a carpenter, partitioned off the entire house, so that half a dozen families might be lodged in it, the screens and partitions creating an illusion that each unit was living in a home with privacy for food, sleep and washing.

It was said that he bathed at the street-tap and fed himself on cooked rice, which was distributed as charity in a nearby temple. He was known to have declared to everyone concerned: "The true *Sanyasi* has no need to live on anything more than the leavings of God." He made himself out to be an ascetic. He collected the rent on the second of each month, took away the entire amount and placed it in Sarayu Street post-office bank. It was said that he never paid any rent for his room in Anderson Lane. The story was that he had advanced a small loan to the owner of the house, which multiplied with interest and became an unrecognizable figure to the borrower in due course. When his wife died the old man moved in to occupy the room in his debtor's house at such a low rent that he could stay there for over twenty years working off the loan.

The very first time Srinivas met him he saw the old man bathing at a street-tap, while a circle of urchins and citizens of Anderson Lane stood around watching the scene. They were all waiting for the tap to be free. But the old man had usurped it and held his place. Srinivas felt attracted to him when he saw him spraying water on the crowd as an answer to their comments. The crowd jeered: he abused it back; when they drew nearer he sprayed the water on them and kept them off, all the while going through his ablutions calmly. Srinivas asked someone in the crowd: "What is the matter?" "Look at him, sir, this is the same story every day. So many of us wait here to fill our vessels, and he spends hours bathing there, performing all his prayers. Why should he come to the tap built for us poor people? We can't even touch it till he has done with it."

"Perhaps he has no other place."

"No place!" a woman exclaimed. "He is a rich man with many houses and relations!" At the mention of houses, Srinivas pricked up his ears. He was desperately searching for a house: all his waking hours were spent on this task.

The old man came out of his bath dripping, clad only in a loin cloth. He told the crowd: "Now go and drain off all the water you like. I don't care." Srinivas felt it might be useful to ingratiate himself in his favor and asked: "Do you do this every day?" The old man looked at him and asked: "Who are you?"

"It is a profound question. What mortal can answer it?"

"You are joking with me, are you?" the old man said, briskly moving off. Srinivas watched the wet old man going away angrily. It seemed to him, watching his back, that the chance of a lifetime was receding from him. An irresistible piece of jocularity was perhaps going to place a gulf between him and this man, who might have provided a solution to his housing problem. "Half a moment, please," he cried and ran after him. "I have an answer for you. At the moment I am a frantic house-hunter." The other halted; his face was changed. "Why didn't you say so? I will give you a house if you are prepared to abide by all the rules I mention. Make up your mind. I don't want to meet indeterminate souls."

"What is your rent?" asked Srinivas.

"Tell me what you will pay. I have one for seventy-five, one for thirty, fifty, ten, five, one. What is it you want?"

"I will tell you presently. But perhaps you might first like to go home and dry yourself."

"Home! Home!" he laughed. "I have no home. Didn't I tell you that I am a *Sanyasi,* though I don't wear ocher robes? Come, come with me. I live in a small room which a friend has given me." He went through the lane, pulled out a thin key knotted to his sacred thread, turned it in the lock and opened the door of a small room. It was roofed with old cobweb-covered tiles, with a window, one foot square, opening at the top of the wall; there was another window opening on the road. He stooped in through the narrow doorway. Srinivas followed him.

"Sit down," said the old man. "You have to sit on the floor. I have not even a mat." Srinivas sat down, leaning against the wall. A few children from the main house came and stood by the doorway, looking in. The old man was spreading out his wet clothes on a cord tied across the wall. He opened a small wooden box and took out a dry dhoti and towel, a box containing ingredients for marking his forehead, and a rosary. He proceeded to decorate his forehead with a symbol, looking into a hand-mirror. The children stood in the doorway, blocking it. The old man turned from the mirror with a hiss. "Get away. What are you doing here? Do you think a fair is going on?" The children turned and ran away, shouting mischievously, "Grandfather is angry." Srinivas felt hurt by the old man's conduct. "Why are you hard upon those children?"

"Because I don't want them. Children are a bane. I must tell this fellow not to let them loose on me."

"They called you grandfather," Srinivas said.

8

"They will call you uncle presently. How do you like it? I am only a tenant here. I hate all children. I have had enough trouble from my own children; I don't want any more from strangers. Are you in the habit of praying?"

Srinivas fumbled for a reply. "Not exactly——"

"Well, I am. I am going to pray for about fifteen minutes. You will have to wait." Srinivas settled down. The other took out his beads, shut his eyes, his lips muttering. Srinivas watched him for a moment and felt bored. He sat looking out. Someone was passing in and out of the main house. Children were dashing to and fro. The old man said, without opening his eyes: "If you are a lover of children you have plenty to watch. All the children of the town seem to be concentrated in this street." After this he continued his silent prayers.

Srinivas reflected: "Who will know I am here, cooped up in a cell with a monstrous old man? If I ceased to breathe at this moment, no one would know what had happened to me. My wife and son and brother——" His thought went back to the home he had left behind. His elder brother could never understand what he was up to. "He has every right to think I am a fool," he reflected. "Man has no significance except as a wage-earner, as an economic unit, as a receptacle of responsibilities. But what can I do? I have a different notion of human beings. I have given their notions a fair trial." He thought of all those years when he had tried to fit in with one thing or another as others did, married like the rest, tried to balance the family budget and build up a bank balance. Agriculture, apprenticeship in a bank, teaching, law—he gave everything a trial once, but with every passing month he felt the excruciating pain of losing time. The passage of time

9

depressed him. The ruthlessness with which it flowed on—a swift and continuous movement; his own feeling of letting it go helplessly, of engaging all his hours in a trivial round of actions, at home and outside. Every New Year's Day he felt depressed and unhappy. All around he felt there were signs that a vast inundation was moving onward, carrying the individual before it, and before knowing where one was, one would find oneself senile or in the grave, with so little understood or realized. He felt depressed at the sight of his son: it seemed as though it was an hour ago that he was born, but already he was in Second Form, mugging history and geography and dreaming of cricket scores.

"What exactly is it that you want to do?" his brother asked him one day.

"The answer is late in coming, but you will get it," Srinivas replied, feeling rather awkward. The question of a career seemed to him as embarrassing as a physiological detail. His brother was the head of the family, an advocate with a middling practice—a life of constant struggle with rustic clients and magistrates in that small town Talapur, where he had slipped into his position after his father's death. His father had been an advocate in his time and had had a grand practice, acquired extensive property in the surrounding villages, and had become a very respectable citizen. The family tradition was that they should graduate at Malgudi in the Albert Mission College, spend two years in Madras for higher studies in the law, and then return each to his own room in their ancient sprawling house.

This suited Srinivas up to a point. But he always felt suffocated in the atmosphere of that small town. His wife had to put up with endless misery at home through his ways, and his little son looked ragged. They put up with his ways for a considerable time before shooting the question at him. He remembered the day clearly even now. He had settled down in his room with a copy of an Upanishad in his hand. As he grew absorbed in it he forgot his surroundings. He wouldn't demand anything more of life for a fortnight more, and then he observed his elder brother standing over him. He lowered the book, muttering "I didn't hear you come in. Finished your court?" And his brother asked: "What exactly is it that you wish to do in life?" Srinivas flushed for a moment, but regained his composure and answered: "Don't you see? There are ten principal Upanishads. I should like to complete the series. This is the third."

"You are past thirty-seven with a family of your own. Don't imagine I am not willing to look after them, but they will be far happier if you think of doing something for their sake. They must not feel they are unwanted by you. Don't think I wish to relieve myself of the responsibility." It was a fact: his elder brother looked after the entire family without making any distinction. "Such a question should not be fired at me again," he said to himself after his brother had left the room. He tried to get reabsorbed in the Upanishad he was reading. His mind echoed with the interview: perhaps something had been happening in the house. His mind wandered from one speculation to another; but he gathered it back to its task:

"Knowing the self as without body among the em-
bodied, the abiding among the transitory, great and
all-pervading——"
said the text before him. On reading it, all his domestic worries and all these questions of prestige seemed ridic-

ulously petty. "*My* children, *my* family, *my* responsibility—must guard *my* prestige and do *my* duties to *my*
family—Who am I? This is a far more serious problem
than any I have known before. It is a big problem and I
have to face it. Till I know who I am, how can I know
what I should do? However, some sort of answer should
be ready before my brother questions me again——"

The solution appeared to him in a flash. He knew what
he ought to do with himself. Within twenty-four hours
he sat in the train for Malgudi, after sending away his
wife and son to her parents' house in the village.

.   .   .   .   .

The old man came out of his prayer and said: "Would
it be any use asking who you are?"

"I'm from Talapur and I am starting a paper here——"

"What for?" asked the man suspiciously.

"Just to make money," Srinivas replied with a deliberate cynicism which was lost on the old man. He looked
pleased and relieved. "How much will it bring you?"

"Say about two thousand a month," Srinivas said and
muttered under his breath: "Is this the only thing you
understand?"

"Eh, what?"

"Come along, show me a house——"

They started out. The old man elaborately locked up
his cell, and took him through a sub-lane to the back of
Anderson Lane. As he came before a house he cried to
someone who was driving a nail in the wall: "You! You! ...
Do you want to ruin my wall? I will give you notice to
quit if you damage my house——"

Srinivas received a very confused impression of the whole house. It had a wet central courtyard with a water-pipe, and a lot of people were standing around it—four children, waiting to wash their hands, three women to draw water, and three men, who had eaten their food, were waiting also to wash their hands. In addition to these there was a little boy with a miserable puppy tied to a string, waiting to bathe his pet. On seeing the old man, one woman turned on him and asked: "Ah, here you are! Can't you do something about this dog? Should it be washed in the same pipe as the one we use for our drinking water?" The young boy tugged his dog nearer the tap. Somebody tried to drag it away, and the boy said: "Bite them——" At which the dog set up a bark and wriggled at the end of its tether, and people grew restless and shouted at each other. The old man tried to pass on, without paying attention to what they were saying. One of the men dashed up, held him by the elbow and demanded: "Are you going to give us another water-tap or are you not?"

"No—you can quit the house——"

"It is not how you should talk to a tenant," said the other, falling back.

The old man explained to Srinivas: "I tell you, people have no gratitude. In these days of housing difficulties I give them a house—only to be shouted at in this manner——"

"It must be heart-breaking," agreed Srinivas. The old man looked pleased and stopped before a doorway in a dark passage and said: "This is going to be your portion. It is an independent house by itself." He turned the key, flung the door open; darkness seemed to flow out of the room. "It only requires a little airing. . . . Nobody to help me in any of these things. I have to go round and do everything myself. . . ." He hurried forward and threw open a couple of window shutters.

"Come in, come in," the old man invited Srinivas, who was still hesitating in the passage. Srinivas stepped in. The walls were of mud, lime-covered, with an uneven and globular surface; bamboo splinters showed in some places—the skeleton on which the mud had been laid. The lime had turned brown and black with time. The old man ran his hand proudly over the wall and said: "Old style, but strong as iron. Even dynamite couldn't break it——"

"That's obvious," Srinivas replied. "They must have built it in the days of Mohenjodaro—the same building skill——"

"What is that?"

"Oh, very rare specimens of building thousands of years ago. They have spent lakhs of rupees to bring them to light . . ."

"Walls like these?"

"Exactly." The old man looked gratified. "How wise of them! It is only the Europeans who can understand the value of some of these things. We have many things to learn from our ancients. Can our modern cement stand comparison with this?" He waited for an answer, and Srinivas replied: "Cement walls crumble like rice-flour when dynamite is applied."

"You see, that is why I look after my houses so carefully. I don't allow any nail to be driven into a wall—— The moment I see a tenant driving a nail into the wall . . . I lose myself in anger. I hope you have no pictures——"

"Oh, no. I have no faith in pictures."

"Quite right," said the old man, finding another point of agreement. "I don't understand the common craze for covering walls with pictures."

"Most of them representation of Gods by Ravi Varma."

"His pictures of Gods are wonderful. He must have seen them in visions, that gifted man——" remarked the old man.

"And yet some people who know about pictures say that they aren't very good or high-class——"

"Oh, they say it, do they?" the old man exclaimed. "Then why do people waste their money on the pictures and disfigure their walls? I have not seen a single house in our country without a picture of Krishna, Lakshmi and Saraswathi on it——"

"Lakshmi, the goddess of wealth, must patronize every home, Saraswathi, the goddess of intelligence and learning, must also be there. Well, don't you talk so lightly of these; you would get no rent or not have the wit to collect it, if it were not for the two goddesses. So be careful——"

"That is a very clever interpretation," the old man said, and added a Sanskrit epigram to support the same idea.

Srinivas found that his house consisted of a small hall, with two little rooms to serve for kitchen and store. . . .

"This is my best flat. I have refused it to a score of people. Such a clamor for it! Quite spacious, isn't it?" the old man asked, looking about. "How big is your family?"

"We are three."

"Oh, you will be very comfortable, I'm sure. There was once a person who lived here with his eleven children."

He pointed out of the window. "You have a very fine view from here. See the plant outside?" A half-withered citrus plant drooped in a yard-wide strip of garden outside. "You must see it when it is in bloom," he added, seeing that the plant didn't make much of an impression on his prospective tenant. "You have a glorious view of the temple tower," he said, pointing far off, where the gray spire of Iswara temple rose above the huddling tenements, with its gold crest shining in the sun.

"But—but," Srinivas fumbled. "What about water—a single tap?"

"Oh, it is quite easy. Only a little adjustment. If you get up a little earlier than the rest———. All a matter of adjustment. Those others are savages———"

On the very first day that he moved in with his trunk and roll of bedding a fellow tenant dropped in for a chat. He was a clerk in a bank, maintaining a family consisting of his father, mother and numerous little brothers and sisters, on a monthly income of about forty rupees. He paid a rent of two rupees for one room in which his entire family was cooped up. The children spent most of their time on the pyol of a house at the end of the street. Now, ever since Srinivas had come this man looked happy, as though Srinivas had settled there solely to provide him with a much-needed sitting-room. He spent most of his time sitting on Srinivas's mat and watching him. He had been the very first tenant to befriend Srinivas. He said: "Do you know why the old devil agreed to give this to you for fifteen rupees?"

"No."

"Because nobody would come here. It's been unoccupied for two years now. A tenant who was here hanged himself in that room, a lonely bachelor. Nobody knows much about him. But one morning we found him swinging from the roof——"

Srinivas felt disquieted by this information. "Why did he do that?"

"Some trouble or other, I suppose; a moody fellow, rather lonely. Every day the only question he used to ask was whether there were any letters for him. He died, the police took away his body, and we heard nothing further about it. One or two tenants who came after him cleared out rather abruptly, saying that his ghost was still here." Srinivas remained thoughtful. The other asked: "Why, are you afraid?"

"Not afraid. I shall probably see it depart. And even if it stays on, I won't mind. I don't see much difference between a ghost and a living person. All of us are skin-covered ghosts, for that matter." Since his boyhood he had listened to dozens of ghost stories that their cook at home used to tell them. The cook dared Srinivas, once, to go and sleep under the tamarind tree in the school compound. He went there one evening, stayed till eight with a slightly palpitating heart, softly calling out to the ghost an appeal not to bother him in any way. "I think I shall be able to manage this ghost quite well," he said.

"I think good people become good ghosts and bad fellows—I dread to contemplate what kind of ghost he will turn out to be when our general manager dies."

"Who is he?"

"Edward Shilling—a huge fellow, made of beef and whisky. He keeps a bottle even in his office room. I am his personal clerk. God! What terror it strikes in me when the buzzer sounds. I fear some day he is going to strike me dead. He explodes 'Damn,' 'Damn' every few minutes. If there is the slightest mistake in taking dictation, he bangs the table, my heart flutters like a——'' He went on talking thus, and Srinivas learnt to leave him alone and go through his business uninterrupted. At first he sat listening sympathetically; but later found that this was unpractical. Though the man had numerous dependents, he had less to say about them than about his beefy master. His master seemed to possess his soul completely, so that the young man was incapable of thinking of anything else, night or day. He seemed to have grown emaciated and dazed through this spiritual oppression. Srinivas had learnt all that was to be learnt about him within the first two or three days of his talk with him. So, though he felt much sympathy for him, he felt it unnecessary to interrupt his normal occupation for the sake of hearing a variation of a single theme.

He was setting up a new home and he had numerous things to do. He took the landlord's advice and got up at five o'clock and bathed at the tap before the other tenants were up. He went out for a cup of coffee after that, while the town was still asleep. He discovered that in Market Road a hotel opened at that hour—a very tiny restaurant off the market fountain. It meant half a mile's walk. He returned directly to his room after coffee. He prayed for a moment before a small image of Nataraja which his grandmother had given him when he was a boy. This was one of the possessions he had valued most for years. It seemed to be a refuge from the oppression of time. It was of sandalwood, which had deepened a darker shade with years, just four inches high. The carving represented Nataraja with one foot raised and one foot pressing down a demon, his four arms outstretched, with his hair flying, the eyes rapt in contemplation, an exquisitely poised figure. His grandmother had given it to him on his eighth birthday. She had got it from her father, who discovered it in a packet of saffron they had brought from the shop on a certain day. It had never left Srinivas since that birthday. It was on his own table at home, or in the hostel, wherever he might be. It had become a part of him, this little image. He often sat before it, contemplated its proportions, and addressed it thus: "Oh, God, you are trampling a demon under your foot, and you show us a rhythm, though you appear to be still. I grasp the symbol but vaguely. You hold a flare in your hand. May a ray of that light illumine my mind!" He silently addressed it thus. It had been his first duty for decades now. He never started his day without spending a few minutes before this image.

After this he took out his papers. He was about to usher his *Banner* into the world, and he had an immense amount of preparatory work to do. He had a thin exercise-book and a copying pencil. He covered the pages of the exercise book with minute jottings connected with the journal. The problems connected with its birth seemed to be innumerable. He did not want to overlook even the slightest problem. He put down each problem with a number, and on an interleaf against it put down a possible solution. For instance, problem No. 20 in his note-book was: "Should the page be made up as three column with 8-point type or double column with 10-point? The latter will provide easier reading for the eye, but the former would be more true to its purpose, in that it will give more reading matter. Must consult the printer about it." He made the entry: "Problem 20: The answer has been unexpectedly simplified. The printer says he favors neither two columns nor three columns; in fact, he has no arrangement whatever for printing in columns. Nor has he anything but 12-point in English—a type that looks like the headings in a Government of India gazette. He insists upon saying that it is the best type in the whole country: no other press in the world has it. I fear that with this type and without the columns my paper is going to look like an auctioneer's list. But that can't be helped at this stage." On the day his printer delivered the first dummy copy, which had to go up before a magistrate, his heart sank. It was nowhere near what he had imagined. He had hoped that it would look like an auctioneer's list, but now he found that it looked like a handbill of a wrestling tournament. One came across this kind of thing at week-ends, the thin transparent paper with the portraits of two muscular men on it, the print soaking through. It had always seemed to him the worst specimen of printing; but then the promoters of wrestling bouts could not be fastidious. But *The Banner*? He said timidly to his printer: "Don't you think we ought to——"

The printer said with a smile: "No," even before he completed his sentence. "This is very good, you cannot get this finish in the whole of South India." He spoke so very persuasively that Srinivas himself began to feel that his own view might not be quite correct. The printer was a vociferous, effusive man. When he took a sheet from the press he handled it with such delicacy, carrying

it on his palms, as if it were a new-born infant, saying:
"See the finish?" in such a tone that his customers were
half hypnotized into agreeing with him. He never let anyone look through the curtain behind him. "I don't like
my staff to watch me talking to my customers," he often
explained. He spoke of his staff with a great pride and
firmness, although Srinivas never got a precise idea of
how many it included, nor what exactly lay beyond that
printed curtain, on which was represented a purple lion
attacking a spotted deer. Srinivas could only vaguely con-
jecture how many might be working there. All that he
could hear was the sound of the treadle. Of even this he
could not always be certain. Some days the printer appeared in khaki shorts, with grease spots on his hands,
and explained: "The best dress for my type of work. I'm
going on the machine today. You see, I solve the labor
problem by not being a slave to my workmen. When it
comes to a pinch, I can do every bit of work myself, including gumming and pasting——"

His help was invaluable to Srinivas. He felt he was
being more and more bound to him by ties of gratitude.
The printer declared: "When a customer enters our
premises he is, in our view, a guest of the Truth Printing Works. Well, you think, *The Banner* is yours. It isn't.
I view it as my own."

He acted up to this principle. In the weeks preceding
the launching of *The Banner* he abandoned all his normal
work: he set aside a co-operative society balance-sheet,
four wedding invitations, and a small volume of verse, all
of which were urgent, according to those who had ordered
them. He dealt with all his customers amiably, but to no
purpose. "You will get the proofs positively this evening,
and tomorrow you may come for the finished copies.

Sorry for the delay. My staff is somewhat overworked at the moment. They've instructions to give you the maximum co-operation." With all this suaveness he was not to be found in his place at the appointed hour. He threw a scarf around his throat, donned a fur cap, and was out on one or the other duties connected with *The Banner*. He arranged for the supply of paper, and he went round with Srinivas canvassing subscribers. The very first thing he did was to print a thousand handbills, setting forth the purpose and nature of *The Banner*. He had spent four nights and days devising the layout for it. Finally he decided upon a green paper and red lettering; when Srinivas saw it his heart sank within him. But the printer explained: "This is the best possible layout for it; it must catch people's eye. I won't bill you for it except some nominal charge for paper." He also printed a dozen tiny receipt books. He scattered the green-and-red notices widely all over the town, into every possible home; and then followed it up with a visit with the receipt book in hand. He worked out the annual subscription at about ten rupees, and managed to collect a thousand rupees even before the legal dummy was ready.

Srinivas was convinced that he could never have got through the legal formalities but for his printer. He had always disliked courts and magistrates; and he was really fearful as to how he would get through it all. The dummy to be placed before the magistrate was ready. Srinivas implored him: "Please make another copy. Is this the paper we are going to use?"

"Oh, you don't like this paper! Norway bond—I've refused it to some of our oldest customers, you know—it is the strongest parchment in the market."

"But the ink comes through."

"Oh, we will check that. I have put a little extra ink on this because magistrates usually like the title to be very dark. They like to carry some printer's ink on their thumbs, I suppose," he said. "You had better leave this magistrate business to me."

He walked into the hall of the court at Race Course Road nonchalantly, adjusted his cap, stood before the court clerk, and handed up his application.

"Can you swear that all your statements in this are true?"

"Yes, I swear."

"You declare yourself the printer of *The Banner*?"

"Yes, I'm the printer." The clerk scrutinized the paper once more. As he was standing there, the printer took out of his pocket a pod of fried groundnut, cracked its shell, and put the nut into his mouth. Srinivas was shocked. He feared he might be charged with contempt of court. The printer's eye shone with satisfaction; he put his fingers into his pocket, took out another bit, and held it out for Srinivas under the table. Srinivas looked away, at which the printer cracked it gently and ate that also. All around there were people: lawyers sitting at a horse-shoe table, poring over books and papers or wool-gathering; policemen in the doorway; prisoners waiting for a hearing at the dock. Srinivas felt that they were going to be thrown out—with that printer of his cracking nut-shells. They were standing immediately below the magistrate's table. But the printer was deft and calm with his nuts, and it passed off unnoticed. The clerk fixed his gaze on Srinivas and asked: "Your name? You declare yourself the editor and publisher of *The Banner*?"

23

"Yes."

"Are you speaking the whole truth?"

"Absolutely." The clerk picked up the papers and handed them up to the magistrate, who seemed to be looking at nothing in particular. The magistrate's lips moved, and the clerk asked: "Will you promise to avoid all sedition and libel?"

The printer quickly answered: "On behalf of both of us, we promise." The magistrate's lips moved again; the clerk asked: "Are you going to deal in politics?"

Once again the printer answered swiftly: "No, it is a literary magazine." The magistrate slightly nodded his head and then the clerk pressed a couple of rubber stamps on the papers, and the magistrate signed on the dots indicated by him. It was over. The permission was secured.

Before they crossed the court compound Srinivas protested: "Why did you say it was going to be literary? Far from it. I shall certainly not avoid politics; while I don't set out to deal only in politics, I can't bind myself——"

"You go on with politics or revolution or whatever you like, but you can't say so in a court; if you do, they may ask for deposits, and you will have all kinds of troubles and worries. You know, I have achieved an ambition in life: I've always wanted to crack nuts and eat them in a court—something to foil the terrible gloom of the place. I have done it today."

His brother's letter reached him, addressed to the office. He had not written home ever since he came to Malgudi. His brother wrote:

"I am very pleased to know your whereabouts through your paper, the first issue of which you have been good enough to send me. I have read the explanations you have given in your first editorial, but don't you think that you have set yourself an all too ambitious task? Don't you have to give some more reading for the four annas you are demanding? As it is, the magazine is over too quickly and we have to wait for a whole week again. And then, will you allow me this criticism? You are showing yourself to be a pugnacious fellow. Almost every line of your paper is an attack on something. You give a page for politics—and it is all abuse; you don't seem to approve of any party or any leader. You give another page for local affairs, and it is nothing but abuse again. And then a column for cinema and arts—and even here you deal hard knocks. Current publications, the same thing—what is the matter with you? Though different articles are appearing under different initials and pen-names, all of them seem to be written remarkably alike! However, be careful; that is all I wish to say. It wouldn't at all do to get into libel suits with your very first effort."

Srinivas pondered over this letter, sitting in his office. He admired his brother for detecting the similarity in all the contributions: all of them were written by himself. Heaven knew what difficulties he went through, on one side, churning up the matter for the twelve pages, and on the other keeping in check the printer, who threatened to overflow on to the editorial side. Not content with appointing himself the dictator in matters of format and business, he was trying to take a hand in the editorials also, but

Srinivas dealt with him tactfully and nicely. He could not pass a copy downstairs without feeling like a schoolboy presenting a composition to his master. He waited with suspense as the printer scrutinized it before passing it on: "You wouldn't like me to advise you here, I suppose?"

"No," Srinivas said, meaning it but trying to make it sound humorous.

"Well, all right. But you see, sir, that film was not produced at Bombay, but at a Calcutta studio."

"Oh! In that case——" Srinivas hastily snatched it back and scrutinized it again. "Sorry for the blunder——"

"It is quite all right—natural," replied the printer expansively, forgivingly, as if to suggest that anyone who was forced to write about so many things himself was bound to commit such foolish mistakes. Srinivas did not very much like the situation, but he had to accept it with resignation. It was true: he was putting his hand to too many departments. But there was no way of helping it. He could not afford to engage anyone to assist him. And his program was more or less as follows: Monday, first page; Tuesday, second page; Wednesday, cinema and arts; Thursday, correspondence and main editorial; Friday, gleanings, comments and miscellaneous. This virtuous calendar was constantly getting upset, and all the items jammed into each other, and he found himself doing everything every day, and all things on Friday, the printer shouting from the bottom of the staircase for copy every five minutes. He flung the matter down the stairs as each page got ready, and the printer picked it up and ran in with it. Or if he had a doubt he shouted again from the bottom of the staircase. At four o'clock the last form went down and then the major worries were over. The treadle was silenced at six, and peace descended suddenly on the community at Kabir Lane.

The intellectual portion of the work was now over, signified by the passing of the editor down the stairs; after which he stepped into the press to attend to the dispatch of copies. The printer lent him a hand in this task. Five hundred copies of *The Banner* were all over the floor of the printer's office. They squatted down and gummed, labeled and stamped the copies with feverish speed, and loaded them on the back of a very young printer's devil, who ran with his burden to the post office at the railway station, where it could always be posted without late fee till 8 p.m.

This brought him up against the R.M.S. It took him time to understand what R.M.S. meant. But he had to grow familiar with it. He received a letter in his mail-bag one day saying: "You are requested to see the under-signed during the working hours on any day convenient to you." He was writing his editorial on the new housing policy for Malgudi. Plenty of labor from other districts had been brought in because the district board and the municipality had launched a feverish scheme of road development and tank building, and three or four cotton mills had suddenly sprung into existence. Overnight, as it were, Malgudi passed from a semi-agricultural town to a semi-industrial town, with a sudden influx of population of all sorts. The labor gangs, brought in from other districts, spread themselves out in the open spaces. Babies sleeping in hammocks made of odd pieces of cloth, looped over tree branches, women cooking food on the roadside, men sleeping on pavements—these became a common sight in all parts of Malgudi. The place was beginning to look more and more like a gypsy camp.

Srinivas made it his mission to attack the conditions in the town in every issue. The municipality feared that they were being made the laughing-stock of the whole country, and decided to take note of the editorials appearing in *The Banner*. And they revived an old plan, which they had shelved years ago, of subsidizing the development of a new town on the eastern outskirts. It was gratifying to the editor of *The Banner* to see the effect of his words! He felt that after all something he was saying had got home. He had the pleasure of reflecting on these lines when he received a note from the municipality: "The president would like to meet the editor at any time convenient to him on any working day." He opened the next and read that the R.M.S. would like to meet him. "God! How many people must I go and meet? When have I the time?" On working days and other days he had to sit in the garret and manufacture 'copy'; if there was the slightest delay the smoothness of life was affected. That life went on smoothly was indicated by the purring of the treadle below. All went well as long as that sound lasted. The moment it paused he knew he would hear the printer's voice calling from the bottom of the staircase: "Editor! Matter!" He worked under a continuous nightmare of not being able to meet his printer's demand. That meant continuous work, night and day, all through the week, and even on a Sunday. He seldom approved of what he wrote and would rewrite and tear up and rewrite, but it was always the printer's call that decided the final shape.

"When I'm so hard-pressed for time I can't be bothered in this way," he remarked to himself, and tossed away the

28

two letters to a farther corner of his table, where they lost their individualities in a great wilderness of paper. He had learnt to deal with the bulk of his correspondence in this way. "Till I can afford to have a secretary and an assistant editor and a personal representative, an accountant, office boy, and above all, a typewriter—all correspondence must wait," he said to his papers. Every post brought him a great many letters. He flung away unopened everything that came to him in long envelopes. He shoved it away, out of sight, under the table. He knew what the long envelope contained: unsolicited contributions, poems, essays, sketches. It was surprising how many people volunteered to write, without any other incentive than just seeing themselves in print. And then an equal number of letters demanding to be told what had happened to their contributions; and why there was no reply, even though postage was enclosed. "It is not enough, my friend," Srinivas said to them mentally, "I must have a fair compensation for looking at your handiwork; that is why I don't open the envelope. Any time you are free you can come and collect it from under my table."

And then there were letters from readers, marriage invitations from unknown people, sample packets of ink powder and other things for favor of an opinion, and copies of Government and municipal notifications on thin manifold paper. The last provided him with a miscellany of unwanted information: "Note that from the 13th to 15th the railway level-crossing will be closed from 6 a.m. to 6 p.m.," said one note.

"Well, I note it for what it is worth; what next?" Srinivas asked. The municipality sent him statements of average rainfall and maximum and minimum temperatures; somebody sent him calendars, someone else the information that a grandchild was born to him. "Why do they think all this concerns me?" he at first asked, rather terrified. But gradually he grew hardened and learnt to put them away. Most of his correspondence was snuffed out in this manner; but not the R.M.S. and the municipal chairman.

Very soon he had another letter from the R.M.S. "Your kind attention is drawn to our previous letter, dated . . . and an early reply is solicited."

"Don't imagine I'm a member of your red-tape clan," he said, putting away the letter once again. The municipal chairman also wrote again, but he had changed his subject matter. "I have pleasure in enclosing copy of our Malgudi extension scheme, for favor of your perusal. . . . You will doubtless see that the question engaged our attention even as far back as 1930. The question had to be shelved owing to practical difficulties . . ." And so the letter continued.

He glanced through the scheme. It visualized a garden city at the eastern end of the town, with its own market, business premises, cinema, schools and perfect houses. Somebody had evidently been dreaming about the town. He went through it feeling happy that *The Banner* had roused the municipal conscience to the extent of making it pull something off a shelf. He studied the pamphlet carefully, and it provided him matter for an article under the heading: "Visions on the Shelf."

The R.M.S. turned out to be more aggressive in their subsequent correspondence. "Our repeated efforts to contact you have borne no fruit. Please take note that by posting your journal in a mass at the last clearing time you are causing great dislocation and blocking the R.M.S. work. It would facilitate R.M.S. work if the dispatch were distributed throughout the day, if possible throughout the week." Reading this, Srinivas was aghast at their ignorance. Did they imagine that the bundles were ready all through the week?

He could not resist writing an immediate reply: "Sir, Friday 8 o'clock is our posting time at present. If we acted up to your suggestion it would result in something like the following: at 12 midday we should be posting the fourth page, at 1 p.m. the sixth page, at 5 p.m. ninth and tenth, 7 p.m. eleventh and at 8 p.m. twelfth page. Since our readers would doubtless have a great objection to receiving the journal piecemeal we are forced to post the journal in its entirety at 8 p.m. Posting the journal on other days is not practicable, since no part of it is ready on those days." To which he received the reply: "It would be considered a favor if you will kindly meet the undersigned on any day during working hours." This brought the question back to the starting-point, and he did what he did with the first letter—obliterated it, and the R.M.S. continued to suffer.

Chapter Two

H E HURT his thumb while pinning up a set of proofs. He put away the paper to suck the drop of blood that appeared on his thumb, and sat back. He cracked his fingers: they felt cramped, the tips of his fingers were discolored with the printers' ink transferred from rugged proof sheets. His joints ached. He realized that he had been sitting hunched up for several hours correcting proofs. He rose to his feet, picking up the proofs, folded them and heaved them downstairs with the shout: "Proofs" directed toward the printer. He paused for a moment at the northern window, looking at a patch of blue sky, and turned away. He paced up and down. He was searching for the right word. He had been writing a series: "Life's Background." The entire middle page had been occupied with it for some numbers. He had tried to summarize, in terms of modern living, some of the messages he had imbibed from the Upanishads on the conduct of life, a restatement of subjective value in relation to a social outlook. This statement was very necessary for his questioning mind; for while he thundered against municipal or social shortcomings a voice went on asking: "Life and the world and all this is passing—why bother about anything? The perfect and the imperfect are all the same. Why really bother?" He had to find an answer to the question. And that he did in this series. He felt that this was a rather heavy theme for a weekly reading public, and he was doing his best to word it in an easy manner, in terms of actual experience. It was no easy task. And that entire Thursday he spent in thinking of it, pacing up and down, pricking himself with the pin through absent-mindedness; he roamed his little attic, round and round like a sleepwalker, paused at the farthest window to listen to the rumble of Sarayu. It seemed ages since he had gone to the river. He resolved to remedy this lapse very soon. When he came to the window he could hear the uproar emanating from the tenements below—he always spent a few minutes listening to the medley of voices. He wished he could open the window and take a look at the strife below, just to see what exactly was troubling them, but the owners of the tenements had their legal injunction against it. His mind dwelt for a brief moment on landlords.

Awaiting the right sentence for his philosophy, he had spent several hours already; he must complete the article by the evening if he was to avoid serious dislocation in the press. Tomorrow there were other things to do. He suddenly flung out his arm and cried: "I have got it, just the right——" and turned toward his table in a rush. He picked up his pen; the sentence was shaping so very delicately; he felt he had to wait upon it carefully, tenderly, lest it should elude him once again: it was something like the very first moment when a face emerges on the printing paper in the developing tray—something tender and fluid, one had to be very careful if one were not to lose it forever. . . . He poised his pen as if he were listening to some faint voice and taking dictation. He held his breath, for fear that he might lose the thread, and concentrated all his being on the sentence, when he heard a terrific clatter up the stairs. He gnashed his teeth. "The demons are always waiting around to create a disturbance; they are terrified of any mental concentration." The printer appeared in the doorway, his face beaming. He came in, extending his hand:

"Congratulations! I bring you jolly news. Your wife and son are waiting downstairs."

Srinivas pushed back his chair and rose. "What! What!" He became incoherent. He ran out on the landing and looked down: there he saw his wife and son standing below, with their trunks and luggage piled up on the ground.

"Oh!" he cried. "Oh!" he repeated louder. "Come up! Come up!" He felt foolish and guilty.

His wife was struggling hard to keep a cheerful face. She came in and stood uncertainly near the only chair in the room, with his son behind her. She looked weary with the journey; her face was begrimed with railway smoke. With considerable difficulty she essayed a smile. The printer said effusively: "Take a seat, madam. You should not keep standing." It was evident that she was very tired, and she immediately acted on this advice. She sat down at the table and viewed it with bewilderment.

"Why? Why have you all come so suddenly? Why didn't you write to me?"

"I wrote four letters and my father wrote two," she said quietly. He looked helplessly at the printer. He knew what it meant. He must have put them in the company of unopened letters. The boy said: "Grandfather wrote to this address—" "Because we didn't know any other address," his mother finished the sentence. There was a certain strain and artificiality in the air, and the printer turned without a word and went downstairs muttering: "I will send the boy to fetch some coffee and tiffin."

Now his wife burst into a sob as she asked: "What is the matter with you? Why do you neglect us in this way? You have not written for months; what have I done that I should be treated like this?" Her voice was cracked with sorrow. Srinivas was baffled.

"No, no, look here, you should not have worried. I was very busy these months. Being single-handed and having to do everything myself——"

"But just one postcard. You could at least have told us your address. You treated me as if I were dead and made me the laughing-stock of our entire village. I have had to write to you four times to ask if I may come——"

The boy said: "Grandfather got your address from a copy of the paper." The boy spoke as if they had been doing a piece of detective work. "Oh, I see. But such a lot of letters come here. Sometimes it happens——" he meandered.

His wife stopped crying, surveyed the room, and asked: "Is this where you live?"

"Oh, no. I have a house. Let us go there."

His eye fell on the sheet of paper on the table. He couldn't afford to leave it now. He asked: "How did you find your way here? It must have been difficult."

"We arrived here at the station at two o'clock, and for over three hours we went about searching for you, and then a student brought us here." Her voice shook, and she was on the point of crying once again. She gulped down a sob and said:"This little fellow, Ramu, he was like an elder. I never knew he could take charge of me so well." She looked proudly at her son. Srinivas cast him a smile and patted his back. He scrutinized his son: he seemed to have grown an inch or two since he saw him last. The coat he wore was too small for him, appearing to stop at his waist, his sleeves stopped four inches beyond the wrist, the collar was frayed: he had neglected his family. He cast a look at his wife: she wore a very inferior discolored cotton sari, patched here and there. "Am I guilty of the charges of neglect?" he asked himself. "Family duties come before any other duty. Is it an absolute law? What if I don't accept the position? I am sure, if I stick to my deeper conviction, other things like this will adjust themselves."

There was a moment's silence as he ruminated over this question. His wife had already risen, ready to start out. He muttered: "Just a minute," gripped his pen, dipped it in ink and wrote: "Notes for article for third week. Family life: Did the philosopher mean family life's all-absorbing nature when he cried for relief from its nightmare? Family preoccupation is no better than occupying oneself solely with one's body and keeping it in a flourishing condition. Man is condemned to be charged with neglect either here or in the heavens. Let him choose where he would rather face the calumny."

He had completed the sentence when the printer came in again, blowing out the remark: "I say, Srinivas, you are trying them too much, I fear, keeping them waiting!" Srinivas put away his pen, explaining apologetically: "I had to note down something at once; otherwise I'm in danger of losing it forever." Now a boy entered, bearing plates and cups on a tray. The printer said: "Take your seat, madam, have some coffee."

"No, no," she protested. "I'm not in need——" She was shy and inarticulate in the presence of the printer. Ramu watched the scene with dislike and boredom. He kept throwing at the tray hungry side-glances, hoping that his mother's refusal would not lead to the removal of the tray.

Noticing it, the printer said: "Come on, young man," and handed him a plate; he then rose, saying to Srinivas: "Please persuade your wife to take something. She has had a tiring journey." He went down the steps. Srinivas held a plate to his wife. "Come on——"

"Hotel food! I can't," she said. She was brought up in a very orthodox manner in her little village. "And I can't eat any food without a bath first. It'd be unthinkable." The boy tried to say through his full mouth: "Mother has been fasting since yesterday—wouldn't take anything on the way."

"Why?" asked Srinivas.

"Should you ask?" she replied.

"What foolish nonsense is this?" Srinivas cried. He stood looking at her for a moment as if she were an embodiment of knotty problems. He knew what it was: rigorous upbringing, fear of pollution of touch by another caste, orthodox idiocies—all the rigorous compartmenting of human beings. He looked at her with despair. "Look here, I don't like all this. You eat that stuff. What does it matter who has prepared it, as long as it is clean and agreeable? It is from a Brahmin hotel. Even if it isn't, you have got to eat it, provided it is clean and the sort of thing you eat. We have all been eating it, and I assure you we have neither felt poisoned in this life nor lost a claim for a place in heaven. You could share the same fate with us, I think." He pressed a plate into her hand and compelled her to accept it. The boy added: "It is quite good, Mother, eat it."

Having been used to the spacious courtyards and halls of their village home, his wife stood speechless when she beheld her home at the back of Anderson Lane. The very first question she asked was: "How can we live here?"

"Oh, you will get used to it," Srinivas replied.

"But what small rooms and partitions!"

"Oh, yes, yes. He is a rapacious rascal, our landlord. You are welcome to tackle him whenever you like."

"But what a locality! Couldn't you get——?"

"Yes, it is a horrible locality. But a lot of men, women, and children are living here; we are one of them."

Meanwhile they found Ramu missing. Looking about, Srinivas saw him engaged in a deep conversation with a boy of his own age, living in an adjoining block of rooms. They saw Ramu open his friend's wooden box and dive into it and bring out something. "He seems to know already where everything is kept in that house," Srinivas said. "Ramu, come here," he called. His son came up with his friend behind him. "This is our house," Srinivas told him. Ramu seemed very pleased to hear it. "Do you like it?" Ramu looked about, looked at his friend, and they both giggled. "What is your friend's name?"

Ramu said: "I don't know. Can I go to the same school as he, Father?"

"Certainly; yes, yes," Srinivas said.

It seemed to have excited the entire community that Srinivas's wife had arrived. Everybody seemed relieved to see Srinivas's home-life return to a normal shape. They said: "Your husband was paying a rent here unnecessarily. Your part of the house was always locked up all day long. He doesn't seem to have cared for anything except his work." Even the old landlord turned up to see her. He said: "I'm an elder, listen to my advice. I have experience of life enough for four of you. You should never leave your husband's side, whatever happens. Make yourself comfortable. Don't drive nails into the wall; I don't like it."

Srinivas found domestic duties an extra burden. What a round of demands. He could clearly see that his wife was being driven to despair by his habits. This was the first time that he was in sole charge of his wife and son, and he found that it gave him a peculiar view of them. All along in the joint family home they had been looked after by others, and he had no occasion to view his wife as a sole dependent. But now he found that it was so with a vengeance. At every turn he found he was violating some principle or other of domestic duty. "This is going to leave me no time for attending to the paper," he often reflected. He secretly admired those hundreds and hundreds of people who did so much in the world, in spite of a domestic life, even with many more to make demands upon them. "There is perhaps some technique of existence which I have not understood," he told himself. "If I get at it I shall perhaps be able to manage things better. Am I such an idiot that I cannot manage these things better?" he often reflected. "Here I am seeking harmony in life, and yet with such a discord at the start of the day itself." His troubles began then. Somehow his wife didn't seem to like the idea of his waking up so early and going out for coffee. "When you have a house, why should you go out for coffee? What will people say if they find the master of the house going out for coffee?"

"You are the master of the house," he replied jokingly, "so it doesn't matter if I go out."

"Don't joke about it," she said, annoyed with him. "Don't you see, people will think it odd?" It seemed to him an appalling state of affairs to have no better guiding lamp in life than other people's approval—which they so rarely gave. He felt, with an extravagant seriousness, that a whole civilization had come to an abrupt stalemate because its men had no better basis of living than public opinion. He raved against their upbringing. His wife as a child must have pleased her grandmother by her behavior, and been rewarded for it. A child's life was reduced to a mere approved behavior in the midst of father, mother, grandmother and uncles; and later in life parents-in-law, husband, and so on and on endlessly till one had no opportunity to think of one's own views on any matter, till it grew into a mania as in his wife. She didn't want him to get up and go out early in the day, lest it should upset the neighbors; she didn't want to raise her own voice in her own house, lest the neighbors should think of her as a termagant; she wouldn't send the little fellow out to play with some children in the neighborhood because they were too ragged, and there were still others who might think her plebeian. He himself wondered that he had observed so little of her in their years of married life. He suffered silently, since he kept his opinions to himself and ruminated upon these questions in the garrets of *The Banner.*

The moment he stepped past the threshold of his home he had to face an annoyed inquiry: "Do you forget that you have a home?"

"What is the matter?" he asked, going on to his coatstand, removing his coat or upper-cloth, and putting it on the hook. He found his son already asleep on a mat in the front room while his wife sat in a corner reading some obscure novel. It was unnecessary for him to ask "What is the matter?" He knew that it must be the same set of causes over and over again: first and foremost his late-coming; secondly, his lack of interest in home-management; thirdly, his apparent neglect of his child; fourthly, insufficient money; and so on and so on—stretching on to infinity. He didn't receive a reply, and he preferred not to press his question further, for he saw outlined against the opposite window the bank clerk's mother, doubtless waiting to follow the progress of the exchanges between them. He passed on to the dining-room, where a couple of leaves were spread out ready. "Why can't you sit down and eat when you are hungry," he said, "instead of sitting up like this for me?"

"I certainly can't do that," she retorted, put away her novel, and rose without a smile, carrying the lamp in her hand. The leaf spread under the window was for him. He sat down before it; his fingers were ink-stained and cramped.

"Please wash your fingers," she implored, "that ink may be poison."

"I've tried. I should have to scrub off my skin. That stain won't go. I seem to be born with it," he said, feeling pleased with the idiom. The lamp was placed in the middle doorway so that there should be light both in the front room, where the child was sleeping, and in the kitchen. She served him rice, remarking apologetically: "Don't blame me if you find the dinner bare. I couldn't get even the simplest vegetable."

"That's all right," he said. "You know I don't bother about these things."

"But it does no good to be swallowing bare rice morning and night. I don't know what has happened to all the vegetable sellers. I can't find anyone to go up to the street-end and get it. I tried to persuade Ramu to go and buy three pies worth of coriander leaves, but he came back without them."

"He is such a child," Srinivas said, throwing a look at the sleeping form in the shadowy hall. His wife was argumentative about it: "But who else is there to go, if he can't?"

"Why don't you go out and do the shopping yourself? It will give you such a nice outing, too!" Srinivas said.

She looked up at him, puzzled whether to take his remark literally or as a joke. And finally she said: "I don't know— but if someone escorts me I could go and do the shopping; it would be the best thing to do."

Chapter Three

S RINIVAS HAD just cleared his table of a bundle of proofs. He had finished writing his editorial and some of the miscellaneous contributions and letters to the editor. He cracked his aching fingers, leaned back in his chair, got up and paced a few steps up and down, and then stood in the doorway, looking at the lane. He was surprised to see his neighbor, the bank clerk, walking down the lane. He called out his name: "Ravi! Ravi!" The other looked up and hesitated. Srinivas said: "Come up and see *The Banner*." The other came up, looking timidly around. He asked: "Am I not disturbing you?"

"Not now," Srinivas replied. "I'm fairly free. What brought you here? Have you no office?" The other seemed reluctant to notice so many questions. He merely pursed his lips, drew up the pin-cushion, and started pulling out the pins and rearranging them. Srinivas observed him for a while and asked: "How is your boss?"

"Bad as ever," he replied. "Today I wanted an hour off, and how he shouted when he heard it. My ear-drums are still trembling."

"He let you off?"

"Oh, yes. He exhausted himself so much that he banged the table and said 'Damn it. You are persistent. But don't do it again,' and so I'm here." He laughed. "It is his usual way of blessing any idea that I conceive. I've grown used to it."

"Rarely do people come up this way," Srinivas said testingly.

Ravi pushed away the pin-cushion, picked up a paper-weight, and tried to make it stand on its top before answering: "You doubtless wish to know why I'm here. I came to look for someone I lost sight of ages ago, as it seems." Srinivas smiled and didn't wish to press the question further. He scented some complexity. Meanwhile Ravi picked up a pencil, snatched a piece of paper, and after plying the pencil for a few minutes, pushed the paper across. "Well, this is the person," he said. It was a perfect pencil sketch of a girl of about nineteen: the pencil outline was thin and firm, etched finely like an image in the mind. A couple of flowers in her hair, a light caught by a gem on her ear-ring, and a spot of light caught by the pupil of her eye. Srinivas became breathless at the sight of it. "I say— this is——" He sought and fumbled for a correct expression, but could get nothing more than: "This is wonderful. I never knew you could draw so well."

"Drawing's not required in a bank," Ravi replied. He picked up the picture, gazed at it, tore off an edge and rolled it away.

"Don't tear it," Srinivas cried, snatching it back. He gazed at it. "I almost feel like returning the smile on her lips!" he exclaimed.

"That's her expression," Ravi said enthusiastically. "She always smiled very slightly, but you know—what a power it had!"

"Who is she?"

"Why go into all that now?" Ravi said with a sigh. "It was some years ago. I saw her one evening coming out of Iswara's temple——"

"What were you doing there?"

"I was very religious then. For months I went there with-

50

out noticing anything, but that day I saw her, suddenly, as in a vision; she stood framed on the threshold of the temple; there were just six stars in the sky, and the gray tower rose among them. She had a flower in her hair, and a silver tray balanced ever so elegantly on her palm—so tall and slender. I don't know how to describe——I saw her just as I was about to go into the temple—I stood arrested on the spot."

The boy brought in coffee. Srinivas pushed a cup across to the other. They sipped their coffee in silence, while the treadle groaned below and a hawker's voice rang along the street. Ravi asked: "Would you like me to continue my story?"

"Yes, yes, certainly."

"I used to meet her regularly after that at the temple. I started to make an oil portrait of her at home at the end of each day. It is an unfinished picture now, because I suddenly lost sight of her."

"Oh, you didn't know where she lived?"

"Yes, I knew. They were in Car Street."

"Did you visit them?"

"Oh, no; they would have thrown me out. Her father was a severe-looking man. I used to hurry off whenever I saw him standing at his gate; but I passed that way several times every day."

"What was her name?"

He shook his head sadly. "I don't know, I couldn't ask."

"You were friends?"

"I don't know. We were friends in the sense that she was used to seeing me at the temple, and once she gave me a piece of coconut offered to the gods. Oh! How I treasured it! But how long can a piece of coconut keep?"

"Was she married?"

51

"I don't know. I didn't ask. Oh, what excitement it was for me, following her back home every day at a distance of about ten yards. Not a word passed between us, but I was there every day at the temple, and she looked for me, I think. And at her gate she just turned her head slightly and passed in; and I ran straight off to my house and worked on the picture, though it was so difficult without sufficient light."

"I never knew you were an artist," Srinivas declared.

"I'm not. I'm only a bank clerk. In those days it was different. I was a student in college. My father was in good health and was a flourishing lawyer. Nobody bothered about what I did in those days—all the family responsibility came on me rather suddenly, you know, when my father was stricken with paralysis."

"What happened to the picture you were working on?"

"Nothing. I had to drop it. She disappeared one day; and with that the picture ended, and I put away my paint-box forever. The picture is still there at the bottom of a lumber box."

"What happened to the girl?"

"I missed her one evening at the temple, and then I waited there till late in the evening; I still remember what a fool I must have looked to passers-by. I waited there till about eight p.m. and went up to Car Street. Their house was dark. I later learned that they had left the town. I lost all trace of them for years. Just today as I sat at my table I saw through the window someone looking like her father going by in a car and at once I left the office to find out if they were back here. I have been all over the town this afternoon, looking here and there. You know this is the first sketch I've done after that day." He added, half humorously: "Now that you have that sketch you will keep it with you and keep your eyes open. If ever you see her you must——"

"Oh, yes, certainly, I will tell you."

Ravi's eye lit up with joy at the mention of this possibility. He leaned over the table and gripped Srinivas's arm and said: "You will tell me, won't you? You will save me. I promise I will draw hundreds of sketches; only tell me that she is here—that you have seen her—"

After that Ravi began to drop in at the office now and then, just to ask for news. It was Srinivas's greatest dread lest anyone should disturb him on a Friday—the day on which the journal emerged in its final shape. Srinivas was in a state of acute tension on that day, and he dreaded hearing any footsteps on the creaking wooden staircase. But Ravi seemed to choose just those days. Directly his office closed he came there, crossed the threshold, grinning a little nervously. Srinivas looked up with a very brief lifeless smile and returned to the papers on his table, as Ravi seated himself on a stool at the other end of the room. He felt annoyed at this interruption, and he wanted to say aloud: "Why do you pester me, of all days, today?" But, as a matter of self-discipline, he tried to smother even the thought. Some corner of his mind said: "Don't be such an uncivilized brute. He is suffering silently. It is your duty, as a fellow-being, to give him asylum." And he looked up at him and murmured: "Office over?" "Yes," the other said, and he timidly added: "How is the sketch?" Srinivas put away the pen and looked at him with a smile and then took out of a drawer a cardboard file, in which he carefully preserved the sketch. He brought it out and gazed at it, and that transformed the entire situation. The light emanating from the eyes of the portrait touched with an exaltation the artist sitting before him and gave him a new stature. He was no longer a petty, hag-ridden bank clerk, or an unwelcome, thoughtless visitor, but a personality, a creative artist, fit to take rank among the celestials.

Srinivas knew what silent suffering was going on within that shabby frame. He knew that an inspiration had gone out of his life. He had no doubt a home, mother, and brothers and sisters, but all that signified nothing. His heart was not there, any more than it was in the bank. Srinivas felt pity for him and murmured as if apologizing to him: "You see, this is a day of pressure and so——" And the other replied: "Yes, yes, I shall be very quiet. Don't disturb yourself; I just came to know how you were faring," which was false, since Srinivas very well knew that he came there only in the hope of news about his lost love; and Srinivas knew that that was the meaning of the question: "How is the sketch?" though he pretended to treat it at its face value, and handed the other the sketch and returned to his duties. For a long hour or more Ravi sat there, gazing at the pencil sketch in the fading evening light, as Srinivas grew more and more sunk in his papers and work.

When the final proof had gone Srinivas got up, saying: "I'm going down to the press." Ravi handed him back the sketch. Srinivas locked it up in his drawer again, and they went downstairs. The printer looked at him with an irrepressible curiosity. Srinivas explained: "A friend of mine, my neighbor." And the printer ostentatiously said: "Come in, please, come in, you are welcome." There on the floor were heaped copies of *The Banner* waiting to be folded and posted. The editor sat down, along with the printer and his urchin, to accomplish this task. The treadle continued to grind away more copies, the printer shouting from where he was: "Boys, go on slowly—watch the ink."

And this made Srinivas wonder, as he again and again wondered, how many people might be slaving at the task of turning out *The Banner* beyond that purple screen. For he never could pluck up enough courage to peer into that sanctum, since he always heard the printer declare with considerable emphasis: "That is the one point on which I'm always very strict—the best of my friends and relations have not seen inside there. For instance, you have never seen my machine-room, sir, and how much I appreciate your respecting my principles: I've pointed out your example to hundreds of my customers." A statement which made Srinivas keep away from that room more than ever. He remembered that at Chidambaram temple there was a grand secret, beyond the semi-dark holy of holies, beyond the twinkling lights of the inner shrine. He had always wondered what it might be; but those who attempted to probe it too deliberately lost their sight, if not their lives. There was a symbolism in it: it seemed to be expressive of existence itself; and Srinivas saw no reason why he should grudge the printer his mysterious existences and mazes beyond the purple curtain.

Ravi sat in a chair scanning the page of a copy of *The Banner*, while the others were busily packing and gumming. The printer threw him a look once or twice, and then held up a folded paper to him: "Mister—I have not the pleasure of knowing your name—"

"Ravi."

"What a fine name. Mr. Ravi, will you please apply this

gum lightly here, and press it?" Ravi did as he was told. And the next stage for him was to share the task with the others, and he received no small encouragement from the printer. "That's right. We must all pull together. Why do I do this when my business should be over with the printing of the copies? It is because I treat it as a national duty; it is neither the editor's nor anybody else's; it is the country's, and every man who calls himself a true son of the country should do his bit for it." Srinivas felt that this was a flamboyant sentiment. "No, no, nothing so grand about it, I assure you. It is just a small weekly paper, that is all. It is not right to call everything a national service." The printer brushed him aside with: "Modesty has done no good to anyone in this world, as I told a customer only this morning. He started raving over some slight delay in the matter of a visiting card. I told him, 'You can offer me a lakh of rupees, but that will not tempt me to do anything other than *Banner* work on *Banner* press day.' "

Srinivas wended his way home through the dark, ill-lit lanes. Ravi followed him silently. "Isn't it very late for you?" Srinivas asked. "It is all the same," the other remarked. "I really enjoyed being in your office. In fact, I love this whole place." He pointed at the soft stabs of feeble, flickering light emanating from door chinks and the windows of humble homes, the only light available here, since the municipal lighting stopped at Market Road. "I like this lighting. I feel like doing an entire picture with half-lights and shadows some day; I don't know when."

His aged mother waited at the door anxiously. "Ravi!" she exclaimed anxiously. "Why are you so late?" His youngest brother and sister clung to his arms as he turned into his portion of the house without a word.

With a copy of the latest *Banner* rolled in his hand Srinivas entered his home. His wife sat by the lamplight reading her novel. He held his latest copy to her with the remark: "I hope you will find something to interest you at least this week." She hastily opened it, ran her eyes through and put it away with: "I will read it later," and she went in to get his dinner ready. She had accommodated herself to his habits fairly well now, and accepted his hours without much grumbling. But she was an uncompromising critic of his journal. She always glanced through the copy he brought in and said: "Why don't you put in something to interest us?"

"If you keep on reading it, you will find it interesting," he said, and loathed himself for appearing to be so superior. He felt that in all the welter of economic, municipal, social and eternal questions he was threshing out he was making the journal somewhat heavy and that he was putting himself one remove from his public. This was a pathological mood that seized him now and then, whenever he thought of his journal. He was never very happy on the day his journal came out. He ate his dinner silently ruminating over it. His wife stooped over his leaf to serve him. She had fried potato chips in ghee for him and some cucumber soaked in curd; she had spent the day in the excitement of preparing these and was now disappointed to see him take so little notice of them. She watched him for a moment as he mechanically picked up the bits and stuffed them into his mouth. He was thinking: "There is some deficiency in *The Banner*. I wish I knew what it was. Something makes it not quite acceptable to the people for whom it is intended. There is a lot of truth in my wife's complaint." She watched him for a moment and asked: "Do you remember what you have just been eating?" He came to himself with a start and smiled uncomfortably. She could not be put off with that. She insisted: "Tell me what you have eaten off that corner." He looked at the corner of the leaf helplessly and answered: "Some fried stuff." "Yes—what vegetable?" He puckered his brow in an effort to recollect. He knew how much it would hurt his wife. He felt rather pained. "I'm sorry, I was thinking of something else. Was it raw plantain?"

She lightly patted her brow with her hand and said: "Raw plantain! What an irony! Here I have spent the whole evening ransacking my money-box and procuring you potato for frying, and you see no difference between it and raw plantain. Why should we take all this trouble if it makes so little difference?" He looked up at her. By the dim light he saw that her face was slightly flushed. Clearly she was annoyed at his indifference. He felt angry with himself. "I don't know the art of family life. There is something lacking in me as in the journal, which leaves a feeling of dissatisfaction in people's minds." He saw that unless he was careful he might irritate her. He merely said: "Don't make much of all this," and cut her short. He went through his meal silently, washed his hands, sat down on his mat with *The Banner* held close to a lamp; he glanced through it again, line by line, in order to decide what changes he should adopt for the next issue. A corner of his brain was noticing the noise in the kitchen: his wife scrubbing the floor, the clanking of vessels being restored to their places, and the blowing out of the kitchen lamp and finally the shutting of the kitchen door. She paused before him for a moment and then went to her bed and lay down beside their sleeping son. Srinivas noted it and felt pity

58

for her. He viewed her life as it was: a lonely, bare life. He had not the slightest notion how she was spending her days: she probably spent them awaiting his return from the office. She was justified if she felt her grievances were there. "I have neglected her lately. It seems ages since I touched her, for when all is said and done a husband-wife relationship is peculiar to itself, being the most tactile of all human relationships. Perhaps she is wilting away without the caress and the silly idiom softly whispered in the ear." He hesitated for a moment, undecided whether to follow up this realization. But he put away the question for the moment to finish the work on hand, and reached out for a tablet on which to note down his points.

Srinivas decided to spend the next day completely at home. The day after the issue of the journal must be a holiday. "I must remember I'm a family man," he told himself. Next morning he surprised his wife by lying on in bed. His wife woke him up at seven-thirty. "Don't you have to get up?"

"No, my dear sir!" he said. "It is a holiday. I won't go near the office today." She let out a quiet little cry of happiness. "Will you be at home all day?"

"Absolutely." She called: "Ramu, Ramu," and their little son came in from somewhere. "What is it, Mother?"

"Your father is not going to his office today."

"Why, Father?" he asked, looking at him dubiously. Srinivas had no ready answer to give. He was really very pleased to see the effect of his decision. "Well, now run off; I will sleep for half an hour more and then you will know."

The boy picked up his top and string and ran out again. Srinivas shut his eyes and let himself drown in the luxury of inactivity. Mixed sounds reached him—his wife in the kitchen, his son's voice far off, arguing with a friend, the clamor of assertions and appeals at the water-tap, a peddler woman crying "Brinjals and greens" in the street—all these sounds mingled and wove into each other. Following each one to its root and source, one could trace it to a human aspiration and outlook. "The vegetable seller is crying because in her background is her home and children whose welfare is molded by the amount of brinjals she is able to scatter into society, and there now somebody is calling her and haggling with her. Some old man very fond of them, some schoolboy making a wry face over the brinjal, diversity of tastes, the housewife striking the greatest measure of agreement, and managing thus—seeing in the crier a welcome solution to her problems of housekeeping, and now trying to give away as little of her money as possible in exchange—therein lies her greatest satisfaction. What great human forces meet and come to grips with each other between every sunrise and sunset!" Srinivas was filled with great wonder at the multitudinousness and vastness of the whole picture of life that this presented; tracing each noise to its source and to its conclusion back and forth, one got a picture, which was too huge even to contemplate. The vastness and infiniteness of it stirred Srinivas deeply. "That's clearly too big, even for contemplation," he remarked to himself, "because it is in that total picture we perceive God. Nothing else in creation can ever assume such proportions and diversity. This indeed ought to be religion. Alas, how I wish I could convey a particle of this experience to my readers. There are certain thoughts which are strangled by expression. If only people could realize what immense schemes they are components of!" At this moment he heard over everything else a woman's voice saying: "I will kill that dirty dog if he comes near the tap again."

"If you speak about my son's dog I will break your pot," another voice cried. "Get away both—I've been here for half an hour for a glass of water." Now they formed to him a very different picture. A man's voice ordered: "I will remove this tap if you are all going to——" It was the voice of the old landlord and quietened the people. One heard only the noise of water falling in a pot. Next moment the old man appeared in the doorway, peeped in and called: "Mister Srinivas. Oh, still sleeping? Not keeping well?" He walked up to Srinivas lying in bed and stood over him: "I thought you would be getting ready to go out." He sat down on the floor, beside his bed, and said: "I tell you, I sometimes feel I ought to lock up all my houses and send away all those people. They seem to be so unworthy of any consideration."

"What consideration do you show them?"

"I've given them a water-tap which they have not learnt to use without tearing each other. I sometimes feel so sick of seeing all these crudities that I blame God for keeping me in this world so long."

"If it makes you so sick, why don't you put up a couple of taps more?"

"Give them twenty more taps, they would still behave in the same manner," he said irrelevantly. "I have known days when people managed without any tap at all; there used to be only a single well for a whole village. It doesn't depend upon that, but people have lost all neighborliness in these days, that is all." He went on with further generalizations. Srinivas felt that it would be useless to remain in bed any longer; he got up, rolled up his bed, and picked his green-handled toothbrush and paste from a little wallshelf and unscrewed the toothpaste top. The old man remarked: "What is the world coming to? Everybody has taken a fancy to these toothbrushes; they are made of pig's tail, I'm told. Why should we orthodox, pure Aryans go in for these things? Have you ever tried Margosa or Banyan twigs? They are the best and they were not fools who wrote about them in the *Shastra*. They knew more science than any of us today—you see my teeth." He bared his teeth. "How do you like them?"

"Most of them are missing," Srinivas said.

"Never mind the missing ones, but they stayed long enough when they did. And do you know what I've used?" Srinivas didn't wait for him to finish his sentence, but made his way toward the bathroom.

He stayed in the bathroom just a little longer, hoping that the old man would have left by then. But he found him still there when he returned, sitting just as he had left him. He came rubbing a towel over his face, and the old man asked: "What are these towels, looking like some hairy insect? Must be very costly."

"H'm, yes, if you are still thinking of your own days," said Srinivas.

"You are right. Do you know, I used to buy twenty towels to a rupee, the Malayalam variety? I'm still using some of them I bought in those days."

"It was due to bargains like yours that no industry ever found it possible to raise its head in our country."

"You are right," said the old man without comprehending the other's statement. "They should not try to rob us of all we have with their prices." Srinivas moved to the windowsill, on which was fixed a small looking-glass; there was a small wooden comb beside it. He ran it through his graying hair mechanically as by immemorial custom, wondering what comment this was going to provoke in the old man. It was not long in coming. He said with a cynical leer: "Fancy men parting and combing their hair like women! How beautiful and manly it was in those days when at your age you had only a very small tuft and shaved off the head. That's why people in those days were so clearheaded."

"Yes, but we don't get the same amount of co-operation from our barbers these days. That is the worst of it," said Srinivas. "And so we are compelled to go from stupidity to stupidity."

The old man laughed at the joke and said: "You have not yet asked my purpose in visiting you today." "Just a minute," Srinivas said and went into their small kitchen. His wife was at the little oven, frying a rice-cake. Her eyes seemed swollen with smoke. But she seemed to be in great spirits. She was sitting with her back to him, humming a tune to herself as she turned the cake. The place was fragrant with the smell of burning ghee. Srinivas stood in the doorway for a moment and listened. "That is a nice bit of singing," he said. She turned to him with a smile. "I'm making these cakes for you. Don't drink up your coffee yet." He had never been given tiffin in the morning except today, and he understood that she was celebrating his holiday. He was disturbed for a moment by the thought that his holiday pleased her so much more than his working—when all his pride and seriousness were bestowed on the latter. "Your meal will be late today," she explained. "I'm going to give you *Aviyal* for your dinner; Ramu has gone out to the market to buy the vegetables for it." A stew of over a dozen vegetables; Srinivas was very fond of it: his mother used to feed him with it whenever he came home during vacation in those days: how the girl remembered his particular taste in all these things and with what care she tended him now. He was touched for a moment. "But all this puts an additional burden on one in life," he told himself. He asked: "I've a guest; can you manage some coffee for him?"

"Yes, who is he?" He held the door slightly open for her to see through. "Oh, that man!" she exclaimed. "Why has he come? Have you not paid the rent?" She added: "Not enough coffee for two." Srinivas said: "Hush! Don't be so cantankerous. Poor fellow! Put out the sitting planks."

The old man was overjoyed when he heard the invitation. He became nearly incoherent with joy. He was torn between the attraction of the offer and shyness. For the first time Srinivas observed that the man could be moved by shyness. "No, no, I never eat anywhere. Oh, don't trouble yourself about it . . . No, no . . ." he said, but all the same got up and followed Srinivas into the kitchen. He grinned affably at Srinivas's wife and commented flatteringly: "I have always told a lot of people to come and observe this lady for a model. How well she looks after the house. I wish modern girls were all like her." Srinivas gently propelled him to a plank, on which he sat down. He observed from his wife's face that she was pleased with the compliment, and Srinivas felt that the old man's coffee was now assured him. His wife came out with a tumbler of water and two leaves and set them in front of them. She then served a couple of cakes on each leaf, and the old man rubbed his hands with the joy of anticipation. At a signal from Srinivas he fell to; and Srinivas wondered how long it was since the other had had any food. "What do you eat at nights?" he asked testingly. The old man tore off a piece of cake and stuffed it in his mouth and swallowed it before he answered, shaking his head: "I'm not a youth. Time was when I used to take three meals a day—three full meals a day in addition to tiffin twice a day. Do you know——"

"That's remarkable," agreed Srinivas admiringly. "But now what do you do?"

"I'm a *Sanyasi*, my dear young man—and no true *Sanyasi* should eat more than once a day," he said pompously. He ate the cakes with great relish. When a tumbler of coffee was placed beside him he looked lovingly at it and said: "As a *Sanyasi* I have given up coffee completely, but it is a sin not to accept something offered," he said.

"You are right," Srinivas replied, and added: "So drink it up now." The old man raised the tumbler, tilted back his head, and poured the fluid down his throat; he put down the tumbler and wiped his mouth with the back of his hand. He shook his head appreciatively and murmured: "If somebody is going to make coffee as good as this, it will prove very difficult for people like me who wish to give it up." Srinivas's wife acknowledged the compliment with a smile and asked, half peeping out of the doorway: "When are you going to give us another tap?"

"Oh!" cried the old man. "How many people ask me this question every morning!"

"I have to fill up every vessel at three in the morning, and even then people try to be there earlier," she said. The old man made a noise of sympathy, clicking his tongue, got to his feet and passed on to the washing-room without a word. After cleaning his hands and face he went on to the front room and sat down on the mat. Srinivas still sat on the plank, saying something to his wife, and the old man's voice reached him from the hall. "Just one small piece of arecanut, please; cannot do without it after eating anything —one bad habit which I'm not able to conquer. . . ."

Srinivas asked his wife: "Have you a piece of arecanut anywhere?" His wife muttered: "The old man is making himself a thorough guest today, although he is so indifferent about the water-tap." She went over to a cupboard, took out a small wicker-basket and gave Srinivas a pinch of spiced arecanut. Srinivas transferred it immediately to his mouth. "Fine stuff," he said.

"It's not for you!" she cried. She handed him another pinch and said: "Let him demand them immediately if he wants betel leaves also."

Srinivas felt himself in a leisurely mood—the sort of relaxation he had never experienced for months now. "Even an oven is given its moments of rest to cool," he told himself. "It's senseless to go on working and forgoing this delicious feeling of doing nothing," he muttered to himself, as he carried the pinch of arecanut to his guest. The old man sprinkeld it on his tongue and shut his eyes in an ecstasy of relish. "You don't want betel leaves and lime or tobacco?" "Oh, no," the old man replied with a shudder. "Do you want to see me make a fool of myself, with my lips reddened with betel juice at my age!" He seemed to view it as a deadly sin, and Srinivas left it at that and began to wonder what he should do next. The old man now said, looking up at him, moving away a little on the mat: "Won't you sit down for a moment?" Srinivas remained silent, wondering if he could conjure up some excuse which might be both truthful and tactful and free him of the other's company. But the old man followed up: "You have not yet asked me what business brought me here so early in the day. I have come here on a definite business." Srinivas sat down beside him, leaned on the wall and stretched his legs, saying: "Do you mind my stretching before an elder?" "Not at all. It is your house as long as you pay the rent regularly," he replied. He bent over and said: "Do you know, I have a granddaughter of marriageable age?"

"I heard only recently that you had a daughter. How is it none of them come this way?"

"Oh——" he wriggled in despair. "Don't go into all that now. I have a granddaughter, that is all I wish to say. I would forget my daughter, if possible. That is an ungrateful brood," he said.

"How many sons and daughters have you?" Srinivas persisted relentlessly. The old man glared at him angrily for a moment and asked: "Won't you leave that subject alone?"

"No," Srinivas replied, "I have got to know. I'm not prepared to hear about your granddaughter unless you tell me first about your daughters and sons."

"Oh, if that is so I will tell you. I have three sons and two daughters; one daughter is in this town—the other daughter is in Karachi: I'm not concerned with her, because her husband is a customs officer, and she thinks it is not in keeping with her status to think of her father and the rest of us. It is over twelve years since she wrote. She pretends that she is of Persian royal descent, I suppose, and not an ordinary South Indian." He laughed at his own joke and continued: "Why should I care? I don't. It saves me postage to forget her. Sometimes her mother used to fret about her, and for her sake I used to waste a postcard now and then. But since the old lady's death I have forgotten that daughter. . . . I'm not talking about my second daughter."

"You have not told me anything about your two sons."

"Oh, won't you leave them alone? Why do you trouble a *Sanyasi* like me with such reminders?"

"Where are they?" Srinivas asked.

"In heaven or hell, what do I care?" the old man replied. "I refuse to talk about them: they are all an ungrateful, rapacious brood; why talk of them?"

"Has this second daughter of yours a daughter?" At the mention of the granddaughter his eyes glittered with joy. "You are absolutely right. Oh, what an angel she is! Whenever I want to see her I go to the Methodist girls' school, where she reads, talk to her during the recess, and come away." His tone fell to cringing: "I wish to see her married. I have set apart five thousand rupees for her marriage. Let them produce a good husband for her, and the amount will go to her; and they must manage the wedding celebrations as well as the dowry within that amount."

"What is your son-in-law?"

"He is a teacher in the same school."

"So you are bound to see him also when you go there?"

"H'm, I never go in. I call her up from outside, see her for a moment, and go away. I don't talk to that fellow nor to that wife of his."

"What did they do?"

"They neglected their mother and wouldn't spend even

an anna when she was ill. I had to pay the doctor's bill—one hundred and seventy-five rupees—all myself. Not an anna was contributed by any of them. Do you know how much the old woman doted on them? I was always telling her that she was spoiling them. But she wouldn't listen. After her death I cut off the entire brood completely. I have no use for ungrateful wretches of that type. Do you agree with me or not?" Srinivas slurred over the question. The old man said: "For this granddaughter of mine, why don't you find a bridegroom? I may die any moment. I'm very old, and as they say in *Gita*——" He quoted a Sanskrit verse from Bhagavad-Gita regarding mortality. He shrank his eyes to small slits and begged: "I want to see this girl married."

Srinivas said: "I don't know what I can do."

"My tenant in that portion—Ravi, isn't he your friend? I have often seen him going with you. I observe all things. Why don't you persuade him to give me his horoscope? I think he will be a good match for this girl."

Srinivas could hardly believe his ears. At the sound of Ravi the entire picture of his complicated life flashed across his mind and he didn't know what to say. "Why have you pitched on Ravi?"

"Because I have observed him, and he is in a respectable job."

"But he has a very large number of dependents."

"Yes, that's a fact. But I shall probably reduce his rent and give him another room. What can we do about his people? We will see about it all later. But will you kindly speak to him about my granddaughter and get me his horoscope? Ever since I saw him I have been thinking what a perfect match he would be for the girl. Tell him that the girl is beautiful and reads in sixth form." Srinivas promised to do his best, without much conviction.

The printer sat down on the stool before Srinivas's table and said: "I rather liked the friend you brought in the other evening—who is he?" Srinivas told him about him. He took out the sketch and passed it on to the other for his scrutiny, saying: "Do you know, there are very few in India who can do that with a pencil?"

"Fine girl," the printer agreed, shaking his head, as if appreciating a piece of music or a landscape. "Who is she?"

"God knows. They were in Car Street, and they are no longer there. That's all he knows. He lost sight of her, and will not draw till he finds her again. He drew this because he thought they were back here." The printer pondered over it deeply. "What a fool to be running after an unknown girl—a man must shut his eyes tight if it proves useless to look any longer. That's my principle in life." This was the first time Srinivas had heard the other talk in this strain. He had known very little of his family life, except that sometimes he referred to his home, away there by a cross-road in the New Extension, containing a wife and five children. Srinivas opened his lips to ask something and hesitated; the printer seemed to read his mind, and said with a smile: "I'm not such a bad husband, sir, as you may think!" He tossed the picture across the table and said: "I thought there was something funny about that young man —these artists are futile: they can neither get along with their jobs properly nor forget a face."

"But," Srinivas said, "I wish he could get that girl back, if it is only to make him go on with his drawing."

"You think it is so important!" asked the printer. "Why, I can get a score of fellows to do this sort of thing." He scrutinized it again, making an honest effort to see what there might be in it. "Well, anyway, it is not his profession; what is there to sorrow about?" Srinivas stared at him for a moment and rapped the table with his palm as if to get the other's fullest attention. "Don't you see what a great artist we are losing? He is an artist; don't you see that?"

"Oh!" the other exclaimed, as if the truth were dawning upon him for the first time. "Oh!" He added: "Yes—you are right." He looked at the sketch intently as if comprehending it better now. "You just leave him to me; I will tackle him; you will see him drawing these pictures one after another till you cry 'Enough. No more!' "

A few days later, going down to the press one evening, he saw Ravi sitting in a chair opposite the printer. Srinivas was rather surprised. Ravi, who would usually come up and occupy his stool, had now been short-circuited by the printer. By the look on the artist's face Srinivas understood that they had been in conclave for a long while. The moment Srinivas appeared the artist rose, gripped his arm and cried, pointing at the other: "Oh, he knows, he knows!" His voice trembled with joy and his hands shook. The printer said, with his eyes twinkling: "He has promised to come and draw a picture of my little son tomorrow evening. Would you like to have any done for you?"

When he went home the artist accompanied him. The printer saw them off at the door, effusively as ever. His parting word to the artist as they stepped into the street was: "The baby will be ready to receive you at seven o'clock sharp. Fourth cross-road, New Extension. I will wait at the gate."

The artist chatted happily all the way. "Tomorrow I must leave home pretty early—a couple of hours at the printer's house and from there on to the office direct. I shall be just there in time; I hope that child is sketchable. What sort of child is he; have you seen?"

"No," replied Srinivas. "And what else did he tell you?"

"Oh, my friend. I never knew I was so near help. All that I want is just another look at that girl, and that will transform my entire life. I never knew that our printer was a man who could be so helpful. What a fine man he is!" Srinivas didn't like to pursue the matter further and remained silent. He somehow felt disinclined to speak about the printer. When they passed the last crossing in Market Road and turned down Anderson Lane he ventured to ask: "What would be your reaction if someone seriously proposed his daughter to you?" "I would kick him," the other replied promptly and recklessly. Srinivas left it at that, feeling that he had discharged the duty laid upon him by the old man.

The old man appeared just as he was hurrying to his office. He turned the corner of the street, and the old man hailed him from under the street tap where he had been bathing. "Mister Editor! Oh! Mister Editor," he called from the tap, and his cry rang past a ring of spectators waiting for the tap to be free. Srinivas turned and wished he could clear the entire street at a jump. But it was not possible. The old man came up to him, dripping with water. He shook his head disapprovingly. "No, no, you must not be so very inconsiderate to an old man." Srinivas tarried and said: "I'm in a hurry."

"Who is not?" asked the old man promptly. "Every creature is in a hurry, every ant is in a hurry, every bird is in a hurry, every fellow I meet is in a hurry, the sun is in a hurry, the moon is in a hurry—all except this slave of God, I suppose." Srinivas was too much engrossed in his own thoughts to say anything in reply. He said: "Now I will be off. I will see you this evening." And he tried to cover the rest of the street at one stride. But the old man would not let him go. He almost cantered behind him and caught up with him. He was panting with the effort. His chest heaved. Srinivas felt that if the old man dropped down dead on the spot, the responsibility would be his, and made a quick decision to change his route from that day. The old man panted: "Have you forgotten that I have such a thing as a granddaughter?"

"I haven't," said Srinivas. "I remember your request. But the time is not yet."

"Are you going to tell me that you have not seen the boy?" Srinivas paused to consider if he might make such an evasion. But the old man went on: "Don't say that, because some evenings ago I saw you both going home. Didn't you turn the street together? I may be old, but not too old to see by street light when there is something to see." Srinivas felt exasperated. "Why is this man plaguing me like this?" He had left home a few minutes earlier in order to clear up some heavy work in the office. He looked hard at the old man and said: "The boy doesn't seem to be in a mood to marry anyone, that is all."

The old man gripped his arm and said: "Do you think I believe a word of what you say?" He gazed on Srinivas's face with his eyes half covered with water drops and attempted to express a merry twinkling at the same time: "Young fellows are always shy about marriage. They will not say so. In fact, do you know, when they came and proposed I should marry, I tried to hide myself in the paddy barn on the wedding day. I was just twelve——"

"But he is twenty-eight——"

"Bah! What an age!" the other commented. "What can a fellow decide at twenty-eight? And why have they left him unmarried for so long? All this is due to the idiotic things they say about child marriage. I was eleven when I married and my wife nine, and yet what was wrong with our marriage?"

Srinivas said: "I will positively come and see you tonight in your room. I promise. I'm in a hurry now."

"All right, go; I like people who attend to their duties properly. Don't forget that I have a granddaughter!" Srinivas almost broke into a run for fear he might be stopped again.

The artist dropped in one afternoon, went straight to his stool, drew it near the window, turned his back on Srinivas and sat looking out. Srinivas was, as usual, submerged in his papers; his mind noted the steps on the creaking staircase, but he did not like to interrupt himself or allow his

74

mind to speculate about the visitor. He went on writing and correcting without lifting his head. He laid his pen aside, rolled up a manuscript, and flung it downstairs. He returned to his seat, leaned back and asked: "Ravi, are you asleep or awake?"

"Neither. I'm dead," the other replied and came nearer, dragging the stool. He planted the stool right in front of the table and cleared his throat as a prelude to a harangue. Srinivas knew he would have to listen to a great deal now. He kept himself receptive. He felt it was his duty to give every possible encouragement to the other, now that he had shown an inclination to go on with his drawings. As a sort of lead he asked: "Well, how far are you progressing with your sketch?" Ravi leaned over and asked: "Of that child?" indicating his fingers down the staircase. "Don't you see that I have avoided him and come up direct?"

"Not finished it yet?"

"It will never be finished," he replied in a hushed voice. "But I dare not tell him."

"Why? What is wrong?"

"It is an awful subject. I won't go on with it."

"But I hear that you go there every day."

"Yes, yes, every day I go and sit before the child, study it for about an hour in the hope of discovering even the faint-est thing to hold on to. But I definitely give it up. Nothing is right about it: all its lines are wrong; its expression is awfully dull and lifeless. It is a pity!"

"But the poor fellow is hoping every day that you are going to do it!"

"That is why I'm trying to avoid him, though I've got to see him. How am I to manage it? I can't tell him about his child, can I?"

75

"No, no, that'd hurt any parent."

"I wish I could get the view of a parent. You haven't seen the child?" Srinivas didn't answer: his mind went off on another line. He wondered if he should tell the printer. "No," he told himself. "There's no sense in interfering in other people's lives. . . ." His mind perceived a balance of power in human relationships. He marveled at the invisible forces of the universe which maintained this subtle balance in all matters: it was so perfect that it seemed to be unnecessary for anybody to do anything. For a moment it seemed to him a futile and presumptuous occupation to analyze, criticize and attempt to set things right anywhere.

As an example: here was the printer telling Ravi imaginary stories about his ability to find the other's sweetheart. Ravi's head was in the clouds on account of those stories; and here was the artist helping the printer also to keep his head in the same cloud-land with promises of sketching his child: these two seemed to balance each other so nicely that Srinivas felt astounded at the arrangement made by the gods. If only one could get a comprehensive view of all humanity, one could get a correct view of the world: things being neither particularly wrong nor right, but just balancing themselves. Just the required number of wrongdoers as there are people who deserved wrong deeds, just as many policemen to bring them to their senses, if possible, and just as many wrongdoers again to keep the police employed, and so on and on in an infinite concentric circle. He seized his pen and jotted down a few lines under the heading "Balance of Power." He was occupied for fully fifteen minutes. He said: "Don't mistake me, Ravi, I had to jot down some ideas just as they came, otherwise I'd lose them forever." He felt thrilled by the thought that he stood on the threshold of some revolutionary discoveries in the realm of human existence—solutions to many of the problems that had been teasing his mind for years. He merely said: "You see, I'm getting some new ideas which may entirely change our *Banner*."

Chapter Four

THE EXPECTED revolution in *The Banner* came in another way. On a Friday, when the editor flung down the manuscript with: "Matter"—the shout came back from the bottom of the staircase: "Editor, you have to spare me a few minutes today," and the printer came upstairs. His face didn't have the usual radiance; he leaned over the table and said: "Your forms are not going in."

"What's the matter?"

"My men have gone on a strike today."

Srinivas was aghast. He jumped to his feet, crying: "We can't let down our subscribers."

"Yes, I know," said the printer. "We've got to do something—I don't know: labor trouble—we are helpless against labor everywhere."

"How many?" Srinivas asked, hoping that at least now he'd know how many worked behind that purple curtain.

"All of them are on strike," replied the printer, and shattered his hope. "All of them: the entire lot. They gave no signs of it and went on a lightning strike at midday; even the first form for the day had gone on the machine. They walked out in a body." Srinivas's mind once again wondered how many workers could form a strike, and his speculations lashed vainly against that purple-dotted curtain.

He looked helplessly down the stairway and ruminated over the hollow silence that reigned in the treadle-room. The printer pushed away a few papers and seated himself on the edge of the table. Srinivas's head was buzzing with alternative suggestions. His mind ran over all the available presses in the town: the Crown Electric, the City Power, Acharya Printing, Sharpe Printing Works, and so on and so forth. He had gone the round once before, when starting the journal, and recollected what a hopeless task it had proved to get any press to undertake the printing of his journal. There was a press law which terrified most printers: they understood very little of it, but always seemed to feel it safer not to go near a periodical publication: they had not enough confidence to read the articles and judge whether they would land themselves in trouble or not (the printer being a willy-nilly partner, by virtue of the Government's order, in all that an editor or publisher might do). They avoided trouble by confining themselves to visiting cards, catalogues and wedding invitations. Everywhere Srinivas got the same reply: "Journal? Weekly. Oh! Sorry, we are not sure we should be able to print the issues in time. Oh, sorry we cannot undertake——" It was only this printer who had said at once: "Leave it to me. I will manage somehow." Going round the town in search of a printer Srinivas had wasted nearly a week, and was weary of the stock reply. He had gone up and down, and accidentally met this man at the Bombay Anand Bhavan in Market Road, where he had gone in for a cup of coffee. Srinivas had by now almost decided to give up all ideas of printing his work in Malgudi, as he sat gloomily in the noisy hall of the Bombay Anand Bhavan, sipping his coffee. He was attracted to his future printer by his voice, a rich baritone, which hovered above the babble of the hall, like a drone. Srinivas understood little of what he had been saying, since he spoke in Hindi and could be easily mistaken for a North

Indian, with his fur cap and the scarf flung around his neck. He sat in a chair next to the proprietor at the counter and seemed to be receiving special attention, by the way waiters were carrying him plates and cups and pressing all sorts of things on him. Apparently he said something amusing to everyone who went near him, since everyone came away from him grinning. He seemed to be keeping the whole establishment in excellent humor, including the fat proprietor. Srinivas was so much struck by his personality that he asked the boy at his table: "Who is that man?"

"He is our proprietor's friend. He prints all our bill-books and invoices."

"What!"

"Prints——"

"Has he a press? Where?"

Next moment he had left his half-finished cup of coffee on the table and gone over to the counter. He looked at the printer and asked: "I wish to talk to you."

"To me? Well, I'm all attention."

"Will you kindly come with me for a minute? Let us sit over there."

"Oh, yes." He descended from the counter with great dignity. He appeared to take charge of Srinivas immediately, although he had come at the latter's invitation. It was as if he were arranging a grand reception. He cried something to the proprietor in northern Indian accents and then called someone and sent him running upstairs. He sent someone else running in another direction. He kept the whole place spinning around. His voice commanded people hither and thither and held itself monarch above the din. People turned their heads and stared at them. Presently he said, with an elaborate note of invitation in his voice, pointing at the staircase: "This way, please." Srinivas felt embarrassed and uttered a mild protest, which the other brushed aside gently and said: "You will be more comfortable there; we can talk quietly." Srinivas began to be troubled by an uneasy feeling that he had perhaps given a totally false and grand impression of himself. Perhaps the other was completely mistaken. He proceeded to say at once, stopping half-way up the step: "You see, it is nothing so——" The other would not allow him to proceed. He categorically said: "I know all that. Please go up."

They came to a cosily furnished room upstairs—a very special room as a board hung outside it said: "For ladies and families only." Srinivas halted before it, finding another excuse: "We are neither ladies nor families. How can we go in?"

"These rules are not for me," the other said. He unhooked the board and handed it to a passing server and said: "Take it to the Saitji and tell him not to send up any ladies or families or anyone into that room while I'm there, and come back." The servant hesitated, at which the other went over to the landing and cried down: "Sait Sab," and was eloquent in some northern language. After that he led Srinivas into the special room, drew up a cushioned chair for him and seated him on it. He then proceeded to give elaborate orders to a server who was waiting at the door. The table was presently littered with plates and cups, and he would not allow Srinivas to speak a word till they had had their repast. After that he called a servant to clear the table. He ordered *pans* and cigarettes. He lit a cigarette, blew out the smoke, leaned back in his chair, and said: "Well, sir, I'm at your service

—what can I do for you?" Srinivas was stunned by all this hospitality. He said: "You are extremely kind to me." The other asked: "Do you think so?" with such earnestness that Srinivas felt constrained to explain: "I'm, after all, a stranger."

"There are no strangers for Sampath."

"Who is Sampath?" asked Srinivas, rather puzzled.

"Speaking," the other said, as if into a telephone. Srinivas looked up at him for a moment and cried: "Oh!" and burst into a laugh. The other joined unreservedly. He said: "I tell you, sir, I'm an optimist in life. I believe in keeping people happy. I have not the pleasure of knowing your name." "My name is——" The other cut him short. "It is immaterial to me. I don't want it—what am I going to do with your name?"

"Shall I at least state my business?"

"If it pleases you."

"I'm the editor of an unborn journal. Can you print it?"

"Do you want me to print it?"

"Yes."

"Well, in that case I've nothing to say. Customers are God's messengers, in my humble opinion. If I serve them aright I make some money in this world and also acquire merit for the next."

"All the printers in this town seemed to be afraid of taking up my journal."

"The worst lot of printers in any part of the world is to be found in this town," Sampath said.

"They seem to be always afraid of breaking the law."

The other said: "By the look of you I don't think you would wish to see me in jail, but if ever you, as the editor, get into trouble it will be my business to share your trouble. When a person becomes my customer he becomes a sort of blood relation of mine: do you understand? But, first of all, let us go to the press."

That was Srinivas's first entrance into Kabir Lane: it was within a few minutes' walk of the hotel. After twisting their way through some lanes Sampath went a little ahead, stepped on his threshold, and said: "You are welcome to the Truth Printing Works, Mr. Editor." The treadle was grinding away out of sight. The printer pointed out a seat to Srinivas and then cried: "John! John!" There was no response. The machine was whirring away inside, but there was no sign of John.

"Boy! Boy!" he cried.

"Yes, sir," answered a thin, youngish voice, and the machine ceased.

The curtain behind the printer parted and a head peeped out—of a very young fellow. He waited for a moment, watching the back of his employer, and then withdrew his head and disappeared softly. Presently the rattle of the machine began again. "Well, sir, I thought I could introduce my staff to you, but they seem to be——"

"Oh, don't disturb them; let them go on with their work. How many have you there?"

The printer turned and took a brief look at the curtain behind him and said with an air of confidence, jerking his thumb in the direction of the other room: "I tell you, labor is not what it used to be. We have to go very cautiously with them. Otherwise we invite trouble. Well, sir, I'm at your service. Here is a sample of my work."

86

He opened a cupboard and threw down on the table a few handbills, notices, pamphlets and letter-heads. He held up each one of them delicately with a comment. "I don't like this, sir," he said, holding up a letter-paper. "I don't approve of this style, but the customer wanted it. Printing is one of the finest arts in the world, sir, but how few understand it!"

At this moment there appeared at the door a middle-aged man wearing a close coat and turban. His face was rigid, and with a finger he was flicking his mustache. At the sight of him the printer jumped out of his seat and dashed toward him with a lusty cry of welcome: "What an honor this is today for Truth Printing."

"I'm tired of sending my clerk and getting your evasive answers. That is why I have come myself."

"What a blessing! What a blessing!" cried the printer and took him by the hand and pulled him to a chair. "I don't want all this," the other said curtly. "Are you going to give me your printed form today or not? I must know that immediately."

"Of course you are getting it," said the printer, turning and going back to his seat. "Meet our editor. He is going to print his weekly here." The other looked at Srinivas condescendingly, his second finger still on his mustache, his face still rigid, and asked: "What sort of weekly—humorous or——" Srinivas turned away, looked at the printer, and asked with cold, calculated indifference: "Who is he? You have not told me."

"Haven't I?" cried the printer, almost in a panic. "He is our District Board President, Mr. Soma Sundaram. I'm one of the few privileged to call him Mr. Somu." Mr.

Somu's face slightly relaxed and a suspicion of a smile appeared somewhere near his ears. He said rather grimly: "You promised me the printed speech ten days ago, and I don't think you have started it at all; the function is coming off on Wednesday."

Sampath explained to Srinivas: "He is opening a bridge, five miles from here, across the Sarayu—a grand function. Do you know that it is going to transform our entire Malgudi district? This is going to be the busiest district in South India. Do you know what odds he had to face, with the Government on one side and the public on the other?" Mr. Somu added: "Mr. Editor, public life is a thankless business. If you knew how much they opposed the scheme!"

"It is a history by itself," Sampath continued. "It is all in his speech. It is going to create a sensation."

The other pleaded: "But please let me have it in time."

Sampath said: "My dear sir, I don't know what you think of me, but I treat this bridge-opening as my own business. When a customer steps over this threshold all his business becomes mine: if you have trust in Sampath you will be free from many unnecessary worries." The other was completely softened by now. He wailed: "I have come to you, of all printers in this town, doesn't it show you how I value your service?" Sampath bowed ceremoniously, acknowledging the sentiment. "With the function only five days ahead, you have not yet given me the proof," began the other.

"Don't I know it? There is a very special reason why I have not given you the proof yet. You will not get it till a day before the function—that's settled."

"Why? Why?" Sampath took no notice of the question.

He rummaged among the papers in a tray and brought out a manuscript. He opened the manuscript and said: "Now listen. Ladies and gentlemen," as if addressing a gathering. It was a masterly declamation, giving a history of the Sarayu bridge and all its politics. The idea of putting up a bridge over the Sarayu was as old as humanity. Sarayu was one of the loveliest rivers in India, coming down from the heights of Mempi Hills and winding its way through the northern sector of Malgudi, an ornament as well as a means of irrigating tens of thousands of acres. The preamble consisted of a long dissertation on the river Sarayu, followed by a history of the whole idea of bridging it, starting with a short note by a Collector, Mr. Frederick Lawley (later Sir Frederick), in a District Gazeteer nearly a century old and culminating in Mr. Somu's own enthusiasms and struggles. It was a hotch-potch of history, mythology, politics and opinion. It was clear that several hands had written that speech for Mr. Somu.

The district board president's face was beaming by this time. He listened appreciatively to his own speech, nodding his head in great approbation. He constantly looked up at Srinivas in order to punctuate the reading with an explanation. "You see, it refers to the Government note issued at that time. Oh! Public life is a thankless business. Do you know what they tried to do when the voting was demanded? Sometimes people stoop to the lowest means to gain their ends. . . ." It was quite half an hour before Sampath put down the speech and leaned back in his chair. He let out a slight cough before saying: "Mr. Somu, do you now see why I can't give you the proof until a day before the show?" The president scratched his head and tried to make out what the reason could be. He turned to

Srinivas and said: "Don't you think that the speech is very good?" Srinivas simpered noncommittally, and the district board president looked greatly pleased. He begged: "Sampath, if you will kindly give it to me in time, I can go through it and make any additions."

"That's one of the reasons why I'm holding up your proof. I don't want you to touch up the speech, which is very good as it is. And then, do you note that your reference in the third paragraph to your predecessor in office cannot yet be printed?"

"Why so?"

"In my view you may have to put everything into the past tense, and I don't want to waste paper and stationery. Don't you know that he has had a heart attack and is seriously ill?"

"I didn't know he was so bad," said the president, pausing.

"I can't take risks, sir. You would have got the two thousand printed copies delivered to you twelve days ago. I even set up a page, but then I heard that Mr. So-and-so was ill. I at once put it away and sent my boy running to ascertain how he was."

"It is very considerate of you."

"Thank you, sir. I've a great responsibility as a printer, sir. If there is any blunder in the speech it is the printer who will be laughed at, sir."

"True, true," the other agreed, completely carried off his feet.

"I never delay unnecessarily, without sufficient reason. You may rest assured of it," Sampath said in a tone full of resentment. The president said: "I'm so sorry, Mr. Sampath. I didn't mean to——"

"Pray don't mention it," Sampath said. "You are perfectly within your rights in hustling me. It is your duty. Your speech will be in your hands in time, sir," he said formally. The other was too pleased to say anything. He showed signs of making his exit, and Sampath clinched it for him by saying: "I will go with you a little way."

When he was gone Srinivas found himself all alone and surveyed the room—a small table and chair blocking the doorway, which was curtained off, beyond which lay a great mystery. The sound of a machine could be heard. He felt tempted to part the curtain and peep in. But he dared not. He turned over in his mind the recent scene he had watched between the printer and his customer, and he felt greatly puzzled about his future printer. He speculated: "Suppose he does the same thing with the weekly when it is out?" He felt a little uneasy, but told himself presently: "I have no right to disbelieve what I have heard and seen. He may have genuine feelings for the president's predecessor. All the same, I must take care that some such thing doesn't happen to the weekly on the due date. If I don't accept his services, where is the alternative? Anyway, God alone must save me——" Just at this moment the printer returned, apologizing profusely for his absence, and said: "Sir, let us get on with your journal."

It went smoothly on until today—until this moment when Sampath came to announce the strike which had taken place among his men. For Srinivas the world seemed to be coming to a sudden end. He was facing the most disgraceful situation in his life. What explanation was he to give to those hundreds of subscribers? He looked at his table littered with proofs and manuscripts; only the editorial and one or two other features remained to be set up today. His editorial entitled "To all whom it may concern," dealing with a profound subject—the relation between God and the State—was almost finished: he had only another paragraph to add, after ascertaining how much space was available on the page. Now he pushed across the manuscript and asked: "Will this fill up the first page or can I add another paragraph?" The printer scrutinized it, measured the lines. "Make your paragraph short, and we can squeeze it in. If you have something important to say, how can we omit it?"

"Thank you; wait a moment," said Srinivas. He seized his pen and dashed off the concluding paragraph: "If you are going to reserve a seat for various representatives of minorities, you could as well reserve a seat for the greatest minority in the world—namely, God. A seat must be reserved for Him in every council and assembly and cabinet: then we shall perhaps see things going right in the world." The printer read it and said: "Well, sir, I am beaten now. I can't make out a line of what you have written. However, it is none of my business. But how are we going to print it?"

"I will help you. Do it somehow."

"How is it possible, sir?" He remained brooding for a while and then said, with a great deal of determination in his voice: "Well, sir, I will do my best, if it costs me my life. I can't be defeated by my men, the ingrates, I gave them a bonus last year. But I don't think we can catch tonight's train: we shall probably have the bundles ready for tomorrow morning."

"But that will mean a day's delay," wailed Srinivas.

"Don't you think, Mr. Editor, that your readers would prefer it to not getting the journal at all?" He looked at his watch and said: "We've only three hours for the night train. Impossible, even if we employ supernatural powers. Now, sir, give me the stuff, and I will start."

Srinivas was very happy to see Sampath in his usual spirits again. "Come on, I will help you in the pressroom."

"No, sir, I have never heard of any printer using an editor to assist him. No, sir, I should make myself the laughing-stock of the entire printing community. Please stay where you are." He hastily got up and went out. Srinivas picked up the pages of his manuscript and followed him without a word.

Downstairs the printer flung off his coat, and took out a blue overall which had lain folded up in a cupboard. With elaborate care he put it on and tied up the strings, rolled up his sleeves, smiled, and without a word parted the purple-dotted curtain and passed in. Srinivas hesitated for a while, wondering what he should do. He wondered how far he could make bold to push that curtain aside and follow. Sampath's oft-repeated compliment that he had told many people the editor had never seen beyond the curtain rang in his ears. But he told himself: "I'm not going to be beaten by a compliment." This seemed a golden chance to enter the great mystery. He felt on the verge of an unknown discovery, and let his impulse carry him on. He pushed through the curtain, a corner of his mind still troubled whether he would find himself thrown out next moment.

He found himself in a small room with no window whatever, in which stood a treadle, a cutting machine, a stitching machine, and a couple of type-boards. The printer was standing before one of them with a composing stick in his hand. He looked at Srinivas very casually and said: "Would you like to try your hand at type-setting?"

"With pleasure," said Srinivas, and the other took him to a type-board, put a stick in his hand and spread out a manuscript on the board. "You just go on putting these letters here—all capitals here, and the lower-cases you will find here. If you can get used to seeing objects upside down or right to left, you will be an adept in no time."

The printer's page was set up, corrected and printed off at midnight. Srinivas for his share produced an uproarious proof-sheet. The printer corrected it. "I think it will be immensely enjoyed by your readers if you print a page of your own as it is," he remarked, laughing heartily at all the inverted letters and the unpronounceable words that had filled the page.

It was 4 a.m. when the printing of the issue was completed. A cock crew in a neighboring house when the treadle ceased, and Srinivas went on to learn the intricacies of the stitching and folding apparatus. His fingers felt stiff and unwieldy when he knelt on the floor and wrote the addresses on labels and wrapped them round the copies drying on the floor. His eyes smarted, his temples throbbed, and the sound of the treadle remained in his ears, as the copies were gathered into bundles. The trains were passing Malgudi in an hour's time. The printer had become less loquacious and even a little morose through lack of sleep. His voice was thick and tired as he said: "Even that boy has joined the strikers! Fancy! I'm afraid we shall have to help ourselves." He heaved a bundle on to his shoulder. Srinivas followed his example

94

and took up the second bundle. They put out the lights, locked the front door and started out. There was already a faint light in the eastern sky, more cocks were crowing in the neighborhood; cows and their milkmen were on the move, and the town was stirring. As they were about to turn into Market Road a figure halted before them. It was Srinivas's wife accompanied by her very sleepy youngster. "What are you doing here at this hour?" Srinivas asked. She was visibly taken aback by the sight of her husband, carrying a load on his shoulders. "What are you doing at this hour? One might mistake you for a robber!" she cried, as her son hung on to her arms, almost asleep. "I was so worried all night." "Well, go home now. I'm quite well. I'll come home and tell you all about it."

At the railway station Sampath woke up the station-master and left the bundles in his charge to be sent up with the guards of the two trains. The station-master protested, but Sampath said: "It is no pleasure for us to come here at this hour, but, sir, circumstances have forced us. Have pity on us and don't add to our troubles. You are at perfect liberty to throw these out. But please don't. You will be making hundreds of people suffer; just tell the guard to put these down at the stations marked and they will be taken charge of."

There was still a quarter of an hour for the first train to arrive, and they decided to trust the station-master and go home. The thought of bed seemed sweet to Srinivas at this moment. At the big square in Market Road, Sampath paused to say "Good night or good morning or whatever it is, sir. This is my road to New Extension and bed."

"To say that I'm grateful to you——" began Srinivas. "All that tomorrow," said the other, moving away. He cried: "Just a moment," and came back. "Oh, I forgot to show you this, Editor; I printed and put this slip into the middle page of every copy." And he handed him a green slip. Srinivas strained his aching eyes and read by the morning light: "Owing to some machine breakdown and general overhauling, *The Banner* will not be issued for some time. We beg the forgiveness of our readers till it is resumed."

"You have done this without telling me——"

"Yes, I set it up while you were busy and I didn't like to bother you with it."

"But, but——"

"There is no other way, Editor. We can't repeat our last night's performance next week or the week after that. The readers have got to know the position; isn't that so? Good night or good morning, sir." He turned and went away, and Srinivas dully watched him go, his brain too tired to think. He heaved a sigh and set his face homeward.

The following days proved dreary. Srinivas left for his office punctually as usual every day. He took his seat, went through the mail, and sat till the evening making notes regarding the future of *The Banner*. Sampath was hardly to be seen. The room below was locked up and there was no sign of him. Srinivas hardly had the heart to open his letters. He could anticipate what they would contain. He did not have a very large circle of readers; but the few that read the paper were very enthusiastic. They complained: "Dear Editor: It's a pity that you should be suspending the journal. Our weekend has become so blank without it." He felt flattered and unhappy. His brother wrote from Talapur: "I was quite taken aback to see your slip. Why've you suspended your journal indefinitely? Have you found it financially impossible? Is that likely to be the secret?" Srinivas felt indignant. Why did these people assume that a journal was bound to land itself in financial difficulties—as if that alone were the chief item? He wrote back indignantly a letter saying that financially it was all right, quite sound, and nobody need concern himself with it. He folded the letter and put it in an envelope. He put it away for posting, and went on to answer another letter and to say that *The Banner* would resume publication in a very short time; he wrote the same message to another and another. They piled up on one side of his untidy table. It was midday when he finished writing the letters. He looked at them again, one by one, as if revising, and told himself: "What eyewash and falsehood! I'm not going to post these." He tore up the letters and flung them into the wastepaper basket. His letter to his brother alone remained on the table. He went through it and was now assailed by doubts. He put it away and took out his accounts ledger. This was an aspect of the work to which he had paid the least attention. He now examined it page by page, and great uneasiness seized him. He picked up a sheet of paper and wrote on it: "Mr. Editor," addressing himself, "why are you deluding yourself? An account book cannot lie unless you are a big business-man and want to write it up for the benefit of the income-tax department. *The Banner* ledgers have no such grandeur about them. They are very plain and truthful. You have neglected the accounts completely. Your printer alone

97

must be thanked for keeping you free from all worries regarding it. He was somehow providing the paper and printing off the sheets and dispatching copies. You received the money orders and disposed of the receipts in every eccentric way—sometimes paying the legitimate bills, more often paying off your rent and domestic bills. The printer has been too decent to demand his money, and so let it accumulate, taking it only when he was paid. I've a great suspicion that all his trouble with his staff was due to *The Banner,* it being almost the major work he did, and without getting any returns for it. If it is so, Mr. Editor, your responsibility is very great in this affair. You have got to do something about it. I remain, yours truthfully, Srinivas."

He folded it and put it in an envelope, pasted the flap, and wrote on it: "To Mr. Sampath, for favor of perusal." He put the letter in his pocket and got up. He took his upper cloth from the nail on the wall, flung it over his shoulders and set out. He locked the room and went downstairs, his heart missing a beat at the sight of the bright brass lock on the front door of the press. He crossed Kabir Lane and entered the Market Road. It was midday and the sun was beating down fiercely. A few cars and buses drove along the road, stirring up the hot afternoon dust. The languor of the afternoon lay upon the place. Some of the shops in the market were closed, the owners having gone home for a nap. The fountain of the market square sparkled in the sun, rising in weak spurts; a few mongrels lay curled up at the market gate, a couple of women sat there with their baskets, a workman was sitting under a tree munching a handful of groundnuts he had bought from the women. Srinivas felt suddenly drowsy, catching the spirit of the hour himself. It was as if he were breathing in the free air of the town for the first time, for the first time opening his eyes to its atmosphere. He suddenly realized what a lot he had missed in life and for so long, cooped up in that room. "The death of a journal has compensations," he reflected. "For instance, how little did I know of life at this hour!" He toyed with the idea of going to the river for a plunge. "I had nearly forgotten the existence of the river." He hesitated, as he came before the National Stores. He would have to turn to his right here and cross into Ellaman Street if he were going to the river, but that would take him away from his destination, which was Sampath's house at New Extension. He had two miles to go along the South Road. He felt suddenly very tired and his head throbbed faintly through the glare from the bleached roads; a couple of cars and lorries passed, stirring up a vast amount of dust, which hung like mist in the air. He saw a jutka coming in his direction, the horse limping along under the weight of the carriage. He called: "Here, jutka, will you take me to Lawley Extension?" The jutkaman, who had a red dhoti around his waist and a towel tied round his head, with nothing over his brown body, was almost asleep with the bamboo whip tucked under his arm. He started up at the call of "Jutka!" and pulled the reins.

"Will you take me to Lawley Extension?" Srinivas repeated. He looked at Srinivas doubtfully. "Oh, yes, master. What will you give me?"

"Eight annas," Srinivas said without conviction. Without a word the jutkaman flicked the whip on the horse's haunch, and it moved forward. Srinivas watched it for a moment, and started walking down the South Road. The jutka driver halted his carriage, looked back and shouted: "Will you give me fourteen annas?" Srinivas stared at him for a second, scorned to give him a reply and passed on. "I would rather get burnt in the sun than have any transaction with these fellows," he muttered to himself. A little later he heard once again the voice of the jutka-man hailing him: "Sir, will you give me at least twelve annas? Do you know how horse-gram is selling now?" Srinivas shouted back: "I don't want to get into your jutka, even if you are going to carry me free," and walked resolutely on. He felt indignant. "The fellow would not even stop and haggle, but goes away and talks to me on second thoughts!" He felt surprised at his own indignation. "There must be a touch of the sun in my head, I suppose. The poor fellow wants an anna or two more and I'm behaving like a——" His thoughts were interrupted by the rattling of carriage wheels behind him; he turned and saw the jutka pulling up close at his heels. The jutka driver, an unshaven ruffian, salammed with one hand and said, rather hurt: "You uttered a very big word, master." Srinivas was taken aback. "I say, won't you leave me alone?" "No, master. I'm fifty years old and I have sat at the driver's seat ever since I can remember. You could give me the worst horse, and I could manage it."

"That's all very well, but what has that to do with me?" Srinivas asked unhappily, and tried to proceed on his way. The jutka driver would not let him go. He cried ill-temperedly: "What do you mean, sir, by going away?" Srinivas hesitated, not knowing what to do. "Why is this man pestering me?" he reflected. "The picture will be complete if my landlord also joins in the fray with petitions about his granddaughter." The jutka driver insisted: "What have you to say, master? I've never been spoken to by a single fare in all my life——" And he patted his heart dramatically. "And this will never know sleep or rest till it gets a good word from you again. You have said very harsh things about me, sir." Srinivas wondered for a moment what he should do. It was getting late for him; this man would not let him go nor take him into his vehicle. The sun was relentless. He told the jutka driver: "I'm a man of few words, and whatever I say once is final. . . ."

"Sir, sir, please have pity on a poor man. The price of grass and horse-gram have gone up inhumanly."

"I will give you ten annas."

"Master's will," said the jutkaman, dusting the seat of the carriage. Srinivas heaved himself up and climbed in, the horse trotted along, and the wheels, iron bound, clattered on the granite. The carriage had its good old fragrance—of green grass, which was spread out on the floor, covered with a gunny sack for passengers to sit upon. The smell of the grass and the jutka brought back to his mind his boyhood at Talapur. His father occasionally let him ride with him in the jutka when he went to the district court. He sat beside their driver, who let him hold the reins or flourish the whip if there were no elders about, when the carriage returned home after dropping his father at the court. Some day it was going to be made quite a stylish affair with shining brass fittings and leather seats, but it remained, as far as he could remember, grass-spread, gunny-sack covered. The driver of that carriage used to be an equally rough-looking man called Muni, very much like the man who was driving now. Srinivas wondered whether it could be the same person. It seemed so long ago— centuries ago—yet it was as if here once again was the same person, his age arrested at a particular stage. Somehow the sight of the hirsute, rough-looking driver gave him a feeling of permanence and stability in life—the sort of sensation engendered by the sight of an old banyan tree or a rock. The smell of the grass filled him with a sudden homesickness for Talapur. He decided to make use of the present lull in activities to visit his ancient home. The driver went on repeating: "The price of gram is—— Master must have mercy on a poor man like me."

At Lawley Extension the driver stopped his horse and grumbled at the prospect of having to go half a mile farther to New Extension. "I clearly heard you say Lawley Extension, master." Srinivas edged toward the foothold. "All right, then, I will get down and walk the rest of the distance." The driver became panicky. He almost dragged him back to his seat pleading: "Master has a quick temper. Don't discredit me," and whipped the horse forward. He went on to say: "If only grass sold as it used to I would carry a person of your eminence for four annas . . . as it is, I heard you distinctly say Lawley Extension. You had better tell me, sir, would anyone quote fourteen annas for New Extension? Please tell me, sir; you are a learned person, sir; please tell me yourself, sir. . . . Horse-gram——"

Sampath's house was at the fourth cross-road; he was standing at the gate of a small villa. Sampath let out a cry of welcome on seeing Srinivas and ran forward to meet him. Srinivas halted the jutka, paid him off briskly, and jumped out of the carriage. "I was not certain of your door number, though I knew the road." Broad roads and cross-roads, fields of corn stretching away toward the west, and the trunk road bounding the east, with the bungalows of Lawley Extension beyond; one seemed able to see the blue sky for the first time here. "What a lovely area!" Srinivas exclaimed.

"Yes, it looks all right, but if your business is in the town it is hell, I tell you. All your time is taken up in going to and fro."

"What a fine bungalow!" Srinivas exclaimed.

"Yes, but I live in the back-yard in an outhouse. The owner lives in this."

He led him along a sidewalk to the back-yard. On the edge of the compound there was an outhouse with a gabled front, a veranda screened with bamboo trellis, and two rooms. It was the printer's house. Srinivas felt rather disappointed at seeing him in his setting now, having always imagined that he lived in great style. The printer hurriedly cleared the veranda for his visitor; he rolled up a mat in great haste, kicked a roll of bedding out of sight, told some children playing there: "Get in! Get in!" and dragged a chair hither and thither for Srinivas and a stool for himself. Srinivas noted a small table at the further end littered with children's books and slates; a large portrait hung on the wall of a man with side whiskers, wearing a tattered felt hat, with a long pipe sticking out of a corner of his mouth. His face seemed familiar, and Srinivas was wondering where he might have met him. The printer followed his eyes and said: "Do you recognize the portrait? Look at me closely." Srinivas observed his face. "Is that your picture?"

"Yes. You don't know perhaps that side of me. But I have not always been a printer. In fact, my heart has always been in make-up, costumes, and the stage—that was in those days. Lately I have not had much time for it. But even now no amateur drama is ever put on without me in it, and what a worry it is for me to squeeze in a little hour at the rehearsal, after shutting the printing office for the day." He became reflective and morose at this thought, then abruptly sprang up and dashed inside and returned in a few minutes.

Srinivas guessed his mission indoors and said: "I'm not in need of coffee now. Why do you worry your people at home?" The printer said: "Oh! Is that so?" and addressed loudly someone inside the house: "Here! Our editor doesn't want you to be troubled for coffee; so don't bother." He turned to Srinivas and said: "Well, sir, I've conveyed your request. I hope you are satisfied." Presently Srinivas heard footsteps in the hall; someone was trying to draw the attention of the printer from behind the door. The printer looked round with a grin and said: "Eh? What do you say? I can't follow you if you are going to talk to me in those signals. Why don't you come out of hiding? Are you a *Ghosha* woman?" He giggled at the discomfiture of the other person at the door, and then got up and went over. A whispered conversation went on for a while and then the printer stepped out and said: "Well, sir, my wife is not agreeable to your proposition. She insists upon your taking coffee as well as tiffin now. She has asked me how I can disgrace our family tradition by repeating what you said about coffee." He looked at the door merrily and said: "Kamala, meet our editor." The person thus addressed took a long time in coming, and the printer urged: "What is the matter with you, behaving like an orthodox old crony of seventy-five, dodging behind doors and going into *Purdha*. Come on, come here, there is no harm in showing yourself." Srinivas murmured: "Oh, why do you trouble her?" and stepped forward in order to save the lady the trouble of coming out. "This is my wife," the printer said, and Srinivas brought his hands together and saluted her. She returned it awkwardly, blushing and fidgety. She was a frail person of about thirty-five, neither good-looking nor bad-looking, very short, and wearing a sari of faded red, full of smoke and kitchen grime. She was nervously wiping her hands with the end of her sari, and Srinivas stood before her, not knowing what to say; an awkward silence reigned. The printer said: "Very well, good woman, you may go now," and his wife turned to go in with great relief, while Srinivas resumed his seat.

In a short while a tender voice called: "*Appa, Appa,*" and the printer looked at the door and said: "Come here, darling, what do you want?" A child, a girl of about four, came through, climbed on to his knee, approached his right ear and whispered into it. "All right, bring the stuff down. Let us see how you are all going to serve this uncle," pointing at Srinivas. The child went in with a smile, and came back with a tumbler of water and set it on the stool; it was followed by another child bringing another tumbler. The second child was slightly older. She complained: "Look at Radhu; she will not let me carry anything." The printer patted their backs and said: "Hush! You must not fight. All of you try and bring one each." He turned to Srinivas and said: "Would you like to wash your hands?" Srinivas picked up the tumbler, went to the veranda steps and washed his hands, drying them on his handkerchief.

Now he found a sort of procession entering—a procession formed by four children, all daughters, ranging from nine to three, each carrying a plate or tumbler of something and setting it on a table and vying with each other in service. The small table was littered with plates. The printer dragged it into position before Srinivas and said: "Well, honor me, sir——"

"What a worry for your wife, doing all this," Srinivas said apologetically.

"She has got to do it in any case, sir. We've five children at home, and they constantly nag her—so this is no extra bother. Please don't worry yourself on that score."

After the tiffin and coffee the printer cleared the table himself and came out bearing on his arm a small child under two years, who had not till then appeared. Srinivas, by a look at the child, understood that it must be the one the artist would not draw. "Is this your last child?" he asked. "Yes, I hope it is," the printer said, and added: "I'm very fond of this fellow, being my first son. I wanted that artist to draw a picture of him. I don't know, he is somehow delaying and won't show me anything——"

"Artists are difficult to deal with. They can't do a thing unless the right time comes for it."

"I thought it would be so nice to hang up a sketch of this boy on the wall. . . ." Srinivas wondered for a brief second if he could tell him the truth, but dismissed the idea. "Well, we will have some entertainment now," he said. He called: "Radhu!" and the young child came up. He said: "Come on, darling, this uncle wants to see you dance. Call your sisters." She looked happy at the prospect of a demonstration and called immediately: "Sister. Chelli ——" and a number of other names till the four gathered. She said: "Father wants us to dance." The eldest looked shy and grumbled, at which their father said: "Come on, come on, don't be shy—fetch that harmonium." A harmonium was presently placed on his lap. He pressed its bellow and the keys. The children assembled on a mat and asked: "What shall we do, Father?" darting eager glances at their visitor. He thought it over and said: "Well, anything you like, that thing about Krishna——" He pressed a couple of keys to indicate the tune. The eldest said with a wry face: "Oh, that. We will do something else, Father."

"All right, as you please. Sing that——" He suggested another song. Another child said, "Oh, Father, we will do the Krishna one, Father."

"All right." And the printer pressed the keys of the harmonium accordingly. There were protests and counter-protests, and they stood arguing till the printer lost his temper and cried arbitrarily: "Will you do that Krishna song or not?" And that settled it. His fingers ran over the harmonium keys. Presently his voice accompanied the tune with a song—a song of God Krishna and the cow-herds: all of them at their boyish pranks, all of them the incarnation of a celestial group, engaging themselves in a divine game. The children sang and went round each other, and the words and the tune created a pasture land with cows grazing under a bright sun, the cowherds watching from a tree branch and Krishna conjuring up a new vision for them with his magic flute. It seemed to Srinivas a profound enchantment provided by the father and the daughters. And their mother watched it unobtrusively from behind the door with great pride.

Srinivas was somehow a little saddened by the per-formance; there was something pathetic in the attempt to do anything in this drab, ill-fitting background. He felt tears very nearly coming to his eyes. Two more song and dance acts followed in the same strain. Srinivas felt an oppression in his chest, and began to wish that the performance would stop; the printer pumping the harmonium on his lap, the bundles of unwashed clothes pushed into a corner, and the children themselves clad uniformly in some cheap gray skirts and shirts and looking none too bright—it all seemed too sad for words. There was another song, describing the divine dance of Shiva: the printer's voice was at its loudest, and the thin voice of the children joined in a chorus. Just at this moment someone appeared in the doorway and said: "Master says he can't sleep. Wants you to stop the music." An immediate silence fell upon the gathering. The printer looked confused for a moment and then said: "H'm— seal up your master's doors and windows if he wants to sleep—don't come here for it. I'm not selling sleep here." The servant turned and went away. Srinivas felt uncomfortable, wondering whether he were witnessing a very embarrassing scene. The printer turned to Srinivas: "My landlord! Because he has given me this house he thinks he can order us about!" He laughed as if to cover the situation. He told the children: "All right, you finish this dance, darlings." He resumed his harmonium and singing, and the children followed it once again as if nothing had happened. It went on for another fifteen minutes, and then he put away the harmonium. "Well, children, now go. Don't go and drink water now, immediately." Srinivas felt some compliment was due to them and said: "Who taught them all this?"

"Myself—I don't believe in leaving the children to professional hands."

Srinivas addressed the children generally: "You all do it wonderfully well. You must all do it again for me another

day." The children giggled and ran away, out of sight, and
the printer's wife withdrew from behind the door. The
printer put away the harmonium and sat back a little, sunk
in thought. The children's voices could be heard nearly at
the end of the street: they had all run out to play. The wife
returned to the kitchen, and the evening sun threw a shaft
of light through the bamboo trellis, checkering the opposite wall. A deep silence fell upon the company. Srinivas
took the envelope out of his pocket and gave it to the
printer, who glanced through it and said: "It's my duty to
see that *The Banner* is out again. Please wait. I will see
that the journal is set up on a lino machine and printed
off a rotary and dispatched in truck-loads every week. For
this we need a lot of money. Don't you doubt it for a
moment. I am going to make a lot of money, if it is only to
move on to the main building and get that man down here
to live as *my* tenant. And if ever I catch him playing the
harmonium here, I will—I will——" He reveled in visions
of revenge for a moment, and then said: "A friend of mine
is starting a film company and I'm joining him. Don't look
so stunned: we shall be well on our way to the rotary when
my first film is completed."

"Film? Film?" Srinivas gasped. "I never knew that you
were connected with any film——"

"I've always been interested in films. Isn't it the fifth
largest industry in our country? How can I or anyone be
indifferent to it? Come along, let us go, and see the studio."

"Which studio? Where is it?"

"Beyond the river. They have taken five acres on lease."

His fur cap and scarf and a coat hanging on a peg were in
a moment transferred on to his person. They started out.

Sampath stopped a bus on the trunk road. The bus conductor appeared very deferential at the sight of him and found places for him and Srinivas. As the bus moved, Sampath asked the conductor: "What sort of collection have you had today?"

"Very good, sir," he said, leaning forward.

"Tell your master that I traveled in his bus today."

"Yes, sir." Sampath turned to Srinivas and said: "This is almost our own service, you know."

"You have printed for them?" Srinivas asked.

"Tons of stuff—every form in their office."

"What will they do now?"

"They will wait till my rotary is ready."

"Why, sir?" the conductor asked, "Is your press not working now?"

"Old machines: they are worn out," he said easily.

The bus stopped at the stand beyond Market Square. They got down. Sampath waved his arm. An old Chevrolet came up, with its engine roaring above the road traffic and its exhaust throwing off a smoke-screen. They took their seats. The driver asked: "Studio, sir?" The car turned down Ellaman Street. ground along uneven sandy roads, and then forded the river at Nallapa's mango grove. People were relaxing on the sands, children played about, the evening sun threw slanting rays on the water. A few bullock wagons and villagers were crowding at the crossing; the bulb-horn of the taxi rasped out angrily, the driver swore at the pedestrians till they scattered, and then the wheels of the taxi splashed up the water and drenched them. Srinivas peeped out and wished that his friend would put him down there and go forward. He was seized with a longing to sit down on the edge of the river, dip his feet in it, and listen to its rumble in the fading evening light. But the Chevrolet carried him relentlessly on till, half a mile off, it reached a gateway made of two coconut tree-trunks, across which hung the sign "Sunrise Pictures." They got out of the car. Sampath swept his arms in a circle and said: "All this is ours." He indicated a vast expanse of space enclosed with a fencing of brambles. Groups of people were working here and there; sheets of corrugated iron lay on a pile; some hammering was going on.

They moved through the lot and reached a brick hutment with a thatched roof. A man emerged from it. He let out a cry of joy on seeing Sampath: "I was not sure if you were coming at all." The orange rays of the setting sun from beyond the bramble fencing touched him and transfigured for a second even that rotund, elderly man, in whose ears sparkled two big diamonds, and whose cheeks came down in slight folds. He was bald and practically without eyebrows, and his spectacle frames gleamed on his brow.

"This is our editor," began Sampath, and Srinivas added: "I've met him before at your press. Is he not Mr. Somu—the district board president?"

"Yes; I relinquished my office six months ago. It is too hard a life for a conscientious man."

"How is that bridge over Sarayu?" asked Srinivas.

"Oh, that!" The other shook his head gloomily. "Somehow the function never came off." Srinivas looked at the printer questioningly. The printer read his thought at once and hastened to correct it: "Not due to me. I printed his speech and delivered the copies in time."

"Oh, what a waste the whole thing proved to be! I must somehow clear off all that printed stuff; gathering too much dust in a corner of the house," said Mr. Somu and added: "Why keep standing here? Come in, come in." He took them in. They sat round a table on iron chairs. Sampath said by way of an opening: "The editor wanted to see the studio."

"I never knew that there was a studio here," added Srinivas.

"There is no encouragement for the arts in our country, Mr. Editor. Everything is an uphill task in our land. Do you know with what difficulty I acquired these five acres? It was possible only because I was on the district board. I've always wanted to serve Art and provide our people with healthy and wholesome entertainment." And Srinivas felt that Mr. Somu could really still keep his bridge speech, which might serve, with very slight modifications, for the opening of the studio. "I'm sparing no pains to erect a first-class studio on these grounds."

"He has an expert on the task, who is charging about a thousand rupees a month."

"Come on, let us go round and see——"

They rambled over the ground, and Mr. Somu pointed out various places which were still embryonic, the make-up department, stage one and two, processing and editing, projection room and so forth.

"When do you expect to have it ready?"

"Very soon. The moment our equipment is landed at Bombay. Well, I am entirely depending upon our friend Sampath to help me through all this business, sir. I want to serve people in my own humble way."

Chapter Five

IN KABIR LANE the old stove-enameled blue board had been taken down. In its place hung the inscription "Sunrise Pictures (Registered Offices)." Over Sampath's door shone the brass inscription "Director of Productions." The director was usually to be found upstairs in Srinivas's garret. Somu was also to be found there several hours a day. Sampath had planted a few more chairs in Srinivas's office, because, as he said, it was virtually the conference room of Sunrise Pictures.

A young man in shirt sleeves, clad in white drill trousers, of unknown province or even nationality, whose visiting card bore the inscription "De Mello of Hollywood" was the brain behind the studio organization. He called himself C.E. (chief executive), and labeled all the others a variety of executives. He was paid a salary of one thousand rupees a month, and Somu had so much regard for him that he constantly chuckled to himself that he had got him cheap. Sampath, too, felt overawed by the other's technical knowledge, and left him alone, as he roamed over the five acres, from morning to night, supervising and ordering people about, clutching in one hand a green cigarette tin. In addition to raising the studio structure and creating its departments, De Mello established a new phraseology for the benefit of this community. "Conference" was one such. No two persons met, nowadays, except in a conference. No talk was possible unless it were a discussion. There were story conferences and treatment discussions, and there were costume conferences and allied discussions. Lesser persons would probably call them by simpler names, but it seemed clear that in the world of films an esoteric idiom of its own was indispensable for its dignity and development. Kabir Lane now resounded with the new jargon. They sat around Srinivas's table, and long stretches of silence ensued, as they remained stock still with their faces in their palms, gazing sadly at paperweights and pincushions. One might have thought that they were enveloped in an inescapable gloom, but if one took the trouble to clarify the situation by going three miles across the river and asking De Mello he would have explained: "The bosses are in a story conference."

And what story emerged from it? None for several days. The talk went round and round in circles and yet there was no story. A few heavy books appeared on the table from time to time. Srinivas suddenly found himself up to his ears in the affair. Sampath piloted him into it so deftly that before he knew where he was he found himself involved in its problems, and what is more, began to feel it his duty to tackle them. It took him time to realize his place in the scheme. When he did realize it his imagination caught fire. He felt that he was acquiring a novel medium of expression. Ideas were to march straight on from him in all their pristine strength, without the intervention of language: ideas, walking, talking and passing into people's minds as images like a drug entering the system through the hypodermic needle. He realized that he need not regret the absence of *The Banner*. He felt so excited by this discovery that he found himself unable to go on with the conference one afternoon. He suddenly rose in his seat, declaring: "I've got to do some calm thinking. I will go home now." He went straight home, through the blazing afternoon. At Anderson Lane he saw his wife sitting in front of Ravi's block, along with his mother and sister. A cry of surprise escaped her at the sight of him. She left their company abruptly.

"What is the matter?" she asked eagerly, following him into their house and closing the main door. He turned on her with amusement and said: "What should be the matter when a man returns to his own house?" She muttered: "Shall I make coffee for you? I have just finished mine."

"Oh, don't bother about all that; I've had coffee. Get me a pillow and mat. I'm going to rest."

"Why! Are you ill?" she asked apprehensively, and she pulled a pillow out of the rolls of bedding piled in a corner. The beds fell out of their order and unrolled on the floor untidily. She felt abashed, muttered "careless fool," and engaged herself in rolling them up and rearranging them, while Srinivas took off his upper cloth and shirt and banian and went to the bathroom. In the little bathroom a shaft of light fell through a glass tile on the copper tub under the tap and sent out a multi-colored reflection from its surface. He paused to admire it for a moment, plunged his hands into the tub, splashed cold water all over his face and shoulders. As he came out of the bathroom he hoped that his wife would have spread out the mat for him. But he found her still rolling up the beds.

"Where is my mat?" he cried. "I have no time to lose, dearest. I must sleep immediately."

"Why have you splashed all that water on yourself like an elephant at the river-edge?"

"I found my head boiling—that's why I have to do a lot of fresh thinking now." He paused before the mirror to wipe his head with a towel and comb back his hair. After that he turned hopefully, but still found her busy with the beds. He cried impatiently: "Oh, leave that alone and give me a mat." She shot him a swift look and said: "The mat is there. If you can't wait till I put all this back . . . I hate the sight of untidy beds." She went on with her work. Srinivas picked up a mat and spread it in a corner, snatched a pillow and lay down reflecting: "How near a catastrophe I have been." He looked on his wife's face, which was slightly flushed with anger. He felt he had come perilously near ruining the day. He knew her nature. She could put up with a great deal, except imperiousness or an authoritarian tone in others. When she was young a music master, who once tried to be severe with her for some reason, found that he had lost a pupil forever. She just flung away her music note-book, sprang out of the room and bade farewell to music. Everybody at her house respected her sensitiveness, and even Srinivas's mother was very cautious in talking to her. Srinivas had, on the whole, a fairly even life with her, without much friction, but the one or two minor occasions when he had seemed to give her orders turned out to be memorable occasions. His domestic life seemed to have nearly come to an end each time, and it needed a lot of readjustment on his part later. He respected her sensitiveness. He told himself now: "Well, I shot the shaft which has hurt her and brought all that blood to her face." He rebuked himself for the slightly authoritative tone he had adopted in demanding the mat. "It's the original violence which has started a cycle—violence which goes on in undying waves once started, either in retaliation or as an original starting-ground—the despair of Gandhi ——" He suddenly saw Gandhi's plea for non-violence with a new significance, as one of the paths of attaining harmony in life: non-violence in all matters, little or big, personal or national, it seemed to produce an unagitated, undisturbed calm, both in a personality and in society. His wife was still at the beds. He felt it his duty to make it up with her. He asked: "When does Ramu return from school?"

"At four-thirty," she replied curtly.

"Come and sit down here," he said, moving away a little to make space for her. She looked at him briefly and obeyed. Her anger left her. Her face relaxed. She sat beside him; he took her hand in his. She was transformed. She sat leaning on him. He put his arm around her and pressed his face against her black sari. A faint aroma of kitchen smoke and damp was about her. He told her softly: "I'm taking up a new work today." He explained to her and concluded: "Do you realize how much we can do now? I can write about our country's past and present. A story about Gandhiji's non-violence, our politics, all kinds of things." He chattered away about his plans.

"This seems so much better than that paper!" she exclaimed happily. "I'm sure more people will like this—that *Banner* was so dull! You will not revive it?"

"Can't say. When Sampath gets a new machine with the money he is going to make——"

"Why should you bother about it?" she asked. "Will this bring you a lot of money?"

"I don't know," he said.

"We must have a lot more money to spend," she said. "We must go and live in a better house," she pleaded.

"I don't know, I don't know," he said, looking about helplessly. "I don't know if I would care to live elsewhere.

I like this place." And he smiled weakly, realizing at once what a hopeless confusion his whole outlook was. He could not define what he wanted. They went on talking till the boy knocked on the door and cried at the top of his voice: "Mother! Mother! Why have you bolted the door?" "Oh, he has come," she cried, and ran up and opened the door. The boy burst in with a dozen inquiries. He flung his cap and books away and let out a shout of joy on seeing his father, and threw himself on him. His mother attempted to take him in and give him his milk and tiffin, but he resisted it and announced: "In our school there was a snake today——"

"Oh, really!"

"But it didn't bite the masters," he added.

"Then what else did it do?"

"I don't know," he said. "I didn't see it. A friend of mine told me about it." His mother took him by his hand and dragged him into the kitchen. Srinivas shut his eyes tight with almost a sense of duty. But his wife presently came out of the kitchen and said: "Take me out this evening. Let us go to the market."

"Oh, but——" Srinivas began. The boy became irrepressible. "Oh, don't say 'but,' Father, let us go, let us go, ask him, Mother. Don't let him say 'but,' Mother. Let us go to a cinema." His mother said: "Yes, why not? I will finish the cooking in a moment and be ready."

"All right," Srinivas said, unable to refuse this duty.

All night his head seethed with ideas and would not let him snatch even a wink. Half a dozen times he interrupted a possible coming sleep to get up, switch on the light, and jot down notes. He got up late next day and rushed to his office. He knew no peace till he was back at his untidy table. He seized his rose-colored penholder, dipped it in the inkpot, and kept dipping it there, as if excavating something out of its bed. The sheets before him filled up, and he became unconscious of the passing of time, till he heard a car stop and the shout from below: "Editor!" He concluded a sentence he had begun, and put away his pen as footsteps approached.

Somu and Sampath sat in their chairs. "We have just come from the studio—took a few test shots with the camera." Sampath pointed at Somu and said: "They have taken five hundred feet of our friend entering the studio. He makes such a fine screen personality, you know." Somu tried to blush and remarked: "It's a good camera, sir, it has cost us forty thousand."

"Forty thousand!" Srinivas exclaimed. The scales of value in this world amazed him. All calculations were in terms of thousands. "Where do they find all this money?" he wondered.

"Everything is ready," Sampath said. "Camera at forty thousand; De Mello costing a thousand rupees a month, and other executives spending ten thousand in all—all waiting; but where is the story?" Srinivas felt that he was somehow responsible for keeping the great engines of production waiting. Sampath added: "If we have a story ready——"

"We can go into production next month." Somu confessed: "I have tried to jot down a few ideas for a story. I don't know if it will look all right." He fumbled in his pocket, but Sampath, stretching out his arm, prevented the other from bringing out his paper, saying at the same time:

"Well, Editor, we rely upon you to give us something today."

Srinivas cleared his throat and said: "Here is an outline. See if you can use it." He read on. The others listened in stony silence. The hero of the story was one Ram Gopal, who had devoted his life to the abolition of the caste system and other evils of society. His ultimate ambition in life was to see his motherland freed from foreign domination. He was a disciple of Gandhi's philosophy, practicing *ahimsa* (non-violence) in thought, word and deed, and his philosophy was constantly being put to the test till in the end a dilemma occurred when through circumstances a single knife lay between him and a would-be assailant; it was within the reach of both; it was a question of killing or getting killed. . . .

Srinivas had not decided how to end his story. The other two listened in grim silence. Somu looked visibly distressed. He looked at Sampath as if for help in expressing an opinion. "It is a beautiful story, Editor. I wish I had the press so that we might print and broadcast it."

"You see," Srinivas explained. "This is the greatest message we can convey, the message of Gandhiji in terms of an experience. Don't you agree?"

"Yes," Sampath replied a little uncomfortably. Somu fidgeted in his seat. There was an uncomfortable pause, and Sampath said: "But we need something different for films."

"Do you mean to say that this cannot be done in a film?" Srinivas asked as calmly as he could. He felt slightly irritated by this cold reception, but told himself: "Take care not to be violent in discussing a story of non-violence. They are entitled to their view." Somu cleared his voice and ventured to mutter within his throat: "You see, we must have romance in the story."

"Romance!" Srinivas gasped. "What sort of romance?"

"You see we are bound to engage a leading lady who will cost us at least two thousand a month, and we have got to give her a suitable role."

Sampath said: "Of course, the type of subject you think of needs much skill and experience in making. Only Russians or Americans would be able to tackle it. I have just been glancing through a book of Pudovkin. De Mello lent me his copy. There is a great deal in it for us to learn, but it will take time. You see, our public——"

"Don't abuse the public, please," said Srinivas.

"We have got to be practical in this business . . ."

Srinivas was amazed at the speed with which they seemed to imbibe ready-made notions (including Pudovkin, whom everyone in the studio mentioned at least once a day: it was a sort of trade-mark).

"I would like to see that book myself," Srinivas said.

"Yes, I will bring it down tomorrow," Sampath said. "You will see what our difficulties are. After all, we are making a start. After we have made three or four films we shall perhaps gain confidence enough to take up a subject like yours, but now we have to move on safe ground." Somu kept up an accompanying murmur, stamping his approval on all that Sampath was saying. Srinivas saw their point, their limitations and their exigencies. He merely said: "Well, I was viewing it differently. Let us consider the question afresh." Somu sat up, his face beamed with relief. He quickly plunged his hand into his pocket and brought out a roll of paper and his spectacle case. He put his glasses on and read too quickly for

Sampath to check him: *"Krishna Leela*—the boyhood of Krishna and his friends, up to his killing of the demon *Kamsa——"* He looked up to add: "I was talking to my grand-aunt, you know how our people are a treasure-house of stories, and she mentioned these stories one by one. You see, we can do wonderful camera tricks, and Krishna will always be popular with our audience. Or if you don't like it"—he went on to the next—"the burning of Lankha by the Monkey-god Hanuman; the disrobing of Draupadi by the villainous gambler Duryodhana; the battle of Kuruk-shetra, and teaching of Bhagavad-Gita; the pricking of the vanity of Garuda—the Divine Eagle, who served as God's couch . . ." And so he continued for over twenty sub-jects, all from the epics and mythology. The grand-aunt, like all grand-aunts, was really a treasure-house, and Somu did not hesitate to draw on it to its fullest capacity.

Sampath briefly dismissed each one of them with: "This subject is not new. Already been done by others; this story has been produced three times over . . ."

"What if it has? We shall do it again," said Mr. Somu.

"The public will run away on hearing the name of the story."

"Oh, what about this then? Has this been done by anyone before? The Burning to Ashes of Kama—God of Love."

Sampath said: "No one has attempted this subject, I'm sure of it. Let us hear the story." Mr. Somu narrated the story, humming and hawing and clearing his throat. "You see, sir," he began, and looked about in a terrified way. like a man who cannot swim when he gets into water.

"Go on, go on," said Sampath encouragingly.

"You see, you know Shiva—"

"Which Shiva? The God?" said Sampath, unable to resist a piece of impishness. "Yes, we all happen to know him fairly well."

Mr. Somu was saying: "You see . . .!" He was still fumbling with "You sees!" and Srinivas felt that the time had come to succor him. He said in a quiet way: "I happen to know the story. Shiva is in a rigorous meditation, when his future bride, Parvathi, is ministering to his needs as a devotee and an absolute stranger. One day, opening his eyes, he realizes that passion is stirring within him, and looking about for the cause he sees Kama, the Lord of Love, aiming his shaft at him. At this, enraged, he opens his third eye in the forehead and reduces Kama to ashes. . . ." Srinivas's imagination was stirred as he narrated the story. He saw every part of it clearly: the God of Love with his five arrows (five senses); his bow was made of sugar cane, his bowstring was of murmuring honey-bees, and his chariot was the light summer breeze. When he attempted to try his strength on the rigorous Shiva himself, he was condemned to an invisible existence. Srinivas read a symbolic meaning in this representation of the power of love, its equipment, its limitation, and saw in the burning of Kama an act of sublimation.

"You are perfectly right, Somu!" he cried, almost reaching out his hand across the table and patting Somu on the shoulders. Somu's face beamed with satisfaction; he looked like a child rewarded with a peppermint for a piece of good behavior.

Sampath declared with great relief: "I'm glad, Editor, you like the subject. Now you will have to go on with the treatment. We will fix up other things."

"The advantage in this is," Somu put in, "there is any

amount of love in the story, and people will like it. Personally, also, I never like to read any story if it has no love in it."

Three days later the front page of most papers announced "Sunrise Pictures invite applications from attractive young men and women for acting in their forthcoming production, 'The Burning of Kama.' Apply with photographs."

Day after day Srinivas sat working on his script. He now seemed to be camping in Kailas, the ice-capped home of Lord Shiva and his followers. Srinivas could almost feel the coolness of the place and its iridescent surroundings. He saw, as in a vision, before his eyes Shiva, that mendicant-looking god, his frame ash-smeared, his loin girt with tiger hide, his trident in his hand; he was an austere god; he was the god of destruction. His dance was in the burial ground, his swaying footsteps produced a deluge. As Srinivas described it, his mind often went back to the little image of Nataraja that he had in a niche at home, before which his wife lit a small oil-lamp every day.

He was sketching out the scenes, and felt it a peculiar good fortune to have been allowed to do this work. He never bothered about anything else. His wife understood his mood and listened attentively to all that he said about it at home. She, too, knew the story, and the talk at home was all about Kama and his fate. Srinivas constantly explained the subtle underlying sense of the whole episode. His son, too, listened with great interest and boasted before his friends that his father knew all about Shiva's burning of the Love God.

At his office, sheet after sheet filled up. Srinivas read and reread the dialogues and descriptions he had written. His mind had become a veritable stage for divine beings to move and act, and he had little interest in anything else. Coffee came to him from time to time, sent up by Sampath. He now left Srinivas alone for a great part of the day so as to enable him to produce the story with the least delay, while he tackled the vast volume of correspondence that resulted from their advertisement in the papers.

Into this delicately arranged world Ravi walked one day. Srinivas's mind noted the creaking on the staircase. Srinivas put away his pen and paper and received him warmly. "Seems years since you visited us. Any progress with any picture?" he asked. Ravi shook his head. "What has happened that I should draw now?" Srinivas took out of his table-drawer the little sketch Ravi had drawn. Ravi looked at it and said: "I can make a full-length portrait in oils, the like of which no one else will have done in India. Give me another glimpse of my subject, and the picture is yours."

Srinivas said: "Like Shiva, open you third eye and burn up love, so that all its grossness and contrary elements are cleared away and only its essence remains: that is the way to attain peace, my boy. I don't know how long you are going to suffer in this manner; you have to pull yourself together."

"Oh, shut up. . . . You don't know what you are talking about. All that I'm asking is another glimpse of my subject, that is all, and nothing more, and you go on talking as if I were asking someone to go to bed with me. Before I am able to open my third eye and burn up love I am myself likely to be reduced to ashes; that is the position, sir; and you want me to draw my pictures with a firm hand!" He laughed grimly and leaned back in his chair. Srinivas looked at him in despair. "Something is seriously wrong with him," he reflected. "He won't be sane unless he paints and he can't paint unless he is sane; he can't be sane unless he finds that girl; and he cannot find that girl unless he can—— Heaven alone knows how many more 'cans' and 'ifs' are going to play havoc with his life." He looked at him despairingly. Ravi remained silent for a moment and suddenly said with tears in his voice: "I have lost my job today."

"Lost it? What do you mean?" Srinivas cried.

"It is all so hopeless," Ravi said. "It is all over . . . I don't know . . . I don't know," he sighed, thinking of all his dependents. "I think it is finished. I have three months' arrears of rent to pay and the school fees of the children, and then and then——"

"Don't worry about all that now," Srinivas said. "Don't lose heart. We will do something. Tell me, what has happened?"

"The clerical staff of our office decided to present a memorial to our general manager, asking for promotions. We were all drafting it in our office when the manager called me in urgently. You know him—that compound of beef and whisky. He had found fault in the spelling of some word in a letter he had previously dictated; some mistake in a proper name; those wonderful names of English people. 'Chumley,' it seems, must be spelt 'Cholmondeley.' Who can understand all this devilry of their language! And he thundered and banged the table and flung the letter at me and asked me to take the dictation again. At this moment the others were coming toward our room to present the memorial. They were nearly thirty, and we could hear them coming. 'What the hell is that noise?' he remarked, and went on with his dictation. Very soon we could hear them outside the door: a scurrying of feet and restless movement outside. I hoped that they would open the door and walk in in a body. We could see their feet below the half-door. We could see them moving up and down and shifting but not coming in. On the other hand, we presently saw them pressing their noses against the frosted glass pane of a window, trying to look in and see if the boss was in a good mood. It was of frosted glass, and though they could not see us we could see them on the other side.

" 'What is all this tomfoolery? What are they up to? Go and find out. Is this a peep-show?' I went out and told them: 'Why do you shuffle and hesitate? Come in and speak to him boldly.' They looked at each other nervously, and before they could decide, the boss sounded the buzzer again and called me in. 'What is it?'

" 'They have come with a representation, sir.'

" 'How many?'

" 'The entire staff, sir.'

" 'Damn!' he exclaimed under his breath. 'I can't see the whole gang here. Ask them to choose someone who can talk for them.' I went out and told them that. They looked at each other and would not choose anyone. They could not come to a decision about it. They were all for edging away and putting the responsibility on someone else. Even the man who held the memorial paper seemed ready to drop it and run away. I picked it up and went in.

" 'They want to come in a body, sir,' I said.

" 'No,' he cried. 'This is not a bloody assembly hall, is it?'

" 'This is the memorial they want to present, sir,' I said, and put it before him. He looked at it without touching it. 'All right, now leave me for a time, and go back to your seats.' He didn't call me again. This note came to me at the end of the day, when I was starting to go home." He took it out of his pocket and held it up. It was a brief typewritten message: "Your services are terminated with effect from tomorrow. One month's salary in lieu of notice will be paid to you in due course."

Srinivas went over next day to Ravi's office to see what he could do. It was a very unprepossessing building in a side street beyond the market square, with a faded board hanging over a narrow doorway: "Engladia Banking Corporation." A peon in a sort of white skirt (a relic of the East India Co. costume at Fort St. George) and a red band across his shoulder sat on a stool at the entrance. On the ground floor sat a number of typists and clerks, nosing into fat ledgers; uniformed attendants were moving about, carrying trays and file-boards. A bell kept ringing.

"Where is the manager?" asked Srinivas.

The servant pointed up the staircase. Srinivas came before a brass plate on the landing, and tapped on the half-door.

"Come in," said a heavy voice.

Srinivas saw before him a red-faced man, sitting in a

revolving chair, with a shining bald front and a mop of brown hair covering the back of his head. He nodded amiably and said: "Good morning," and pointed to a chair. Srinivas announced himself, and the other said: "I'm very pleased to see you, Mr. Srinivas. What can I do for you?"

"You can take back my friend Ravi into your service. It is not fair——"

"You are friends, are you?" the other cut in. He paused, took out his cigarette-case, and held it out. "I don't smoke, thanks," said Srinivas. The other pulled out a cigarette, stuck it in a corner of his mouth, looked reflective and said: "Yes, it is a pity he had to go, but we are retrenching our staff; those are the instructions from our controlling office at Bombay."

"He is the only one to suffer," said Srinivas. "Yes, at the moment," the other said with a grim smile.

Srinivas burst out: "You are very unfair, Mr. Shilling. You cannot sack people at short notice——"

"I'm afraid I agree with you. But the controlling office at Bombay——"

"This is all mere humbug. You know why you have dismissed my friend. Because you think he is an agitator."

"I don't know that I would care to discuss all that now. Other things apart, Mr. Srinivas, there is such a thing as being fit for a job. What can I do with a stenographer who cannot understand spelling?"

"Why the devil do you spell Chumley with a lot of idiotic letters? You cannot penalize us for that."

"You are certainly warming up," the other said, quite unruffled. "I quite agree with you. English spelling needs reforming. But till it is done, stenographers had better stay conventional. You see my point?" He raised himself in his seat slightly, held out his thick hand, saying: "If there is nothing else I can do——"

Srinivas pushed his chair back and rose, and said: "This is not the India of East India Company days, remember, when you were looked upon as a sahib, when probably your grand-uncle had an escort of five elephants whenever he stirred out. Nowadays you have to give and take at ordinary human levels, do you understand? Forget forever that God created Indians in order to provide clerks for the East India Company or their successors."

"Well, you are saying a lot——" The other left his seat and came over to him. "Mr. Srinivas, you are not helping your friend by making a scene here. I don't understand what you are driving at."

"Don't you see how you are treating the man? Can't you see the lack of elementary justice? He has a family dependent upon him, and you are nearly driving him to starvation."

"Now you must really go away, Mr. Srinivas," he said, holding open the door, "Good morning."

His self-possession was a disappointment to Srinivas. He muttered weakly: "Good morning," and passed out. He ran downstairs, past the man in skirt-like dress, out into the Market Road. He paused for a moment at the turning of Market Road to collect his thoughts. A few cyclists rang their bells at him impatiently. The sun was warm—though it was October it still looked like June. Edward Shilling was red as blotting-paper and suffocated with the heat, and yet he sat there in his shirt-sleeves, worked for his controlling office, and kept his self-possession. Turning over what he had said, Srinivas felt he had spoken wildly and aimlessly. "What is it that I've tried to say?" he asked himself. He felt that his ideas arranged themselves properly and attained perspective only when he was writing in *The Banner*. He wished he could sit down and spin out a page under the heading: "Black and White" or "East India Company" and trace Shilling's history from the foundation-stone laying of Fort St. George.

At the Kabir Lane office downstairs, Sampath was in conference with an odd assortment of people—actors, musicians and so on, who had besieged him after the advertisements in the papers. Srinivas stood in the doorway unnoticed, wondering how he was going to have a word with the other. "Will you come out for a minute?" he cried. Sampath got up and elbowed his way out. They stood at the foot of the staircase. "Ravi is done with at his office. We shall have to do something for him now." Sampath was a man of many worries now. This was just one more. He rubbed his forehead and said: "I'm interviewing some of these artists. I will come up in a moment."

Srinivas turned and went upstairs, feeling very confused and unhappy. He felt he would never be able to finish that third scene today. His mind was in a whirl of cross-currents. "I don't know how the poor fellow is going to manage things on the first of next month."

He found Ravi dozing off in a corner, with his head resting on the arm of a chair. He was snoring loudly. Srinivas looked at him for a moment, and went to his table on tiptoe. He had left a sentence unfinished. He mechanically picked up his pen and tried to continue. But his mind wouldn't move. He found that it was impossible to pursue the scenes of Kailas at a moment like this. "I had better put it away and spend my evening in some other way," he told himself. He lifted a fat dictionary (which served as paperweight), and laid the sheets of paper under it.

Ravi opened his eyes, sat up, and yawned. "Did you meet the bully?"

"Yes," Srinivas said. "He didn't seem to be much of one, though. He didn't say 'damn' or bang the table even once."

"Oh, yes, that is a privilege he has reserved for his staff, not for his visitors. He won't take me back, I suppose?"

Srinivas shook his head. "Not a chance. But don't bother; we will do something for you. It has all happened for the best," he said, not feeling very convinced of it. And Ravi at once added: "A benefit which will become known after all my people have perished and I am in the streets; the old devil will drive me out if I don't pay the rent next month."

"God has gifted you with art and he will not let you starve, if you are true to yourself." At the mention of art, Ravi's eyes blazed with anger and he almost let out a hiss. "What is the matter with you, calling me artist and all that bunkum? Go and tell it to those who are likely to feel flattered by it." He subsided into a sort of unintelligible whimper. Srinivas said nothing in reply, but merely held up the old sketch. Ravi looked at it and became somewhat quietened. He gazed at it fixedly and said: "If you think I am an artist on the strength of that——" He added: "She is the real artist and not I. A picture is produced only when she appears. A flash of her eyes can make a picture. I think she could do that even to you. If you saw her you would produce a masterpiece, I'm sure

—a grand canvas. But where is she? Everybody deceives me." He pointed downstairs. "I've even given up asking him about it. I've grown tired."

"But have you done his son's picture for him?"

"Oh, that!" He became reflective. "How can I? When I tell you I cannot draw?"

Presently Sampath came up and went to a chair. He looked tired. "I have interviewed nearly fifty persons today. Not one fit to be seen even in a crowd scene. I don't know why they keep coming like this."

Srinivas scribbled on a piece of paper: "Have you thought of anything for Ravi? If you have, don't speak it out yet." He passed it unobtrusively to Sampath. Sampath looked at it, looked at Ravi, crumpled the paper and threw it away. Srinivas suddenly got up and started to go downstairs. Sampath followed him. On seeing them rise, Ravi, too, got up. "I will be going——"

"Where?"

"I don't know," he said, and moved on to the door.

Srinivas said: "Don't go away yet; I will be back in a moment." Ravi obeyed him mutely and resumed his seat.

At the foot of the stairs Sampath told Srinivas: "I can speak to Somu and take him in the art department. He can become an art director in due course."

"Will he get enough to support him?"

"Yes, about a hundred now——"

"Oh, that's ample; twenty-five rupees more than what he got in the bank——"

"Will he accept it?" asked Sampath. "He doesn't talk to me much nowadays."

"I will make him accept it," said Srinivas. "But don't tell him that it is anything connected with the arts."

"But he will have to take his brush and start work

almost immediately, otherwise it will create difficulties for me with Somu," Sampath said.

"You just take him in somewhere, and we will settle about his future later. For the present take him into your office section. Just for our sakes, please——"

"Yes, I will see what I can do. But it is going to be rather difficult with Somu——"

Srinivas went upstairs and took his seat. He felt there was no use leaving the choice in any matter to Ravi. He assumed a peremptory tone and said: "I've a job at a hundred rupees for you."

"Where? Where?"

"You are good at accounts, aren't you? All you will have to do is to keep the debits and credits in good shape, and they will give you a hundred rupees——"

"Yes, gladly, provided you don't expect me to draw any pictures."

"Not at all. How can we? You have told us of your limitations." Ravi's face shone with relief. He said: "I won't even mind if there is a bully there who will worry me to death."

Sampath dropped in at Srinivas's house one morning. Srinivas cried from bed: "What a rare visit! So early in the day!"

"Just left home early, and I thought I might as well drop in——"

Srinivas hurriedly rolled up his bed. He spread out a mat for Sampath and said: "I will be back in a minute." Before going he called to his son, who was still sleeping.

Ramu opened his eyes and stared at Sampath, at his fur cap and the scarf. "Who are you?"

Sampath grinned and answered: "Uncle Sampath. Have you forgotten me?"

He took off his cap and scarf and lifted the little fellow out of his bed and said: "Now, do you see?" The child rubbed his eyes wide and said: "Oh, you! Oh, you print father's paper."

"Oh, that was in another age," Sampath said, looking wistfully at him. "Won't you give me one type?" Ramu pleaded. "Why one? You can have the entire lot, when I can get at them myself. Anyway, why do you want types?"

"I want to print my name very urgently on my books."

"Oh! What a pity!" Sampath burst into a laugh. "I am never able to face my customers with a straight reply. It's the same story for everyone!" He laughed heartily. Ramu was puzzled. "Why do you laugh?" he asked.

"Yes, you will get your name-slip from a Lino——"

"When?" asked the boy. Sampath scratched his chin thoughtfully, and said: "As soon as possible. Ask your father. It all depends upon him. As soon as we have Shiva and Kama set up before the camera."

"Why before a camera?" the boy asked, rather puzzled.

"We are making a cinema-picture, don't you know?" Sampath asked.

"Yes, will you take me there?"

"Certainly; I will bring a car and take you there some day, provided you read your lessons well. How do you do in your class-work?"

"There is a boy in our class called Sambu who always stands first in all subjects. He is my friend." He added reflectively: "Do you know there was a snake in our school one day, but it did not bite any of the masters?"

"Did it bite any of the boys?" asked Sampath.

"Oh, no," he replied, shaking his head and smiling indulgently. "Boys are not allowed to go near it."

"Oh, that's the rule in your school, is it?" asked Sampath.

"Yes," Ramu replied.

Srinivas returned, bearing a plate of tiffin and a tumbler of coffee, and set them down before Sampath.

"You have put yourself to a lot of trouble," muttered Sampath.

"Oh, stop all that formal courtesy," Srinivas said.

"All right, sir, I'm hungry and the stuff seems to be of rare quality." Ramu watched him for a moment, uttered some comment, and tried to resume his sleep. His father said: "Now, little man, don't try to sleep again. Get up and get ready for your school. It's seven-thirty." At the mention of seven-thirty Ramu sprang up with a cry of "Oh! My teacher will skin me if I am late," and ran out.

When they were left alone Sampath said: "I came here in order to talk to you undisturbed."

"Wait a minute then," Srinivas said, picked up the empty tumbler and plates and carried them away, and returned, closing the middle door.

"Oh, so much precaution is not necessary. It is only about our Somu. I wanted to say something. I don't like to be under any obligation to him. I can't go on at the present rate——"

"What has happened?"

"Nothing definitely, but the trouble is always there. He is the proprietor of the studio, and he is prepared to give us the best service the studio can give."

"Well, it is all right for everybody concerned, isn't it?"

"Please wait till I finish my sentence. Provided he is taken as a studio partner and nothing more; that is, not as the producer and investor. He has been grumbling about it for some days now."

"Why, he seemed quite enthusiastic about it . . ."

"That he is still, but it seems to me that he wants me also to invest. His partnership will take the form of studio service; that is all; for the rest we will have to find the money ourselves."

"Why is he backing out now?"

"It is not backing out——"

"If he is not backing out, what else is he doing, and why are you worried about it?"

Srinivas found this entire financial transaction mystifying; he was trying hard to follow the threads of the problem. Sampath talked for over an hour, and Srinivas gathered from his speech that he needed money for putting the picture into production. "But you must already be spending a great deal."

"But that's all studio account," said Sampath, and once again Srinivas found his understanding floundering. It seemed to him somewhat like relativity—giving brief flashes of clarity which prove only illusory. Now he definitely gave up any attempt at understanding the problem. Srinivas asked point-blank: "So, what? What's to be done now?"

"I must find fifty thousand rupees if I have to produce the picture. This will enable me to go through the picture with a free and independent mind, and when it is done, or rather, even when we are half-way through it, we can realize the entire amount and more by selling the territorial rights for distributors."

Srinivas was pleased to hear this note of hope. Sampath continued: "I've found one or two people who are prepared to join me. I just want another person who will give ten thousand, and that will complete the sum."

"Oh, you know my position," Srinivas said apprehensively.

"Oh, no," Sampath said. "I wouldn't dream of bothering you about it. I'm told that your landlord has a lot of money. Can't you speak to him and persuade him to invest?"

"My landlord! Oh!" Srinivas burst out laughing. He checked himself presently, and quietly said: "He is a great miser. He won't spend even ten rupees on himself."

"That's true. But he will get about twelve and a half per cent assured."

"I don't know if anybody has succeeded in getting any money out of him. He won't spend anything on another water-pipe for us."

"Can't you try?"

"Oh, I have never spoken to him about money. He always calls himself very poor. All the mention he has made of money with me is some five thousand which he's reserved for his granddaughter's marriage; and that, too, he mentioned to me, because he wanted me to recommend her to Ravi." He explained the old man's persistent pursuit of Ravi.

"You won't mind if I meet the old man and talk to him?" asked Sampath.

"Not at all—why should I? But don't say that I sent you there."

When Srinivas passed that way Ravi's aged father, who was blind, somehow sensed him and called to him. It was a most painful experience for Srinivas to go into their house. The single room, crowded with Ravi's younger brothers and sisters, the smoke from the kitchen hanging over the whole place like December mist, the impossible heaping of boxes and bedding and clothes . . . The old man stretched out his hand to feel the hand of Srinivas, fumbled and asked almost in a cry: "What, what did my son do at that office?"

"Nothing; they merely retrenched," replied Srinivas.

"Are you sure? If he has done anything to merit punishment he is not my son." He drew himself up proudly. "Our family has gone on without a blemish on its members for seven generations, do you know?" he asked. "Whatever happens to us we want to preserve a good name in society." The old man went on talking; the ragged children stood around and gaped. Ravi's mother came in and said: "Can't you do something for the boy? He goes out somewhere and returns late every day."

"You get in," thundered the old man. "Get in and mind your business. I don't want you to trouble this gentleman with all your idiotic words."

"It is no trouble," said Srinivas. The lady said: "Oh, you are standing." She told one of the boys: "He is standing, give him a mat."

"I won't bring the mat," said the boy sullenly, and pointed to another and said: "Let him do it. Why should I alone do everything?" The other fellow pounced upon him for making this suggestion. This quarrel came to a stop when the old man thundered at his wife: "Why can't you leave the children alone—always nagging and worrying them?" The lady quietly spread out a mat on the floor and said: "Be seated, please."

"Yes, yes, pray don't keep standing," added the old man. And then: "Yes—— I was saying something, what was it?"

"Family honor," Srinivas felt like saying, but suppressed the impulse and said: "Don't you worry about your son. I will see him fixed up satisfactorily in a new place." He felt consolation was due to the old man.

"What office?" the old man asked.

"Connected with film production——"

"What film production?"

"They have recently started a studio——" and he went on to explain its nature and scope. The old man said emphatically: "That will never do. I wouldn't like my son to work in a place like that, among play-boys and dancing girls. I won't have him go there."

"He is not acting," said Srinivas.

"If he is not, what business has he there?" asked the old man. The lady fidgeted about nervously, fearing what the old man might say at any moment. Srinivas said: "He is not acting—he is going to do quite a respectable piece of work."

"What is that?"

"He is going to be given a start of a hundred rupees, and he may rise very fast."

"I don't care if he is going to earn ten thousand; it is of no consequence to me; tell me what he will have to do to earn his salary." And then Srinivas had to blurt out: "He is an artist—probably will prove to be the greatest artist of the century some day."

"Art! Art!" the old man mimicked offensively. "What does he know of art?"

"Please don't be offended with him," begged the lady. "He doesn't mean to offend you."

"You go in and do your cooking and don't come and interfere with us here," the old man ordered. The lady quietly went in, sighing a little as she went. The children trooped behind her with war cries. Srinivas felt like counting their numbers, but refrained from doing so, since he felt that it might fill him with infinite rage against the old man. The old man said: "Do you know what difficulty I had in finding him a job in the bank? I went from door to door, and how lightly he has thrown it up! And now he wants to pursue art, is that it? What does he know of art? Where has he studied it?"

"He is born with it," Srinivas said.

"Don't put notions into his head, please," the old man said. "I would like him to keep up the family honor and not do anything that may bring it discredit in any way. We have lived without dishonor for seven generations and now this fellow wants to associate with dancing girls and that sort of gang. He will be spoilt. He can't go there, that is certain. Let him beg and cringe and get back to his old office——"

"I saw the manager. It's no use," said Srinivas.

The old man shook his head. "Then he had better try and do something else. For a man with his wits about him, there must be dozens of ways of making a living without becoming a performing monkey."

Srinivas rose to go. He was afraid to open his lips and say anything. Everything connected with Ravi seemed to get into such complications that he wondered how he was going to survive at all.

"Can't you stay a few minutes more?" implored the

old man. "I have nothing to offer you in this bare house. There was a time when in our old house we had fifty guests, and all of them were treated royally. It was a mistake to have left our old house in the village, and it was not my mistake exactly, but my father's. He always—— All right, why should I think of all that now? I was saying—what was I saying before?"

Srinivas was in no mood to help him out of the constant difficulty into which he seemed to be getting. He merely said: "I have got to be going now." He did not wait for further permission from the old man.

When he had gone a few yards from the house, a little girl came up behind and stopped him. She was one of Ravi's numerous sisters. "Mother wants to know if you can give us a loan of ten rupees for buying rice."

"Your mother?"

"Yes, she didn't want to ask before Father, and so sent me on to see you. We have had no rice for two days and we have been trying to eat something else." Srinivas opened his purse and put ten rupees into her hands. "Give it to your mother and tell her not to bother returning it yet . . . and tell her that Ravi will soon be earning enough to keep you all free from worry."

At his office he found Ravi, sitting up as usual in a semi-doze. Srinivas hung his upper cloth on the nail, came to his seat, and said: "Ravi, I had an interesting talk with your father; this is the first time I've met him, you know: an interesting man."

"What did he say?" Ravi asked anxiously. "Did he speak about me?"

"Of course; he is bound to talk about you. Well, I assured him that things will be all right. All that doesn't arise now, since you are well on your way to a new job. . . ." It seemed to be a delicate negotiation, steering him into a job. He had to be put in without much ado, without his own knowledge, so to speak.

"You can go and start duties tomorrow at the office of Sunrise Pictures down below." He added for the sake of safety: "They need someone with experience in accounts. Sampath will help you to pick up the work." Ravi seemed to hear the news without showing any enthusiasm. On the first day when it was mentioned he had seemed so enthusiastic. Today, somehow, his mood had changed. He looked dully at Srinivas and asked: "Why should I work and earn? For whom? For whose benefit? Why can I not be allowed to perish as I am?" Srinivas found that a little peremptoriness always helped him with Ravi. He said: "We can decide all that later. You are free today; probably from tomorrow you will be very busy. Why don't you hear me read out the story to you?" Ravi sat up attentively. Srinivas picked up his manuscript sheets and started reading from the first scene.

Evidence of Sampath's handiwork came to light. The old landlord dropped in quite early one morning and said: "Tell your wife not to trouble to give me coffee or anything every time I come. I have come now on business. I can't catch you unless I come so early." Srinivas called up his wife to bring a tumbler of coffee for the old man. When the coffee arrived the old man's eyes shone with joy. "You are going to force it on me?"

"Yes," said Srinivas, "why not?"

"You forgot, sir, that I am a very old man and a *Sanyasi*, at that; I should never indulge in all this, though I'm inclined that way. It is not good for my soul."

"This is not alcohol, after all—only coffee," said Srinivas.

The old man said: "What if it were alcohol? Does a man's salvation depend upon what he drinks? No, no—it depends upon . . ." He became reflective and paused as if wondering what it really depended on. Srinivas could not resist asking: "On what does it really depend?"

The old man looked very puzzled and said, with his fingers fondly curling round the coffee tumbler: "Shall I drink this off before it gets cold?" He lifted the tumbler, tilted back his head and gulped it off. Srinivas asked: "You would like a piece of arecanut, I am sure, after this?"

"Arecanut? Arecanut, at my age? Oh! But how good of you to think of my needs. Who can ever forget the lovely scented nuts that your wife provides her guests?" He reveled in visions of this supreme luxury. Srinivas got up and put a little bottle containing them in his hands. He looked at it fondly and put it away with a sigh. "A man should not succumb to more than one temptation." He raised his voice in a song and quoted an Upanishad which said: "Food is *Brahman* . . ." A few children came up from Ravi's house and stood in the doorway and watched him with interest. He glared at them and said: "That is what I hate about children—their habit of hanging about and staring at people. After this I'm not going to give my house to anyone who has children. They are a nuisance."

"We have all been children," Srinivas said.

"Yes, yes," the old man agreed. "But what of it? We

146

don't remain children. Leave that vexed question aside. I want to tell you a happy piece of news." He lowered his voice and said: "It seems that that boy is going to get a hundred rupees a month. I always knew that he would rise."

"Who told you?" asked Srinivas.

"Ah, nobody can conceal such things from me. I know everything that goes on in the town," said the old man rather boastfully. Srinivas thought of Ravi with pity once again. This was another unwanted element in his already complicated life. The fates seemed to have chosen him for their greatest experiment in messing things up. Srinivas asked the old man: "Has Sampath seen you?"

"He is a good man," the old man said. "I had not the pleasure of seeing him before. But he came to my humble room and sat there one day. I liked him at first sight. It is always my habit. Nobody can deceive me. I know when I meet a good fellow, and I know when I meet a bad one. Association is an important thing. Otherwise, why should I ever come in search of you and talk to you, though I have not spoken to anyone in all my life, especially if they are my tenants?"

"What did Sampath say?" asked Srinivas.

"Nothing. He showed a desire to learn a few things in Bhagavad-Gita and Upanishads. Somebody seems to have told him that I have perused these things, and he wanted to clear some doubts."

"Oh!" exclaimed Srinivas, picturing Sampath, racked with metaphysical doubts.

"Why do you cry out in such surprise? There are some young men like him even in these days who have spiritual interests. How can we say 'No' to them? He said he

147

would come to me two or three days in a week, whenever he found time. Do you know, he asked what fee he should pay me? I grew very angry with him and told him 'I'm not here to sell my knowledge as a market commodity.' But he said: 'Very well, master. But any piece of learning accepted becomes worthless, ineffectual, unless a man has given a *Guru Dakshina* (master's fee).' What a reasonable argument! Yes, there is that verse." The old man quoted another scripture to prove that learning which has not been properly paid for is like water held in a vessel without a bottom. Srinivas reflected that here was Sampath unfolding yet another surprise. The old man lowered his voice and said: "Do you know, he has agreed to fix up the marriage of my granddaughter with your friend, though you forgot this old man's appeal?"

"I have not forgotten," replied Srinivas. "But——"

"It seems Ravi is working under him and will listen to what he says. I knew that that girl was fortunate and would not get any husband less than one getting a hundred rupees a month. You will keep all this to yourself?" begged the old man, starting to go. "I came here expressly to give you this piece of good news. You are my only well-wisher. Who else is there to feel happy about the good things that happen to me? You make me think less and less of those blighted sons and daughters of mine, those vultures."

Ravi was very rarely to be seen nowadays. He sat making entries in ledgers in the office below. Sampath had managed to put him into the accounts section, transferring his accountant to the art section of the studio. "That's how I have been able to manage this affair with Somu," he confessed to Srinivas.

"But the other man, what can he do in the art department?" asked Srinivas in genuine doubt.

"He will have to do something, otherwise he will lose his job. Do you know, under such a pressure, anybody will turn his hand to anything; that's how I find that most of our actors, musicians, and technicians are produced. You watch; in a short time that fellow will refuse to come back to accounts, because he will have bloomed into an artist, just when Ravi is prepared to do art work. And then I will be faced with a further complication with Somu. Do you know, I'm facing peculiar difficulties with Somu nowadays?"

At this moment Somu himself arrived in a big car. As soon as he entered, he said: "It's so difficult to approach this place, Sampath. We must very soon look out for a good building on the main road itself."

"How is the story progressing, sir?" he asked, turning to Srinivas. Srinivas tried to recapitulate to himself Sampath's account of Somu's partnership complications, and wondered in what way his present question was connected with that report. He found himself getting into a maze once again, and gave up the attempt. He merely replied: "All the scenes will be ready very soon."

"Ah! Ah! That's very good news. We must fix up an auspicious day for cranking. I want to invite our district judge to switch on." Seeing that Srinivas received the suggestion without enthusiasm, he hastened to add: "Of course, you must allow us business people to do things in our own way."

"What's the point in asking the judge to do it?"

Somu turned to Sampath, and said with a very significant wink: "Tell him some time." Sampath rose to the occasion and said: "You will know soon. All this has its own value."

Srinivas turned to go upstairs, back to his work. He had been spending a considerable amount of time at the foot of the staircase with Sampath. They had to do all the talking here because inside Sampath's office, in an ante-chamber, Ravi worked, and they had to talk of certain matters without his knowledge. Srinivas now felt that the time had come for him to beat a retreat, since the foot of the staircase was threatening to become a conference room. Somu stopped him and said: "We must have another story conference shortly to see how far we have progressed."

"You can go ahead with your other plans. I will tell you when it is all ready."

"One thing, mister, I want you to remember. You must not fail to introduce a comic interlude." A slight frown came on Srinivas's face. "I don't see how any comic interlude can be put into this."

"Please try. It would make the picture very popular. People would come again and again to laugh. Personally, do you know, I always like something that makes me laugh."

The old landlord waited for Srinivas at the road-bend, explaining: "I could have come to your house and caught you, but didn't. You are sure to press on me your hospitality, and what will people say? 'This old fellow goes there to snatch a free cup of coffee.' No, sir, I don't want that reputation. I have always had honorable dealings with all my tenants."

"Except in the matter of water-taps."

"Oh! You always have a word about that. All right. I will add a new tap—not one, several—one for each block. Are you satisfied?"

"When?"

"When? Oh! You cross-examine me like a lawyer, sir; that's why people always say 'Beware of people who write!' "

"You have not answered my question," Srinivas said.

"You are very difficult to satisfy," he replied, as if paying a compliment. "If it were any other landlord he would have become distracted—well, I'm not here to talk about all that now. I've an important matter on which to consult you. You are going to your office. Shall I walk along with you?"

"Oh, you will feel bored and tired, coming back all alone," said Srinivas, trying to put him off.

"That shows you don't know me," said the old man. "There is no loneliness for a *Sanyasi* like me. If I keep repeating 'Om,' I have the best companion on a lonely way. Don't you know this *sloka*:

'Wherever my mind, there be your form; wherever my head there be your feet'?"

Srinivas slowed down his pace, and the old man followed him. After several more questions he said: "What do you think of Sampath's film company? What are they doing?"

Srinivas explained as well as he could its various aspects and purposes. "Do you really think it is a very profitable concern?" Srinivas could not easily answer the question. "I'm sorry, I don't know much about that." The old man stopped for a moment to hold him by the arm and say: "Ah, how careful! You don't want to give away trade secrets, is that it?" He gave the other a knowing wink. Srinivas tried not to look portentous, and said: "I will find out, if you like, from Sampath all about it." "No, no, no," the old man cried, alarmed. "Not that way. I don't want you to speak to Sampath about it. I don't want him to think I've been talking about it. He trusted me with a confidence. . . . No, no. I was just thinking that if I invested five thousand at twelve and a half per cent——"

"Why not ten thousand?"

"Why not fifty thousand?" asked the old man. "You seem to imagine I've a lot of cash!" He looked horror-stricken at the thought of someone thinking him rich. "I've only a few coppers kept for the marriage of that child. If it can be multiplied without any trouble it will mean a little more happiness for the child. Sampath is taking an interest in her, and so I thought . . ." He meandered on, and then feeling that he had spoken too much of his finances, shut up suddenly. "Well, I will get back. I thought you might be able to give me some information." He turned abruptly round, leaving Srinivas to go forward alone. Srinivas went to his office, trying to divine what exact technique Sampath was employing with the old man. An indication of it was not long in coming.

Sampath followed him upstairs to his room. "Well, Mr. Editor, I think after all I can make up the capital." Srinivas did not feel it necessary to put any question, since he was listening to something he already knew. He hooked up his upper cloth and went to his chair. Sampath looked at his wrist-watch. Recently a watch had appeared on his wrist, and he constantly looked at it. "I can manage to stay with you for a quarter of an hour more. I've asked some people from the music department to come and meet me."

Apparently he intended to become reflective for those fifteen minutes. "I'm really puzzled, nowadays, Mr. Editor. I shall be obliged if you will enlighten me. What am I in this scheme of things? On one side I interview actors, artists and musicians; I run about for Somu, doing various errands for the studio, and I have the task of our picture, its direction and so on." He swelled with importance. "Now what am I?" He looked so puzzled that Srinivas felt obliged to answer: "Who can answer that question? If you understood it, you would understand everything." He thought that perhaps Sampath's formal studies with the old man had wakened him to new problems. This idea was soon dispelled by Sampath: "Am I the producer of this picture or am I not? It was just to decide this question that I wanted capital. I think I can make up the amount; at any rate your landlord is showing an interest in the proposition." "And also clearing a lot of your philosophical doubts, I suppose?" Srinivas added. Sampath laughed heartily, "Well, sir, believe me, I do wish to know something about Self and the universe. What greater privilege can one have than studying at the feet of a great master?" He shut his eyes reverently and pressed his palms in a salute at the memory of his *Guru*. And Srinivas asked: "And how are you going to fulfil your promise to see his granddaughter married?"

"Oh, that! Well, that is really a problem; I hope"—he lowered his voice—"that our friend downstairs will help us."

"But you have already promised to find him his sweetheart," Srinivas reminded him.

"Oh, yes, yes." He looked agonized at the number of

153

the undertakings that weighed him down. An idea flashed into his mind and he looked relieved. "Probably it was this granddaughter that he used to see at the temple. Who knows? Let us have a look at that sketch, Editor." Srinivas took out the sketch. At the sight of it, with its ray of light reflected off the diamond on the ear-lobe, Srinivas was thrilled and cried out: "Oh, the boy ought to be drawing and painting and flooding the world with his pictures. This is a poorer world without them." He sighed.

"Yes, sir, I agree. Even today if he were prepared to get on to the art department, I would make a place for him there." He scrutinized the picture and shook his head despondently. "No, the landlord's granddaughter is different."

"Have you seen her?"

"Oh, yes, daily. I am coaching her in the arts. Smart girl. I wish Ravi would see sense. But"—he became reflective—"I don't know what we can do if he has set his heart on this type, though a girl in the flesh ought to be worth a dozen on paper. Can't you put some sense into him? I think he will listen to you, and it will please the old man." Srinivas said nothing in reply. Sampath remained gazing at the picture absent-mindedly, and suddenly cried: "This face looks familiar—wait a minute." He got up and ran downstairs and returned, bearing an album under his arm. He opened its leaves, placed it on the table and pointed at a snapshot of a girl pasted in it. Under it was written: "Appln. No. 345, Madras—Name Shanti." Srinivas looked at the face and then compared it with that in the sketch. "Well, it looks very much like it. Have you got her address?"

"Of course; we can call her up. Her face struck me as the

most feasible type for Parvathi." Sampath scrutinized her face very carefully now. "I will send off a telegram!" he cried. "We must give her a mike and camera test at once, and if that is O.K. I am sure she will do very well. We can make a star of her." Srinivas felt happy. "So this means Ravi's worst troubles are over. He will be so glad. Let us tell him." Sampath was hesitant. "Oh, please wait. She may be someone else or she may have some other problems; I think we'd better wait."

"Well, there doesn't seem to be any harm. All that he wants is to take a look at her; that'll ease his mind so much that we can get him to work." Sampath was very lukewarm about that proposition. He shut the album, put it under his arm and started to go. He paused in the doorway to say: "No, Mr. Editor. Please do not tell him anything yet. It's studio business; it's better that such things should not get complicated. You see, we have to move cautiously. As you know, Somu is a funny sort of man, and he may misconstrue the whole thing." He wandered on, Srinivas not comprehending much. When Somu's name cropped up, there were always hints of vast complications, and Srinivas left it all alone.

A story conference met on the day Srinivas mentioned that his writing was completed. Somu was beside himself with joy, and Sampath was stung into fresh activity. De Mello said: "Well, sir, the studio only starts its real work now." He rolled up his sleeves and lit a cigarette and gave an affectionate pat to his green cigarette tin. They sat around Srinivas's table as he began the reading. "Scene one, Kailas—mountain peaks in the background, rolling peaks, with ice gleaming in multicolor——" De Mello interrupted to say: "Oh, don't bother about all that detail; it is the business of the art department. You can just indicate the location."

"Go ahead, Mr. Srinivas," implored Somu, who looked docile and pleased. He seemed quite ready to do Srinivas's bidding at this moment; he was so awestruck by his ability to fill up a hundred-odd foolscap sheets with the story. But he was not prepared to confess his admiration in full. He said: "Writing requires a lot of patience; you must sit down and fill up page after page—a thing which we business men cannot afford to do. That is why we have to depend upon intellectuals like you, sir." He spoke as if he were presenting a casket and reading out the address printed on silk. Sampath cut him short with: "Shan't we go on with the story?" De Mello put down a cigarette stub and pressed his shoe on it. Tobacco smoke hung in the air. Srinivas read on. "Second scene, Parvathi—a young woman of great beauty, with her maids." De Mello interrupted: "How can we be sure till we fix up the actress?" Somu looked despondent. He looked pathetically at Sampath and asked: "Yes. What do you say to that?"

"In Hollywood we never approach the story till we have fixed up the chief artists."

"This is not Hollywood," Srinivas said. "So let us try to find the people who will do the part. . . ."

"But that doesn't pay, Mr. Srinivas. In films the real saleable commodity is the star-value. All other things are secondary." Sampath tried to smooth matters out with: "We will make stars, if the ready-made ones are not available." Somehow this seemed to please the other members of the conference, and Somu and De Mello said almost simultaneously: "That is a very good point, Sampath.

We've got to make stars." To Srinivas it seemed as if they were going to cling to this phrase now and forever. He shuddered to think that they might be going to repeat it like a litany: "Star! Star! We must make a star!" But he realized that the matter was proceeding on correct conference lines. It was the essence of a conference that somebody should say something, and somebody else should say something else, and a third person should throw out a catch phrase for all to pick up and wear proudly like a buttonhole. This was the approved method of a conference, and he could not object to it. And so, although he was being constantly interrupted, he curbed his own annoyance and continued his reading. He felt he was emulating a street preacher he had encountered in his younger days in his town, a man who came to propagate Christianity and lectured to a crowd, unmindful of the heckling, booing, and general discouragement. Srinivas had even seen a grass-seller throwing her burden at the preacher's head, but he went on explaining the gospels. Such a faith in one's mission was needed at this moment. Srinivas persisted: scene after scene with the description, action and dialogue followed; and this continuous drone lulled them into silence. As darkness gathered around his room and voices rose from the tenements below he became lost in his own narration; his listeners seemed to him just shadows. Even De Mello's tobacco fog rose to the cobweb-covered ceiling and paused there. Srinivas read on, inspired by his own vision, though he could not decide whether they were lost in enjoyment of his reading or were asleep. He read with difficulty in the gathering darkness, afraid to get up and switch on the light, lest that should break the spell and set them talking.

Chapter Six

THE NEXT important event was the opening ceremony. A special bus ran from the city to the studio on the other bank of the river. The bus was painted "Sunrise Pictures" along its whole body, and placards were hung out on its sides: "The Burning of Kama—Switching-on Ceremony." It slowly perambulated along the Market Road, and anyone who carried an invitation to the function could stop it and get in.

The invitation was printed on gold-sprinkled cartridge sheets, on which was stamped a map of India, represented as a mother with a bashful maiden kneeling at her feet, offering a sprig of flowers, entitled "Burning of Kama." The maiden was presumably "Sunrise Pictures."

"Is this your idea?" Srinivas asked Sampath, who worked without food and sleep for the sake of the function. Sampath was cautious in answering: "Why, is it not good?" Srinivas hesitated for a moment whether he should be candid or just not answer the question. He decided against expressing an opinion and asked: "What do others say?"

"Everybody says it is so good. Somu was in raptures when he saw it. Our boys did it, you know—something patriotic: we offer our very best to the country, or something like that."

"Your idea?" Srinivas asked. Sampath was rather reluctant to be cross-questioned, and turned the subject to the task of printing: "What a trouble it was getting this through in time! They couldn't fool me. I sat tight and got it through." Srinivas quietly gloated over this vision of Sampath harassed by printers. "I've not been home at all for three nights; I sat up at the Brown Press and handled the machine myself. How I wish I'd my own Press now!" He sighed a little. "No need to worry; we are on the way to getting our big press." He seemed distressed at the memory of printing, and Srinivas obligingly changed the subject. "How many are you inviting?"

"Over a thousand!" Sampath said, brightening. "It is going to be the biggest function our city has seen."

As the bus turned into Nallapa's Grove, far off one saw the bunting flying in the air, made up of flags of all nations, including China, Scandinavia and the Netherlands. One could pick them out by referring to Pears' Encyclopaedia. The bunting was an odd treasure belonging to the municipal council; no one could say how they had come to gather all this medley of ensigns; but they were very obliging and lent them for all functions, private and public, unstintingly. And no gathering was complete unless it was held under the arcade of these multi-colored banners: there were even a few ship's signals included among them.

The vast gathering was herded into studio number one, in which hundreds of wooden folding chairs were arrayed. The switching-on was fixed for 4:20, since at 4:30 an inauspicious period of the day was beginning. The district judge, who was to preside, was not to be seen. They fidgeted and waited for him and ran a dozen times to the gate. Sampath calmed Somu by pulling him along to the microphone and announcing: "Ladies and gentlemen, the president is held up by some unexpected work, but he will be here very soon. Meanwhile, in order not to lose the auspicious hour, the switch will be put on." He himself passed on to the camera on the tripod, and asked: "Ready?" and pressed the switch. The lights were directed on to a board fixed on an easel on which the art department had chalked up: "Sunrise Pictures proudly present their maiden effort, 'The Burning of Kama,'" and they shot a hundred feet of it. De Mello cried "Cut." He had come in a dark suit, his mustache oiled and tipped. Thus they caught the auspicious moment, although the big wicker-chair meant for the president was still vacant.

A committee of astrologers had studied the conjunction of planets and fixed the day for the inauguration ceremony. There had been a regular conference for fixing the correct moment, for as Somu explained to the others: "We cannot take risks in these matters. The planets must be beneficial to us." And he gave three rupees and a coconut, each on a plate, for the Brahmins who had given him the date. The Brahmins officiated at the ceremony now, after deciding what the ritual should be. A couple of framed portraits of Shiva and a saint, who was Somu's family protector, were leaned against the wall, smothered under flowers. The holy men sat before them with their foreheads stamped with ash and vermilion and their backs covered with handspun long wraps. They each wore a rosary around the throat, and they sat reading some sacred texts. In front of them were kept trays loaded with coconut, camphor and offerings for the gods. A few minutes before the appointed moment they rose, lit the camphor, and circled the flame before the gods, sounding a bell. Then they went to the camera and stuck a string of jasmine and a dot of sandal paste on it. De Mello trembled when he saw this. They seemed to be so reckless in dealing with the camera. He felt

163

like crying out: "It's a Mitchel, so—please . . . It cost Rs. 40,000," but he checked himself as he confessed later: "In this country, sir, one doesn't know when a religious susceptibility is likely to be hurt. A mere sneeze will take you to the stake sometimes—better be on the safe side." The priests finished with the camera and then offered him a flower, which he did not know what to do with, but vaguely pressed it to his nose and eyes, and then they gave him a pinch of vermilion and ash, which also worried him, till he saw what others did, and followed their example and rubbed it on his brow. He looked intimidated by these religious observances. It was an odd sight: De Mello in a dark suit, probably of Hollywood cut, and his forehead colored with the religious marking. "It's just as well," Srinivas remarked to himself. "They are initiating a new religion, and that camera decked with flowers is their new god, who must be propitiated." To him it seemed no different from the propitiation of the harvest god in the field. To Somu and all these people, God, at the present moment, was a being who might give them profits or ruin them with a loss; with all their immense commitments they felt they ought to be particularly careful not to displease Him. As he was a champion of this religious sect, there was nothing odd in De Mello's submissiveness before it. Srinivas wished he had his *Banner*. What an article he could write under the heading "The God in the Lens."

And these rituals were being witnessed by an audience of over five hundred with open-mouthed wonder. There was suddenly a bustle: "The president has arrived," and Somu ran out in great excitement to receive him. There was a stir in the audience, and people craned their necks to look at the president. Though they saw him every day, they never failed to see him as the president with renewed interest, and in this setting he was peculiarly interesting. In strode a strong dark man, wearing colored glasses and grinning at the assembly. "I'm sorry," he said loudly. "I was held up by court work. Is it all over?" They propelled him to his wicker chair; he pulled the invitation out of his pocket, to study the items of the program. He looked at the flower-decked camera and the Brahmins and asked: "Is this the first scene you are going to shoot?" Sampath explained to the president and apologized, garlanded him, and gave him a bouquet. "Why are they centering all their affection on him? Have they met here today to fuss about him or to get their film started?" Srinivas wondered. He was struck with the rather pointless manner in which things seemed to be moving. "Subtle irrelevancies," he told himself as he sat, unobserved on an upturned box in a corner of the studio. They presently brought the president to the microphone. He said, with the rose garland around his neck: "Ladies and gentlemen, I know nothing about films, and court work held me up and delayed the pleasure of being here earlier. I don't usually see films—except probably once a year when my little daughter or son drag me there." And he smiled in appreciation of this human touch. He rambled on thus for about an hour; and people looked as though they were subsiding in their seats. He went on to advise them how to make films. "I see all around too many mythological and ancient subjects. We must throw all of them overboard. Films must educate. You must appeal to the villager and tell him how to live, how to keep his surroundings clean; why he should not fall into money-lenders' hands, and so on. The film must not only tell a story but must also convey a message to the ignorant masses. There are problems of cultivation and soil—all these you can tackle: there is nothing that you cannot include, if only you have the mind to be of service to your fellow men. They say that the film is the quickest medium of instruction; we all like to see films; let us see ones that us tell something. You have been too long concerned with demons and gods and their prowesses. I think we had better take a vow to boycott Indian films till they take up modern themes." At this point he was gently interrupted. They had all along wished they could gag him, but it was not an easy thing to choke off a district judge, particularly when he was the president of the occasion. So Sampath and Somu popped up on either side of the judge and carried on a prolonged conversation with him in an undertone. After they withdrew, the judge said: "I'm sorry I forgot to notice"—he fumbled in his pocket and pulled out the invitation—"what story they are starting. Now my friends Somu tells me it is an epic subject. Our epics undoubtedly are a veritable storehouse of wisdom and spirituality. They contain messages which are of eternal value and applicable to all times and climes, irrespective of age, race, or sex and so on. The thing is that they must be well done. India has a lesson to teach the rest of the world. Let us show the world a sample of our ancient culture and wisdom and civilization. Blessed as this district is by a river and jungles and mountains, with these energetic captains at the helm, I've no doubt that Malgudi will soon be the envy of the rest of India and will be called the Hollywood of India." De Mello's voice could be heard corroborating the sentiment with a timely "Hear! Hear!" and resounding applause rang out. The president went to his seat, but came back to the microphone to say: "I'm sorry I forgot again. I'm asked to announce the happy news that there is going to be a dance entertainment by some talented young artists." To the accompaniment of the studio orchestra some new recruits to the studio threw their limbs about and gave a dance program with the studio lights focused on them. Afterward with the president beside the camera, and Somu and Sampath touching the switch, still photos were taken from four different angles. This was followed by a few baskets being brought in, out of which were taken paper bags stuffed with coconuts and sweets, which were distributed to all those present. Sampath went to the microphone and thanked the audience and the president for the visit.

When they were moving out, Srinivas noticed a familiar head stirring in the third row. It was his old landlord, transformed by a faded turban, a pair of glasses over his nose, and a black alpaca coat, almost green with years. Srinivas ran up to him and accosted him. He felt so surprised that he could not contain himself. "Oh, you are here!" The old man gave him his toothless smile. "First time for thirty years I have come out so far—Sampath wouldn't leave me alone. He sent me a car. Where is your artist friend? I thought he would be here."

"Ravi! He must be in the office. He doesn't usually fancy these occasions." The old man looked about for Sampath and called to him loudly. Srinivas slipped away, somehow not wishing to be present at their meeting, feeling vaguely perhaps that Sampath might try to get a check out of the old man at this opportunity.

Srinivas was busy putting the finishing touches to his script. He worked continuously, not budging from his seat from nine in the morning till nine in the evening. Even Ravi, who came in when he had a little leisure, hesitated at the door and turned back without uttering a word. Srinivas worked in a frenzy. He was very eager to complete his part of the work, though he had at the back of his mind a constant misgiving about the final treatment they might hatch out of it, but he ruthlessly pushed away this doubt, saying to himself: "It is not my concern what they do with my work."

Sampath was not to be seen for nearly a week, and then he turned up one evening, bubbling with enthusiasm. A look at him, and Srinivas decided that it would be useless to try to get on with his work. He put away his papers. Sampath began: "She has come!"

"When?"

"Five days ago, and we have been putting her through the tests. De Mello says she is the right type for the screen. She is a fine girl."

"Is she the same as——" asked Srinivas, indicating the old sketch. Sampath smiled at this suggestion. He scrutinized the sketch, remarking under his breath: "Extraordinary how two entirely unconnected people can resemble each other." He laughed heartily, as if it were the biggest joke he had heard in his life. He seemed extraordinarily tickled by it. "Yes, she is somewhat like this picture, but there is a lot of difference, you know. In fact, this is her first visit to this town. She has never been here before. She was born and bred in Madras."

"Where is she at the moment?" asked Srinivas.

"I've found her a room in Modern Lodge. I could've put her up at my house if it was necessary; after all, I find that she is related to me, a sort of cousin of mine, though we never suspected it. Anyway, our problem is solved about Parvathi. She is going to do it wonderfully well. I foresee a very great future for her. We are finalizing the rest of the cast tomorrow; after that we must go into rehearsals."

Srinivas was present at the rehearsal hall in the studio. It was a small room on the first floor, furnished with a few lounges covered with orange and black cretonne, a coir mattress spread on the floor and a large portrait of Somu decorating the wall. On the opposite wall was a chart, showing the life history of a film—starting with the story-idea and ending with the spectator in the theater. The rehearsal was announced for eleven, and Srinivas caught an early bus and was the first to arrive. He sat there all alone, looking at the portrait of Somu and at the chart. A medley of studio sounds—voices of people, hammerings, and the tuning of musical instruments—kept coming up. Through the window he could see far off Sarayu winding its way, glimmering in the sun, the leaves of trees on its bank throwing off tiny reflections of the sun, and a blue sky beyond, and further away the tower of the municipal office, which reminded him of his *Banner*. Its whole career seemed to have been dedicated to attacking the Malgudi municipality and its unvarying incompetence. He felt a nostalgia for the whirring of the wheels of a press and the cool dampness of a galley proof. "When am I going to see it back in print?" he asked himself. His whole work now seemed to him to have a meaning because, beyond all this, there was the promise of reviving *The Banner*. He had not yet spoken to Sampath about what he was to be paid for his work. He felt he could never speak about it. He found on his table on the second of every month a check for one hundred and fifty rupees, and that saw him through the month, and he was quite satisfied. How long it was to continue and how long he could expect it, or how much more, he never bothered.

His wife occasionally, waiting on him for his mood, asked him, and all that he replied was: "You get what you need for the month?"

"Yes. But——"

"Then why do you bother about anything? You may always rest assured that we will get what we need without any difficulty. You will be happy as long as you don't expect more."

"But, but——"

"There are no further points in this scheme of life," he cut her short. And that was the basis on which his career and daily life progressed. "Of course, if *The Banner* could be revived," he reflected, "I could breathe more freely. Now I don't know what I'm doing, whether I'm helping Sampath or Sampath is helping me—the whole position is vague and obscure. The clear-cut lines of life are visible only when I'm at my table and turning out *The Banner*." He had now a lot of time to reflect on *The Banner*. For one thing, he decided to rescue Ravi and get him to work for *The Banner*. "*The Banner* can justify its existence only if it saves a man like Ravi and shows the world something of his creative powers. . . ." He made a mental note of all the changes he was going to make in *The Banner*. He would print thirty-six pages of every issue; a quarter for international affairs, a half for Indian politics, and a quarter for art and culture and philosophy. This was going to help him in his search for an unknown stabilizing factor in life, for an unchanging value, a knowledge of the self, a piece of knowledge which would support as on a rock the faith of Man and his peace; a knowledge of his true identity, which would bring no depression at the coming of age, nor puzzle the mind with conundrums and antitheses. "I must have a permanent page for it," he told himself. "This single page will be the keystone of the whole paper—all its varied activities brought in and examined: it will give a perspective and provide an answer for many questions—a sort of crucible, in which the basic gold can be discovered. What shall I call the feature? The Crucible? Too obvious . . ."

It was so peaceful here and the outlook so enchanting with the heat-haze quivering over the river-sand that he lost all sense of time passing, leaning back in the cane chair, which he had dragged to the window. He presently began to wish that the others would not turn up but leave him alone to think out his plans. But it seemed to him that perverse fates were always waiting around, just to spite such a wish. He heard footsteps on the stairs and presently Sampath and the new girl made their entry.

"Meet my cousin Shanti, who is going to act Parvathi," Sampath said expansively. Srinivas rose in his seat, nodded an acknowledgment, and sat down. He saw before him a very pretty girl, of a height which you wouldn't notice either as too much or too little, a perfect figure, rosy complexion, and arched eyebrows and almond-shaped eyes—everything that should send a man, especially an artist, into hysterics. Srinivas, as he saw her, felt her enchantment growing upon him. Her feet were encased in velvet sandals, over her ankles fell the folds of her azure translucent sari, edged with gold; at her throat sparkled a tiny diamond star. She seemed to have donned her personality, part by part, with infinite care. Srinivas said to himself: "It's all nonsense to say that she does all this only to attract men. That is a self-compliment Man concocts for himself. She spends her day doing all this to herself because she can't help it, any more than the full moon can help being round and lustrous." He caught himself growing poetic, caught himself trying to look at a piece of her fair skin which showed below her close-fitting sheeny jacket. He pulled himself up. It seemed a familiar situation; he recollected that in the story Shiva himself was in a similar plight, before he discovered the god of the sugar-cane bow taking aim. He seemed to realize the significance of this mythological piece more than ever now. And he prayed: "Oh, God, open your third eye and do some burning up here also." "Mankind has not yet learned to react to beauty properly," he said to himself. Shanti, who had by now seated herself on a sofa with Sampath beside her, muttered something to Sampath. And Sampath said: "My cousin says you look thoughtful." She at once puckered her brow and blushed and threw up her hands in semi-anger, and almost beat him as she said in an undertone: "Why do you misrepresent me? I never said any such a thing." She shot scared glances at Srinivas, who found his composure shaken. He said: "Don't bother. I don't mind, even if you have said it," and at once all her confusion and indignation left her. She said with perfect calm: "I only said that we seemed to have disturbed you while you were thinking out something, and he says——" She threw a look at Sampath. Srinivas wanted to cut short this conversation and said rather brusquely: "I have waited here for two hours now. You said that rehearsals were at ten."

"Apologies, Editor," replied Sampath. "Shall I speak the truth? The real culprit is——" He merely looked at his cousin, and she at once said apologetically: "Am I responsible? I didn't know."

"Well, you have taken a little over three hours dressing up, you know," Sampath said. Srinivas noted that they seemed to have taken to each other very well. He said to the girl: "You are his cousin, I hear?"

"I didn't know that when I applied," she said.

"Have you a lot of film experience?" he asked and felt that he was uttering fatuous rubbish. Before she could answer he turned to Sampath and asked: "Have you told her the story?" And he realized that it was none of his business and that he was once again uttering a fatuity. But that fact didn't deter Sampath from building up an elaborate reply of how he had been talking to her night and day of the part she was to play, of how he was constantly impressing upon her the inner significance of the episode, and he added with warmth: "My association with you is not in vain, Editor." He constantly shot side glances to observe the effect of his speech on the lady, and Srinivas listened to him without saying a word in reply, as he told himself: "I don't seem to be able to open my mouth without uttering nonsense."

Presently more footsteps on the staircase, and half a

dozen persons entered, followed by Somu. Somu, who came in breezily, became a little awkward at seeing the beauty, and shuffled his steps, stroked his mustache, and in various ways became confused. "He will also find it difficult to speak anything but nonsense," Srinivas said to himself. The visitors spread themselves around, and Somu said, pointing at a strong paunchy man: "This is Shiva." The paunchy man nodded agreeably as if godhead were conferred on him that instant. He had a gruff voice as he said: "I have played the part of Shiva in over a hundred dramas and twenty films for the last twenty years. I act no other part because I'm a devotee of Shiva."

"You must have heard of him," Sampath added. "V.L.G. ———" Srinivas cast his mind back and made an honest attempt to recollect his name. It suddenly flashed upon him. He used to notice it on the wall of the magistrate's court at Talapur, years and years ago———"V.L.G. in . . ." some Shiva story or other. He almost cried out as he said: "Yes, yes, I remember it: rainbow-colored posters"—that color scheme used to make his flesh creep in those days; and at the recollection of it he once again shuddered. "Yes, it was in *Daksha Yagna*," Shiva said, much pleased with his own reputation. "I always do Shiva, no other part, I'm a devotee of Shiva."

"He gets into the spirit of his role," Sampath said. Shiva acknowledged it with a nod and repeated for the third time: "I do no other role. I'm a devotee of Shiva. Both in work and in leisure I want to contemplate Shiva." True to his faith his forehead was smeared with sacred ash and a line of sandal paste. Srinivas viewed him critically, remarking to himself: "His eyes are all right, but the rest, as I visualized Shiva, is not here. He certainly was without a paunch—the sort of austerity which is the main characteristic of Shiva in the story is missing. And he should not have such loose, hanging lips, all the inconvenient, ungodly paddings of middle age are here—what a pity! Some tens and thousands of persons have probably formed their notions of a god from him for a quarter of a century." As if in continuation of his reflections Sampath said: "When his name is on the poster as Shiva, the public of our country simply smash the box-office." Shiva accepted the compliment without undue modesty. He added in a gruff tone: "So many people were troubling me, and I refused them because I wanted some rest. But when I heard about the starting of this studio I said I must do a picture here," and Somu beamed on him gratefully. Srinivas felt inclined to ask more questions, so that he might clear the doubt at the back of his mind as to what special reason the actor had for conferring this favor on this particular studio; but he left the matter alone, one of the many doubts in life which could never be cleared. V.L.G. took out of his pocket a small casket, out of it he fished a piece of tobacco and put it in his mouth, and then proceeded to smear a bit of lime on the back of a betel leaf and stuffed it also into his mouth. He chewed with an air of satisfaction; and from his experience of tobacco chewers, Srinivas understood that V.L.G. was not going to talk any more, but would be grateful to be left alone to enjoy his tobacco. He seemed to settle down to it quietly and definitely. Others, too, seemed to understand the position, and they left Shiva alone and turned their attention to the man next him—a puny youth, with a big head and sunken cheeks and long hair combed back on his head. "He is going to be Kama," said Sampath. "He has been doing such roles in various films." Srinivas looked at him. He wondered if he might get up and make a scene. "I'm not going to allow the story to be done by this horrible pair." But presently another inner voice said: "If it is not this horrible pair, some other horrible pair will do it, so why bother?" And his further reflections were cut short by the lady remarking as she looked at her tiny wrist-watch: "It's four o'clock. When do we start the rehearsal?"

"As soon as we finish coffee, which is coming now," said Sampath. It was six-thirty when they finished their coffee, and then they unanimously decided to postpone the rehearsals, and got up to go away with relief and satisfaction.

Srinivas was touching up the conversation between the disembodied Kama and his wife. Kama said: "Here I am. Don't you see?" And his wife answered: "Seen or unseen, you are my lord. You are in my thought. I will beg of Shiva to make me also invisible." Srinivas pondered over the sentence: it seemed too cloying for him. "Can't I make it sound a little more natural?" But another part of his mind argued: "You are not dealing with a natural situation. The agony of a wife whose husband is made invisible can be understood only by another in a similar position. What would my wife say if she suddenly found I'd been made invisible? I must find out from her." As he was contemplating this scene, without being able to come to a decision, Sampath came in jubilantly, crying: "I've achieved a miracle." Srinivas said: "I will listen to your miracle presently. But first sit down and answer my question. Suppose you were made suddenly invisible, what would be your feelings?" Sampath thought it over and answered: "I should probably think that the clothes I wear are unnecessary." He laughed and added: "I think it would be a gain, on the whole."

"What do you think your wife would say?" Srinivas asked.

"If she were in her normal mood she would probably break down, but if she were in her ten a.m. mood she might say: 'This is another worry. How I am to manage with an unseen husband God alone knows. But please tell me where you are; don't surprise me from corners.'"

"What is that ten a.m. mood?" asked Srinivas curiously.

"Every day at ten a.m. she is in a terrible temper; just about the time when the children have to be fed and sent to school and shopping has to be done and some lapse or other on my part comes to light, and all sorts of things put her into a horrible temper at that hour, and she will be continuously grumbling and finding fault with everyone. She is always on the brink, and if I don't have my wits about me we might explode at each other damagingly."

"You must try to reduce all her irritations, poor lady!" Srinivas said, much moved by the memory of how she stood behind the door on the day he visited Sampath. He suspected that Sampath hardly went home nowadays, spending all his time in the studio and running about, completely lost in his new interests. So he pleaded with him with special fervor: "You must forgive me if I appear to be presumptuous." He lectured him on family ties and responsibilities, a corner of his mind wondering at the same time what his wife might have to say about his own habits of work; he wondered if Sampath would retaliate. But he was too good to do it. He became rather somber at the end of the lecture.

"Has anyone been complaining about me?" asked Sampath.

"Well, not yet," replied Srinivas.

Srinivas felt that he had encroached too much into personal matters and checked himself. He said: "Now tell me how this dialogue sounds." He read what he had written. Sampath listened to it intently and said: "It's very elevating. Let us try to add a song there." He then passed on to the business that had brought him. "Do you know, your landlord has, after all, agreed to finance our scheme!"

"That's the miracle, is it?" asked Srinivas.

"Isn't it?" Sampath said.

Srinivas declared warmly: "You are a great fellow. People must bow before you for your capacity." "Well, wait, wait," Sampath said grinning. "You can compliment me after I show you the first installment of cash. He is going to give it in five installments. And he wants separate notes for each. He will give me each installment, deducting his twelve and a half per cent interest in advance, but writing up the note for the full amount."

"Oh, God! You have not agreed to it?"

"I have no choice."

"And you are going to deal with his granddaughter's marriage, too?"

"Of course." Sampath lowered his voice and pointed downstairs. "I don't know why that old man has set his heart on him. He has never even spoken to him. I must get at him some time and do something." He looked worried at the thought of Ravi. "Why will he not listen to reason. That girl is bringing five thousand plus twelve and half per cent interest. I think artists should be trained up in more practical ways of thinking. Tomorrow morning we are going to a lawyer's office to write the first note and then he will hand me the money. I'm also mortgaging with him some gold and silver knick-knacks we have at home."

"Your wife's?"

"We have accumulated a variety of silver things during our marriage, you know!" he said with affected lightness. He remained moody for a moment. "That'll help me face Somu's conditions. After that I shall really be able to make a substantial deal. Our rotary is not so far out of reach, sir. I'm really grateful to you for introducing me to the old man; under him I have made tremendous progress in Sanskrit studies. Though it is so difficult to make him talk of his passbook, he readily opens his mind and soul to every spiritual inquiry. It is a pleasure to sit with him and hear him talk." He raised his voice and recited in fluent Sanskrit:

"The boy is immersed in play; the youth, in the youthful damsel; the old, in anxiety; (but) none in the Supreme Being!"

"Do you know, he gives six different interpretations for the same stanza?"

It was getting on toward evening, and Srinivas left his table to go home. There was a car waiting for Sampath downstairs. "I will drop you at home," Sampath said.

"I prefer to walk home."

Sampath got into his seat. "Boy!" he cried, sitting in his

car, and a servant came up, brightly buttoned, wearing a cap. "This is our old office boy—he has come back." The boy smiled affably, and Srinivas recognized the young printer's devil of *Banner* days, transformed by an inch more of height and a white-and-green uniform. "White and green is our studio color," Sampath said. "I've ordered even our paperweights to be made in this color." The boy stood waiting. "Boy, is Master Ravi there? Ask him if he is coming home with me." The boy ran in and returned in a moment to say: "He is not coming now, sir. He says he has work." Sampath said gloomily: "That boy Ravi, somehow he is very reserved nowadays. He is aloof and overworks. I thought I might take him out with me and speak to him on the way and do something about that old man's pet. Well, another occasion, I suppose. You see how smart that little devil is! I knew he would come back. This is only the beginning. I know that all the rest of my staff will also come back: I shall know how to deal with them. Well, good night, sir; I will go home and take the wife and children for a drive. Your advice is very potent, you know." He drove away.

In Anderson Lane, Srinivas noticed an unusual liveliness. Groups of people were passing to and fro. They stood in knots and seemed deeply concerned. But Srinivas was absorbed in his own thoughts. He didn't bother about it. The citizens of Anderson Lane had a tendency to get excited over nothing in particular almost any evening; but what struck him now was the number of persons from other streets who were moving about, and it made him pause and wonder. He found the crowd very thick in one place, in front of the house where his landlord had his room. Young boys chatted excitedly, old men, women, students and adults stood staring at the house. "What is the matter?" he asked a young fellow. Three or four young men and an adult gathered round and started talking at once. The young fellow said: "We were playing cricket in this road. Every day we play here, our team is known as Regal, and we had a match today with Champion Eleven . . ." His voice was a high-pitched shriek. But a higher-pitched shriek of another was super-imposed on it: "But we couldn't complete the match. We could play only half the match today. We won't take it as a draw." Yet another member of the team was eager to add, even before the previous sentence was finished: "The ball went through that window." And they looked at each other guiltily, twirling their little bats in their hands, and said: "The old man is dead." "Which old man?" They pointed sadly at the landlord's room. Srinivas ran in that direction. A constable was there on duty. He would let no one pass. Srinivas pushed his way through the crowd. The crowd watched him with interest. "He is his son," he heard someone remark. "No, can't be; he has no son," remarked another. "They won't let you go there," said another. Srinivas ignored them all and went on. The constable barred his way. The crowd watched the scene with interest. "Go back," the constable said. His face was lined with gloom and boredom. Srinivas did not know what to do. He said: "Look here, constable. I have got to go and see him."

"Our inspector has ordered that no one should be al-lowed to go near the body."

"Just let me. I won't take even five minutes. I wish to have a last look at him. Wouldn't you want to do the same thing in my place?" There was such earnestness in his request that the constable asked: "Are you related to him?" Srinivas thought for a minute and said: "Yes, I'm his only nephew. I live in his house. He is my uncle." And at the same time he prayed to God to forgive him the falsehood. "I can't help it at this horrible moment," he explained to God. The policeman said, his face relaxing: "In that case it is different. I always allow blood relations to go and see, whatever may happen. The inspector reprimanded me once or twice for it, but I told him 'Even a policeman is a human being, after all. Relations are relations . . .' "

Srinivas did not hear the rest of the statement. He went past him and stood in the doorway. The policeman came up, and the crowd pressed forward. The policeman said: "You should not go into that room, sir. You can stand in the doorway and watch. Don't take a long time; the inspector will be back any moment." Srinivas stood and looked in. The old man seemed to sit there in meditation, his fingers clutching the rosary. His little wicker box containing forehead-marking was open, and his familiar trunk was in its corner. Dusk had gathered and his face was not clear. The boys' ball lay there at his feet. Srinivas felt an impulse to snatch it up and return it to the boys, but he overcame it. He felt a silly question bobbing up again and again in his head: "Are you sure he is dead?" he wanted to ask everybody. He felt he had stared at the body long enough. It seemed to him hours, but the constable said: "Hardly a minute; you could have stayed there a little longer. But what can you do? People must die, old people especially." Srinivas passed out of the crowd. They looked on him as a hero. They asked eagerly, thronging behind him: "What, sir, what?" He didn't reply, but went straight home, went straight to the single tap, which was fortunately free, took off his shirt, and sat under it and then went into his house. "A great final wash-off to honor his memory," he told his wife. She told him the rest of the story. "It seems they saw him bathe at the street-tap as usual and saw him go in at about eleven in the morning. But no one saw him again." His son, who had just come in from Ravi's house, added: "We were playing against Champion Eleven, and some rascal of that team shot the ball in; they got up to the window to ask for it and called him to throw up the ball, but——" he shook his head. "I came running home when I heard he was dead. I was the first to tell Mother."

"Your ball didn't hit and kill him, I hope?" said Srinivas with serious misgivings.

"How could it, Father? We were playing the match with a tennis ball. It hits us so many times. Are we all dead?" He added ruefully: "It was their batting, and they are claiming a boundary for it. Is that right, Father?"

The greater part of the next day Srinivas had to spend at the inquest. The *Panchayatdars* (a board of five) sat around a room, examining the post-mortem report. They summoned Srinivas because he had called himself his nephew. They took a statement from him as to when he had seen the old man last, and about his outlook and antipathies and phobias. They summoned Sampath because he was often seen going there. He looked panicky, as if they were going to haul him up for murder. A statement from him was recorded as to why he visited the old man so often. He explained that he was his student and was learning Sanskrit from him. And then they set out a number of exhibits—a savings bank pass-book, a piece of paper on which were scrawled 12½ per cent, 5,000, and the name Sampath. He was asked if he had seen the pass-book before. Sampath said "No." He was asked to explain what he knew about the piece of paper containing his name and the 12½ per cent calculation. He said that he was consulted by the old man regarding some investment calculations, and possibly he had tried to work it out. The *Panchayatdars* pried further and wanted to know what the investment was. Sampath who had by now recovered something of his composure, answered: "How should I know? Occasionally my master would talk of investments generally, and work out hypothetically some figures. I don't know what he had in mind." Two more witnesses had been summoned, the owner of the house where the old man had his room, and his son-in-law. They were questioned very briefly, and then the board adjourned for a moment into another room, and came out to say: "We are satisfied that . . . died seven hours before he was seen, as the doctors think. Death is due to natural causes, old age and debility."

Chapter Seven

THE SOUND of a car moving off reached Srinivas's ears, and at the same moment he heard the cry on the stairs: "Editor! Editor! Editor!" It was such an excited cry that he ran out to the landing. He saw Ravi at the foot of the staircase. "Editor! Editor!" he cried. "Did you see?"

"What?" asked Srinivas.

"Are you free? Shall I come up?" Ravi asked. He climbed up in three bounds. Srinivas moved back to his chair and pointed the other to his usual seat. Ravi wouldn't sit down. He was too excited. He could speak neither in whispers nor in a loud voice and struggled to find a *via media* and made spluttering sounds. He came over to Srinivas's chair, gripped its arms and said: "She— she——" He couldn't finish his sentence. His face was flushed. Srinivas had never seen him so excited. He gently pushed him to a chair and said: "Calm yourself first." But Ravi was not one to be calmed. It didn't seem necessary at the moment. He said: "Give me that sketch." He held out his hand. Srinivas took it out and passed it to him. It seemed to act as a sedative, and Ravi became calmer. "I can do it now; on a big canvas, in oils, if you like." Srinivas felt, amidst the various misgivings in his mind, that this was the moment he had been waiting for all his life.

Ravi was lost in the contemplation of the sketch he had in his hand. He was going into a sort of loud reverie.

"Nobody told me she was here. I didn't know she had come to the studio. How providential! Don't you see the hand of God in it?" Srinivas asked: "Did you speak to her?"

"Yes, yes. I was in the office attending to those damned accounts. I heard footsteps and went on with my work, thinking it was just another of those damned visitors dropping in all through the day. I heard little sandals pit-patting: that itself seemed music to my ears, but as a rule I never look up. But the footsteps approached and stopped at my table. 'Accountant,' the voice called, and I looked up, and there she was. Oh, Editor, it was a stunning moment. I don't remember what she asked and what I said: I fell into a stupor, and she turned round and vanished. I thought it was an apparition, but the office boy was also there, and he says that she asked for Sampath and went away." He was rubbing his hands in sheer joy and pacing up and down. Srinivas watched him uneasily. He felt he should tell him the truth and check him a little. "Ravi, are you sure she is the same?" "What doubt is there? She gets a high light on her right cheek-bone. That is the surest mark. Even if other things are a mistake, nobody can go wrong in this. I challenge——"

"But she says this is her first visit to this town."

"She says that, does she? But I have seen her; I know her, that high light no one else can have."

"Did she recognize you?" Srinivas asked.

"How could she? She never knew me before. I used to see her every day and she might or might not have seen me. How can I be sure?"

"But you have spoken a word or two to her and you used to say she gave you a piece of coconut and so on; isn't that so?"

188

Ravi suddenly thrust out his chest and said, defying the whole world: "I said so, did I? I don't care. What do I care what she or anyone says or thinks? It is enough for me. She is there. Let her not notice me at all. It is enough if I have a glimpse of her now and then. Mr. Editor, you must help me. I will not do these accounts any more. I can't. I hate those ledgers. I want to work in the studio now—in the art department. Please speak to Sampath. Otherwise, I don't want this job at all. I will throw up everything and sit at the studio gate. That will be enough for me." He sat down, fatigued by his peroration. He added: "If you are not going to speak to Sampath, I will." He held the sketch in his hand. Srinivas gently tried to take it back. But the other would not let it go; he gazed on it solemnly, pointed at a spot and said: "You know how long ago I drew this? But you see that high light where I have put it. Go and look at her in the studio; that is her peculiarity. A human face is not a matter of mere planes and lines. It is a thing of light and shade, and that is where an individual appears. Otherwise, do you think one personality is different from another through the mere shape of nose and eyes? An individual personality is——" He was struggling to express his theories as clearly as he felt in his mind. He concluded with: "It is all no joke. High lights and shadows have more to do with us than anything else."

Srinivas undertook a trip to the studio in order to meet Sampath, who seemed to be too busy nowadays to visit his office downstairs regularly. "Mr. Sampath comes only at three," they told him. Srinivas sat down in a chair in the reception hall and waited. Girls clad in faded saris, with flowers in their hair, trying to look bright, accompanied by elderly chaperons; men, wearing hair down their napes and trying to look artistic; artists with samples of their work; story-writers with manuscripts; clerks, waiting for a chance; coolies, who hoped to be absorbed in the works section, all sorts of people seemed to be attracted to this place. De Mello had framed strict rules for admission which were so rigorous that the studio joke was that the reception hall ought to be renamed rejection hall. But hope in the human breast is not so easily quenched. And so people hung about here, without minding the weariness, trying to ingratiate themselves with the clerk and vaguely thinking that they might somehow catch the eye of the big bosses as they passed that way in their cars. The reception hall marked the boundary between two classes—aspirants and experts. But from what he had seen of those inside, Srinivas felt that there was essentially no difference between the two: the only difference was that those on the right side of the reception hall had got in a little earlier, that was all, and now they tried to make a community of themselves, and those here were the untouchables!

The afternoon wore on. The reception clerk scrutinized a leather-bound ledger, entreated a few people who went in to sign their names clearly and fully, threw a word of greeting at a passing technician, and after all this task was over, opened a crime novel and read it, lifting his eye every tenth line to see if there was anyone at the iron gate at the end of the drive.

The hooting of a car was heard, and he put away his book and said: "That's Mr. Sampath." And now there swung into the gate the old Chevrolet with Sampath at the wheel and his cousin by his side. The clerk looked very gratified and said: "Didn't I say he would be here at three o'clock? Shall I stop and tell him?" "No, let him go in, I will follow." The car went up the drive and disappeared round a bend. Srinivas got up, and the others looked at him with envy and admiration. They reminded him of the alms-takers huddled at a temple entrance, a painting he had seen years ago, or was it a European painting of mendicants at the entrance to a cathedral? He could not recollect it. He went on.

He went to the rehearsal hall. Sampath said on seeing him: "Ah, the very person I wished to meet now. I'm putting my cousin through line rehearsals and she has difficulty in following some of the interpretations." She was dazzling today, clad in a fluffy sari of rainbow colors, with flowers in her hair to match. Srinivas thought: "Surely God does not create a person like this in order to drive people mad." She smiled at him, and he felt pleased. "Oh, God, don't spare the use of your third eye," he mentally prayed. She had a fine voice as she asked: "How do you want Parvathi to say these lines?" She quoted from a scene where Parvathi is talking to her maids and confesses her love for Shiva. She says: "How shall I get at him?" and Shanti now wanted to know: "How do you want me to say it? Shall I ask it like a question or a cry of despair?" It seemed a nice point, and Srinivas felt pleased that she was paying so much attention to her role. She spoke naturally and easily, without a trace of flirting or striving for effect. Srinivas said: "It is more or less a desperate cry, and that dialogue line has to lead to that song in *Kapi Raga*. Do you follow?" She turned to Sampath triumphantly and said: "Now, what do you say? We've got it straight from the author!" She said: "All day Sampath has been trying to rehearse me in these lines, saying that they are to be asked like a question. I have been protesting against it, and we did not progress beyond ten lines today. And he wagered ten rupees, you know!" Sampath took out his purse and laid a ten-rupee note in her hand. "Here you are, sweet lady. Now that this question is settled, let us go ahead. Don't make it an excuse for stopping." She picked up the ten-rupee note, folded it and put it in her hand-bag made of a cobra hood. Srinivas observed on it the spectacle-like mark; a shiver ran through his frame unconsciously. He felt it incongruous that she should be carrying on her arm so grim an object. He asked: "Where did you get that? Is it a real cobra hood?"

"Isn't it?" she asked. "I had gone to a jungle in Malabar once on a holiday, and this thing . . ." She struggled to hide something and ended abruptly: "Yes, it was a king cobra. It was shot at once, and then a bag was made of it." She trailed off, and Srinivas did not like to pursue the matter.

Later, when she went away for some costume rehearsals, Sampath said: "My cousin married a forest officer, and they had to separate, you know, and all kinds of things, and then she became a widow. She feels somewhat uncomfortable when she thinks of all that, you know."

"Well, I didn't intend to hurt her or anything. But I was struck by her bag because it seemed such a symbolic appendage for a beautiful woman and for us men to see and learn."

"Yes, yes, quite right," Sampath said. He was more

keen on continuing his narrative. "They were in a forest camp. The cobra cornered her in her room, as she lay in a camp cot in their forest lodge and it came over the doorway, hissing and swaying its hood. She thought that her last hour had arrived, but her husband shot it through a window." Srinivas decided to turn the topic from the cobra. People might come in, and he might lose all chance of talking to Sampath alone for the rest of the day. So he at once said: "I came here to talk to you about Ravi."

"Oh! Yes, I wanted to speak to you, too. It seems he has not been coming to the office for three or four days now. What is he doing?"

Srinivas said: "He is prepared to work in the art section. Why don't you take him in? We ought to do everything in our power to give him the chance, if it will make him draw pictures. It is our responsibility."

In his habitual deference to Srinivas's opinions, Sampath did not contradict him. "If I were free as I was before, I would do it before you finished the sentence. But there are difficulties. I'm now in a place which has become an institution."

"Look here. Are you going to take him in or not? That's what I want to know."

"I will ask Somu. I don't wish to appear to be doing things over his head. After all, he is very important."

Of late, after the old landlord's death, Srinivas noted a new tone of hushed respect in Sampath's voice whenever he referred to Somu.

"All right, talk to him and tell me. I will wait."

"Now? Oh, no, Mr. Editor! Please give me a little time. I don't know what he is doing now." Srinivas looked resolute. "Don't tell me that you can't see him when you like. Surely you shouldn't tell me that." There was in his tone a note of authority which Sampath could not disobey.

"Well, my editor's wishes before anything else—that's the sign of a faithful printer, isn't it?" he said and went downstairs. When he was gone his cousin came up. "I've finished the costume business," she said. "Where is he?"

"I've sent him down on some business." This seemed to Srinivas a golden chance to get her to talk. But he dismissed the thought instantly as unworthy. He wanted at best to ask her: "I heard you were at the office yesterday," but he suppressed that idea also. He knew it would not be a very sincere question. He would ask it only with a view to getting her to talk about Ravi. But even that seemed to him utterly unworthy. He hated the idea of being diplomatic with so beautiful a creature. So he merely asked: "Do you like the part you are going to play?"

"Really?" she said. "I have got to do what is given to me, and I wish to do my best. That's why I get into such a lot of trouble with Sampath over the interpretations. I like to give the most correct one. But we've so little voice in these matters: we shall have to do blindly what the director orders." During her costume trials she seemed to have disarranged her hair and sari ever so slightly and that gave her a touch of mellowness. "What a pleasure to watch her features!" Srinivas thought. "No wonder it has played such havoc with Ravi's life." She didn't pursue the conversation further, but went to a corner and sat there quietly, looking at the sky through the window.

Sampath returned. He looked fixedly at his cousin for a

second. She remained looking out of the window. He beckoned to Srinivas to go out with him for a moment and told him, when they were on the terrace: "I've managed it."

"Thanks very much," said Srinivas. "You will see what wonderful pictures he will draw now . . ."

"Well, I hope so, sir. But I hope he will not create complexities here," he said, glancing in the direction of his cousin.

Ravi's new chief was the director of art and publicity, a large man in a green sporting shirt and shorts, who went about the studio with a pencil stuck behind his ear. He had an ostentatious establishment, a half-glass door, a servant in uniform, and a clerk at the other end of the room. He sat at a glass-topped table on which were focused blinding lights; huge albums and trial-sheets were all over the place. He wore rimless glasses with a dark tassel hanging down. He called this the control room; it was in the heart of the arts and publicity block, and all around him spread a number of rooms in which artists worked, some at their tables and some with their canvases and sheets of paper spread out on the floor.

Sampath walked in two days later, almost leading Ravi by the hand into the hall. "Well, Director of art and publicity, here I've brought you the best possible artist to help you." The director looked him benignly up and down and asked: "Where were you trained?" Ravi was struggling to find an answer when Sampath intervened and said: "Wouldn't you like to make a guess? See his work and then tell me."

"Very well," said the director and rang the bell. His servant appeared. "Three cups of coffee," he called out. Ravi muttered an apology. "No, it's my custom to drink a cup with my assistants at least on the first day," said the director. After coffee he ceremoniously held out his large palm and said: "Your room is over there, I will send you instructions." He pressed a bell again. A boy entered. "Show him room four." Ravi followed him out without a word. His docility pleased Sampath. He said: "Director, he is a good boy. . . . If I may give you a little advice . . ."

"Yes?" began the director, all attention. Sampath wondered for a moment how he could finish the sentence, and then rose to go. "Oh, nothing, you know how best to handle your boys." He went out and completed the sentence at Srinivas's office in Kabir Lane: "If you don't think it strange of me, I'd like to suggest that you give some advice to Ravi——"

"Yes, what about?" Srinivas asked, looking up.

"Well——" Sampath drawled, and Srinivas saw that he was awkward and could not say what he had in his mind. This was probably a very rare sight—Sampath unable to speak freely. "I mean, Editor, I have transferred Ravi as you desired: I want you to do me a little favor in return, that is—well, I suppose, I must say it out. You know Shanti is there. I wish he would keep out of her way as far as possible."

"He may have to see her in the course of his work."

"Oh, that doesn't matter at all. That is a different situation. I'm not referring to that, but don't let him——"

"Pursue her or talk to her, isn't that what you wish to say?" asked Srinivas with a twinkle in his eye. Sampath merely smiled, and Srinivas said: "Well, I don't think he will do anything of the kind, but I will caution him, all the same. Let us hope for the best. In any case, she is a different person. Isn't that so?"

Sampath made a gesture of despair. "Well, who can say how an artist looks at things? I've always been rather bewildered by Ravi's ways."

Srinivas waited for Ravi to come home that night. Srinivas heard him arrive in the studio van and then went over and called softly: "Ravi!" Ravi came out. "If you are not too tired, let us go out for a short stroll." "Very well," he said. A little sister clung to his arm and tried to go out with him. But he gently sent her back with a promise: "I will buy you chocolates tomorrow; go in and sleep, darling——" As they went through the silent Anderson Lane with people sleeping on pyols, talking or snoring, Srinivas wondered how he was to convey the message from Sampath. But he viewed it as a duty. He simply let Ravi follow him in silence for a while. "How do you like your work?" he asked.

"It is quite good," Ravi said. "They leave me alone, and I leave the others alone. I just do what I'm instructed to do. At ten o'clock the van is ready to take me back home, and I come back here. I'm doing a portrait. Come and see it some time, when you are in the studio."

"I'm very happy to hear it," said Srinivas. "What is the subject?"

"My only subject," Ravi said. "I've only one subject on this earth, and I'm quite satisfied if I have to do it. . . ."

"You are not asking for a sitting, are you?" Srinivas asked. In the darkness Srinivas could see Ravi shaking with laughter. "Sitting? Who wants a sitting? It's all here," he said, pointing at his forehead, "and that is enough. I'm doing a large portrait, all in oils—that's a work I'm not paid for, but I'm snatching at it whenever I'm able to find a little time. I'm experimenting with some vegetable colors also, some new coloring matter. My subject must have a tint of the early dawn for her cheeks, the light of the stars for her eyes, the tint of the summer rain-cloud for her tresses, the color of ivory for her forehead, and so on and on. I find that the usual synthetic stuff available in tubes is too heavy for my job. . . ."

Srinivas was somewhat taken aback by this frenzy. At the same time he was happy that a picture was coming. He could hardly imagine what it would turn out to be. He felt it would probably convulse the world as a master-piece, the greatest portrait of the century—to thrill human eyes all over the world. At this moment he felt that any risk they were taking in keeping Ravi there was well worth it. Any sacrifice should be faced now for the sake of this masterpiece. It struck him as a very silly, futile procedure to caution Ravi. A man who followed his in-stincts so much could not be given a detailed agenda of behavior. He decided at the moment not to convey to him Sampath's warning. They had now reached Market Road. It was deserted, with a few late shops throwing their lights on the road, and municipal road lights flickering here and there. The sky was full of stars, a cool breeze was blowing. And it appeared to Srinivas a very lovely night indeed. He felt a tremendous gratitude to Ravi for what he was doing or going to do.

Srinivas bade him good night without saying a word of what Sampath had commissioned him to say. But he decided to take the first opportunity to tell Sampath, since he hated the idea of keeping him under any misapprehension about it. The chance occurred four days later, when Sampath came to his room, ostensibly to discuss some point in the story, but really to ask about Ravi. His discussion of the story did not last even five minutes. He mentioned a few vague objections about the conclusion of some sequence, and ended by agreeing with every word Srinivas said. He then passed direct to the subject of Ravi. "You will not mind my coming back to the subject, Editor," he said. "Which subject?" asked Srinivas, bristling up. "I'm very sorry to worry you so much about it," Sampath said pleadingly. And at once Srinivas's heart melted. He felt a pity for Sampath and his clumsy fears. He looked at him. He had parted his hair in the middle and seemed to be taking a lot of care of his personal appearance. There were a few creases under his eyes. Clearly he was going through a period of anxiety at home, in the studio, about Ravi and about all kinds of things. His personality seemed to be gradually losing its luster. Srinivas wished that Sampath would once again come to him, not in the silk shirt and muslin dhoti and lace-edged upper cloth which he was flaunting now, but in a faded tweed coat with the scarf flung around his neck, and his fingers stained with the treadle grease. He looked at the other's fingers now. The nails were neatly pared and pointed, his fingers were like a surgeon's, and one or two nails seemed to be touched with the garish horrible red of a nail polish. Srinivas was alarmed to note it and asked: "What's that red on your finger?" Sampath looked at his finger with a rather scared expression and, trying to cover it up, said in an awkward jumble of words: "Oh, that cousin of mine; she must have played some joke on me when I was not noticing. She has all kinds of stuff on her table," he tried to add in a careless way. He flushed and looked so uncomfortable that Srinivas dropped the subject, and went on to talk of what was most in the other's mind: "I know you want to tell me about Ravi—well, go on."

"Have you spoken to him about what I said?" Sampath asked.

"I'm not going to," replied Srinivas, with as little emphasis as possible. "Things will be all right; don't worry."

"Listen to my difficulties, please. He is a little conspicuous nowadays. I see him almost every day at the gate; he hangs about the costume section at odd hours."

"Does it mean that he is not doing his work properly?"

"Oh, no, it wouldn't be fair to say such a thing, but he is a little noticeable here and there."

"What is wrong with that?" asked Srinivas.

Sampath took time to answer, because there seemed to be an element of challenge in this question. He said: "There is a studio rule that people should not be seen unnecessarily moving about except where they have business."

"I guarantee you that he won't go where he has no business," Srinivas said, and his reply seemed to overwhelm the other for a moment. He remained silent for a little before he said: "You see, there is this trouble. Even my cousin has noticed it. She said she is oppressed with a feeling of being shadowed all the time. She even remarked: 'Who is that boy? I find him staring at me wherever I go. The way he looks at me, I feel as if my nose were on my cheek or something like that.' "

"Let her not worry, but just look into a mirror and satisfy herself."

"But you see it affects her work if she feels that she is being stared at all the time."

"Sampath, she cannot know she is being stared at unless she also does it—the cure is in her hands. I find her a good girl; tell her not to get ideas into her head, and don't put any there yourself."

When he next paid a visit to the studio Srinivas went over to meet Ravi. He was not in his seat in room number four. He found him coming out of the works department with an abstracted air. He didn't seem to notice anything around him now. "I've been to see you," Srinivas said. He seemed to come back to himself with a start. "Oh, Editor, I'm sorry I didn't notice you here."

"I thought I might see your new picture."

"Oh, that!" He seemed hesitant. "Let me get on with it a little more. I don't like anyone to see it now." They were in the little park. "I am free for about half an hour. Care to sit down for a moment?" he asked. Srinivas followed him. They sat under a bower. De Mello had engaged a garden supervisor who was filling up the place with arcades and bowers and lawns wherever he could grow anything. Ravi sat down and said: "Something must be done about this gardening department. It is getting on my nerves. This horrible convolvulus creeper everywhere. That garden supervisor is an idiot; he has trained convolvulus up every drainpipe. His gardening sense is that of a forest tribesman."

"It looks quite pretty," Srinivas said, looking about him.

"But don't you see how inartistic the whole thing is? There is no arrangement, there is no scheme, no economy.

What can we achieve without these?" He looked so deeply moved that Srinivas accepted his statement and theories without a murmur. And Ravi went on: "Our art director is the departmental head of this gardening section, and he ought to sack the supervisor. But how can we blame him? He is not an artist. You must see the frightful composition he has devised for Parvathi—both her ornaments and settings. He probably wants her to look like a—like a —like a——" He could not find anything to compare her with, and he abandoned the sentence. He said: "He is an awful idiot. But I take my orders from him, and obey him implicitly. Let him give me the worst, the most hideous composition, and I execute it gladly without a murmur: I'm paid for that. But let them stop there!" He raised his voice as if warning the whole world. He waggled his fingers as he said: "Let them stop there. Let them not come near my own portrait: that's my own. I do it in the way I want to do it. No one shall dictate to me what I should do. If I didn't have that compensation I would go mad." Srinivas found that his mood of calm contentment of a few nights ago during the walk had altered; some dark, irresponsible mood seemed to be coming over him. But Srinivas didn't bother about it. "It's all in the artist's make-up," he told himself. Srinivas felt that it was none of his business to pass any comment at the moment. He listened in silence. Ravi said: "My portrait is come to a blind end, do you know? I'm not able to go on with it: that's why I don't wish to show you anything of it now. I'll tell you what has happened. My director called me up a couple of days ago and told me not to go about the studio unless I'd any definite business anywhere. I felt like hitting him with my fist and asking 'Why not?' But I bowed my head and said

'Yes, sir', and I have tried to keep myself in confinement. What's the result? I see so little of her now. I can't get even a glimpse of her. How can I work? Even at the gate, while she comes in, the car has side curtains put up. Do you know where I'm coming from now? From the works department, where I have no business at the moment. But there, if I stand on a block of wood—a gilded throne pedestal of some setting really—I can see the courtyard of the costume section which she crosses. That's helped me to clear a point or two, and I shall be able to add something to her portrait today." A clock struck four, and he sprang up, saying: "I must leave you now, Editor, there is a publicity conference in the directors' room." And he sped away.

On the first of the following month Srinivas was wondering to whom he should pay the rent. He had not long to wonder, for a stranger turned up at 6:30 a.m. and woke him. Srinivas opened the front door and saw a middle-aged man, wearing a close alpaca coat and a turban. He remembered seeing the same turban and coat somewhere else and then suddenly saw as in a flash that he had seen his old landlord wear it on the day he was present at the inauguration of their film. Srinivas concluded there was some connection between this visitor and the old man. He had a pinched face and sharp nose and wore a pair of glasses. "I'm Raghuram, the eldest son-in-law of your landlord. I've come for the rent." Srinivas took him in and seated him on a mat, though he was still sleepy. He wondered for a moment if he might send the man away, asking him to return later, while snatching a further installment of sleep. But his nature would not perpetrate such a piece of rudeness. He sat the man on a mat, and in about fifteen minutes returned to him ready for the meeting.

The stranger said: "My name is . . . and I'm the eldest son-in-law of your late landlord. My father-in-law has assigned this property to my wife, and I shall be glad to have the rent."

"How is it I have never seen you before?" asked Srinivas.

"You see, my father-in-law was a peculiar man, and we thought it best to leave him alone: he must always go his own way. We'd asked him to come and stop with us, but he did what he pleased."

"He used to tell me about you all, but he said he had a daughter in Karachi."

"That is the next sister to my wife. I came early because I didn't know when else to find you." He looked about uncertainly, eagerly awaiting the coming of the cash. Srinivas did not know how to decide. He went in and consulted his wife as she was scrubbing a brass vessel in the back-yard. "The old man's son-in-law is here; he will be our landlord now. He has come for rent. Shall I give it him?"

"Certainly," she said, not liking to be interrupted in this job she liked so much. She would give her consent to anything at such a moment. "Ask him when he is going to give us an independent tap." Srinivas returned, opened an almirah, took out a tiny wooden box, and out of it six five-rupee notes. He put it into his hand. "Do you want a receipt?" he asked. He pulled out a receipt book, filled it up and gave it to Srinivas. Srinivas said: "You have to give us an independent water-tap." "Haven't you got one?

Surely, surely—of course I must give you one, and"—he surveyed the walls and the ceiling—"yes, we must do everything that's convenient for our tenants."

During the day, as he sat working in the office, another visitor came—a younger person of about thirty-five. "You are Mr. Srinivas?" he asked timidly, panting with the effort to climb the staircase. He was a man of slight build, wearing a khaddar *jibba,* and his neck stood out like a giraffe's. Srinivas directed him to a chair. He sat twisting his button and said: "I'm a teacher in the corporation high school. I'm your late landlord's son-in-law. My wife has become the owner of this property. I've come for the rent."

Srinivas showed him the receipt. The visitor was greatly confused on seeing it. "What does he mean by coming and snatching away the rent in this way?" He got up abruptly and said: "I can't understand these tricks! My daughter was his favorite, and he set apart all his property for her, if it was going to be for anyone."

"Your daughter is the one studying in the school?"

He was greatly pleased to hear it. "Oh, you know about it, then!" He went back to the chair. He lowered his voice to a conspiratorial pitch and asked: "I say, you will help me, won't you?"

"In what way?"

He rolled his eyes significantly and reduced his speech to a whisper as he said: "My daughter was his one favorite in life. He mentioned an amount he had set apart for her marriage. Has he ever mentioned it to you?" He waited with bated breath for Srinivas's reply, who was debating within himself whether to speak to him about it or not. Srinivas said finally: "Yes, he mentioned it once or twice," unable to practice any duplicity in the matter. The visitor

205

became jumpy on hearing it. His eyes bulged with eager anticipation.

"Where did he keep this amount?" he asked.

"That I can't say," replied Srinivas. "I don't know anything about it."

The other became desperate and pleaded: "Don't let me down, sir, please help me."

Srinivas looked sympathetic. "How can I say anything about it? He mentioned the matter once or twice—I really don't know anything more."

"I hear that he has all his money in the Post Office Savings Bank. Is it true?" Srinivas had once again to shake his head. He could not help adding: "It is difficult to get any money, even of living people, out of the Post Office Savings Bank!"

"Oh, what shall I do about my daughter's marriage?" the visitor asked sullenly. He looked so concerned and unhappy that Srinivas felt obliged to say: "If he had lived a little longer, I am sure he would have done everything for your daughter. He was so fond of her."

"Just my luck," the other said, and beat his brow. "Why should he have held up his arrangements?" He complained against sudden death, as if it were a part of the old man's cunning, and looked completely disgusted with the old man's act of dying. He got up and said: "I will look into it. Till then, please don't pay the rent to anyone else." He took a step or two, then returned and said: "He used to confide in Mr. Sampath. Do you think he will be any use and tell us something?"

"Well, you can try him. He will probably be downstairs. You can see him as you go."

Toward evening yet another person came: a tall man,

who introduced himself as the eldest son of the old man.

"I know my father wrote a will. Do you know anything about it?"

"Sorry, no . . ."

The man looked pleased. "That's right. He wrote only one will and that is with me. If anyone else starts any stunt about any codicils I shall know how to deal with them. It's a pity you have paid the rent for this month. After this don't pay it to anyone else till you hear from me." Yet another called on him next morning, demanding the rent and a hidden will, and Srinivas began to wonder if he would ever be able to do anything else than answer these people for the rest of his life. "I hear," said this latest visitor, "that he has put everything in the Car Street Post Office Savings Bank. How are we to get at it? He has left no instructions about it." All this seemed to Srinivas a futile involvement in life. "Where were all these people before this? Where have they sprung from?" he wondered.

He decided to get clear of their company and its problems, and started looking for a house. But Malgudi being what it was, he could not get another. He forgot that if such a thing were possible he would not have become a tenant of the old man at all, and so he wasted a complete week in searching for a house. His wife had meanwhile become so enthusiastic about it and looked forward to a change with such eagerness that every evening when he came home her first question at the door was: "What about the house?"

"Doesn't seem to be much use; tomorrow I must try Grove Street and Vinayak Street. And after that——" She became crestfallen. Mentally she had accommodated herself in a better house already, and now it seemed to her impossible to live in this house any more. She found everything intolerable: the walls were dirty and not straight, plaster was crumbling and threatening to fall into all the cooked food; the rafters were sooty and dark, the floor was full of cracks and harbored vermin and deadly insects, and, above all, there was a single tap to draw water from. Srinivas listened to her troubles and felt helpless. His son added to the trouble by cataloguing some of his own experiences: "Do you know, when I was bathing, a tile fell off the roof on my head? There is a pit in the back-yard into which I saw a scorpion go," and so on. They had both made up their minds to quit. The relations of the old man also drove him to the same decision. But no house was available. What could anyone do? He confided his trouble to Sampath. "We shall manage it easily," Sampath said, very happy to be set any new task.

The final version of the will which the old man was supposed to have made proved to be a blessing for the moment. When one of the relatives came next, Sampath neither accepted nor denied knowledge of the matter, and very soon had all of them running after him. "We shall have to convene a lost-will conference," he said. He was nearly in his old form, and Srinivas was delighted to notice it. Through his finery and tidiness an old light came back to his eyes.

He got the half-dozen relatives sitting around Srinivas's table on a Saturday afternoon. They threw poisoned looks at each other; not one of them seemed to be on speaking terms with the others. Sampath said unexpectedly in a voice full of solemnity: "We are all gathered today to honor the memory of a noble master." They could not easily dispute the statement. "I have had the special honor

of being in his confidence. I've had the privilege of learning the secrets of truth. Even in mundane matters, I think,
I was one of the few to whom he opened his heart. . . ."
Here they looked at each other darkly. "I must acknowl-
edge my indebtedness to our Srinivas, our editor, for introducing me to the old gentleman." They once again looked
at each other darkly. He added vaguely: "Let us now pull
together—his relations and sons and friends—and do something to cherish the memory of this great soul; that we
can do by treating each other liberally and charitably."
Srinivas was amazed at Sampath's eloquence. Presently he
came down to practical facts. "He has left us his houses, his
money in the post office, and all the rest that may be his.
No doubt, if he had had the slightest inkling of what was
coming, he might have made some arrangements for the
distribution of his worldly goods. But this I doubt, for after
all, for such a saintly man, worldly goods were only an
impediment in life and nothing more. He used to quote an
old verse:

"When I become a handful of ash what do I care who takes
    my purse,
Who counts my coins and who locks the door of my safe,
When my bones lie bleaching, what matter if the door of
    my house is left unlocked?"

"However, this is a digression. Now it is up to us to decide
what we should do. Here is Srinivas and my other friend
Ravi in a portion of the house in Anderson Lane, among
the tenants I have most in mind. Now the position is that
our editor does not know to whom he should pay the rent."
A babble arose. Sampath silenced them with a gesture and
said: "It's certainly going to someone or everyone; that I
don't dispute. It will certainly be decided very soon, but

till then, where is he to pay the monthly rent, since he is a man who does not like to keep back a just due?"

"That question is settled," said several voices. Sampath made an impatient gesture and then said without any apparent meaning: "Yes, as far as every one of us is concerned. But where is a tenant to pay in his rent till the question is established beyond a shadow of doubt? My proposal is that till this is established my friends will pay their monthly rents into a Savings Bank account to be specially opened." There were fierce murmurs on hearing this, and Sampath declared: "This is the reason why my friend wants to move to another house. He says 'How can I live in a house over which people fight?' " And he paused to watch the effect of this threat on the gathering. They looked bewildered. They need not have been. But somehow, since the remark was delivered as a threat, they were half frightened by it. "You cannot afford to lose an old, valued tenant," Sampath added, driving the threat home.

"No, no, we do not want to disturb him," they all said and looked at each other sourly. "What we want to know is, where is the will?" asked a voice. "I thought we had come here about that. Do you know anything about it?" Now all eyes were fixed on Sampath. He replied simply: "In a delicate matter like this, how can I say anything? I have heard him mention so many things."

"You need not tell us anything of other things. But, surely, you could tell us about the will," they cried. Sampath said decisively: "No. I will not speak of it for two months. By that time whatever there is to be known will be known. Of that I'm certain."

"Here is the copy of the will, registered by my father. Please examine this, Mr. Sampath," said the eldest son.

The others became feverish. Sampath bent over and read out its contents ceremoniously: "I do hereby bequeath . . . and I hold that there is no further will."

"What about my daughter?" "What about my share?" "You certainly were not his dearest one . . ." "Have you forgotten . . ." A babble broke out. "It must be tested in a court and not here," Sampath said. "We do not care to be involved in all this. After all, blood relations may quarrel today and unite the day after. It is none of a stranger's business to get involved in such a matter. We will pay the rent to whoever is justly entitled to it. . . . Meanwhile, whoever thinks that he is entitled to the house, ought to complete all the unfinished business of the old gentleman; he will have to undertake some responsibility; that'll establish his claim."

"What responsibility?" they asked.

Sampath said: "There is a car below; please follow me." He got up. They trooped behind him. They seemed very happy to have the chance of a car ride. They sat crushing each other. Sampath went straight to Srinivas's house. It was like an investigation committee examining the spot. The first thing he said was: "This is the only source of water for four families—imagine!" And then the various families, including Srinivas's, gathered round and mentioned a list of all their requirements.

The result was: in a few days the block of houses in Anderson Lane became transformed: it only meant a little dislocation for Srinivas—having to shift with his family to his office. When he returned he found the walls scraped and lime-washed, tiles changed, floor smoothed with cement, and an independent water-tap planted in his own back-yard; some of the partitions behind Ravi's house were knocked down, and now only three families lived where there had been four or five before. It would not have been easy to investigate and say who was mainly responsible for these changes. All the relations seemed to have vied among themselves to give their tenants amenities. Srinivas's wife was delighted. Sampath said: "So that settles your problem, Mr. Editor. You will have to send your rent to the Savings Bank on the first. They've agreed to it. Meanwhile, the entire gang is going to the court for succession rights. But it's none of our business at the moment."

Chapter Eight

O NE OF the most important sequences. Shiva is in a trance. He opens his eyes and keeps looking at Parvathi. Vague desires stir in him. He looks into his own mind for the reason. Till today he was able to receive her ministrations with absolute detachment, but today he finds himself interested in her. He feels that there is some mischief afoot and looks for the reason, and he espies in a corner the God of Love aiming his shaft at him, and burns him up immediately; then he resumes his meditation.

This was filmed and projected on the screen. They lounged in their comfortable cushion chairs, lit their cigarettes and watched in silence. Somu, Sampath, Sohan Lal, who was buying the picture, De Mello, and a number of technicians in the back row. The operator in his cabin was tired of mechanically throwing the same reel on the screen over and over again. Somu was the first to break the gloomy silence. He asked Mr. Lal: "Well, what do you say, Mr. Lal."

Lal said: "It's no good. I shall be obliged if you will retake it. It is lacking in something."

"It's lacking in pep, if I may put it in a word," added De Mello. "There is a lot of scope for working up this sequence on the right lines. I agree with Mr. Sohan Lal."

"Well, if everyone thinks the scene must be retaken, we've got to do it, that is all. The script will have to be rewritten." They all looked at Srinivas. "Do you think that the scene can be rewritten?"

"How?" asked Srinivas, trying to look as calm and considerate as possible. He felt pity for them, for the hunted look they wore. They were dealing with things beyond them, and the only pressure was commerce. He tried to sympathize with them and suppress the indignation that was rising within him. His question remained unanswered. They looked at each other in a frightened way and whimpered uncomfortably. It was De Mello who plucked up enough strength to say: "Perhaps a dance act will serve the purpose: that will appeal to the public."

"Yes," agreed Sohan Lal. "A dance act would be excellent. This picture needs some entertainment."

"The comedy is there," said Somu, for he was particularly proud of this contribution. Srinivas tried not to hear, for his blood boiled whenever he thought of those comic scenes. He had detached himself from them early; and Sampath and Somu had hatched them between themselves, shot them separately, and cut them up and scattered them like spice all along the story. He found that some of the most sublime moments he had conceived faded into the horseplay of Gopu and Mali and their suggestive by-play. They were the highest-paid comedians on the films, and they propped up any picture by this means. The public always flocked to see them and hear their gags. Somu was highly gratified with his own efforts. To his remark Sohan Lal replied: "Well, that's only comedy. We must have an entertainment item like a dance sequence." And they decided to convert this scene into a dance act, and they at once called up a number of people from various parts of the studio. Srinivas accepted the position with resignation. He only exerted himself to the extent of refusing to write the scene any further. This was one of his favorite scenes. By externalizing emotion, by superimposing feeling in the shape of images, he hoped to express very clearly the substance of this episode: of love and its purification, of austerity and peace. But now they wanted to introduce a dance sequence. Srinivas found himself helpless in this world. He tried not to take a too tragic view of the situation. He wanted to avoid further tortures to his mind, and so leaned over and whispered to Sampath "I'm going. I don't have to explain why?"

"Yes, yes," said Sampath, and Srinivas went out. He walked along the open drive of the studio. So many people, so busily engaged, and going from place to place with a serious preoccupied air for at least ten hours in the day. "With this manner of theirs, why can't they do something worth while?" he reflected and went on. He came to the art and publicity block.

In his room Ravi was busily working on a publicity poster. He was sitting on the ground with a huge board leaning against the wall. He was clutching a brush in his hand. A huge outline of Shanti was penciled, and he was coloring it. It seemed to be an enlargement of the little pencil sketch he had done long ago. Its eyelashes were so full of life, its eyes shone so much with light, and a ray of light reflected off a diamond in the ear; it was colored so elegantly that it seemed a masterpiece worthy to hang in any art gallery. Srinivas stood admiring it.

"How do you like it?" Ravi asked.

"Is this the portrait you mentioned?"

"Oh, no, this is only a poster for a theater gate. The other's in oils and is my own."

"Where is it?"

"There, turned to the wall." Srinivas saw the back of a

217

wooden board in a far-off corner. He made a motion toward it, asking: "May I see it?"

"Oh, no, it'll probably be years before I can let anyone see it . . ." He put away the brush, sat down in a chair and said: "It gives me a feeling of being near her when I do this. I want nothing else in life when I'm doing her picture, even if it is only a poster. Do you think he is quite truthful in saying that she is different?"

"Don't you worry about all that," Srinivas implored.

"I'm not worrying. I see her going home every day, sitting close to Sampath and touching him; they are always together. He doesn't allow me to approach her at all. Does he take me for a fool?" he laughed bitterly. "I'm not going to talk to her, even if she comes and speaks to me. She is pretending she is someone else."

"Don't keep brooding over all that, Ravi; you do your work and forget the rest."

"Practically what I'm doing now. What else should I do? As long as I'm doing a portrait like this, even if it is only a poster, I'm at peace. Let that fellow keep her to himself, I don't care; I've got something better out of her."

All around the room there were preliminary advertisement layouts. One of them said: "Golden opportunity to see God himself." Ravi pointed at the caption and said: "How do you like the lettering? This is the advertisement slogan I'm asked to write out."

"God has never had a worse handling anywhere."

Ravi merely shrugged his shoulders. "What do I care? I just do what I'm asked. If they want me to write 'I'm an unmatched fool,' I will provide the required lettering for it. What do I care? I tell you, we have an art director who is fit only to be a clock-winder in the studio. He cannot even draw a straight line or a curve, but yet he is our boss, and we get our salary only if he approves of our work." He laughed uncontrollably. The veins on his forehead stood out like pipes, and he spoke loudly. He was very careless in his talk and seemed to want to challenge every-body with his remarks. He did not bother either to subdue his voice or speak discreetly. He seemed to have become very garrulous, too. This Srinivas suddenly noticed in him; and he also saw that his complexion was turning yellow and waxen. "I say, you must take care of your health. Why are you neglecting yourself in this way?" Ravi made a wry face at the thought of looking after himself. He got up, looked at himself in a looking-glass on the wall with distaste. "This is the best that can be done about you, my dear chap," he said, addressing himself. "Don't demand further concessions. You are being treated better than you really deserve." And he once again broke into a laugh. He interrupted it to explain: "You see, my director wants a dozen different advertisement posters to be ready, and then we have the actual work on the sets. I go on working here all night nowadays. I have not been home." A shiver ran through him at the thought of his home. "I prefer this place. My father has completely given up talking to me. He becomes so rigid when he hears my voice at home that I fear he will have a seizure some day. Of course, he keeps hectoring my poor mother, and that is the worst of it. But for those young fellows and my mother," he said reflectively, "I should have blasted my so-called home ages ago."

"You aren't free to come out for a moment, I suppose?"

"Where to?" asked Ravi.

"Come to my house. I will give you good coffee and

something to eat. You can rest and return to the studio whenever you want." Ravi revolved the offer in his mind and rejected it. "I have to finish three different styles of this god notice before tonight." And he settled down resolutely.

At home Srinivas's wife said: "Do you know, Sampath's wife was here this afternoon?"

"How did she come all this way? You have not seen her before?"

"No, she managed to come in a car. What a lot of daughters she has."

"Why, do you envy her?" Srinivas asked, and she replied: "What is there to joke about in all this! She came on a very serious business. She wants me to speak to you about her husband."

"What about him?"

"It seems that their household has become impossible. There is that woman who is playing Parvathi. He is always with her."

"He is her cousin."

"It seems they are not cousins. They are of different castes."

"What if they are?" Srinivas asked, thinking what an evil system caste was. She flared up. "Let her be any caste she pleases, but what business has she to come and ruin that family? They were so happy before. Now he doesn't care for the house at all. He is always with her. And it seems now that he is threatening to marry her and set up another household. The poor girl has been crying for days now. You have got to do something about her."

She was so much worked up and became so vehement that Srinivas felt that he ought to speak to Sampath.

Srinivas waited for an opportunity to meet Sampath alone at the studio. He was always with Shanti, except when she went in to dress or into the women's make-up room, when he hung about Sohan Lal, who had still to pay him a lakh and a half. The mastery of the studio was now gradually passing into the hands of Sohan Lal, and Sohan Lal was completely absorbed in arranging the dance act. Sampath was told: "Give me the dance act completed, and I will pay the first half of the agreed amount." And if he received that lakh and a half, Sampath was going to buy up the interests of Somu also and become virtually the owner of the picture; then he would put on hand another picture almost at once. So it was in his interest to complete the dance act as quickly as possible, and night and day he was being dragged hither and thither to complete it. Sohan Lal was dogging his steps, and he dogged the steps of Sohan Lal, and Somu went round and round these two, hoping for the completion of the dance act, when he, too, hoped to get various payments made to him. It was, on the whole, a very intricate mechanism of human relationships. In this maze Srinivas walked about unscathed, because he had trained himself to view it all as a mere spectator. This capacity saved him all the later shocks. He saw, without much flutter, the mangling that was going on with his story. The very process by which they mangled his theme attracted him, and he moved from room to room, studio to studio, through floor-space and setting, laboratory and sound processing and moviola, into the projection room, watching, and he very soon accommodated himself to the notion that they were doing a picture of their own entirely unconnected with the theme he had written.

It was difficult to get at Sampath alone. All the same, when they were passing from their discussion chamber to the second studio to see a test arrangement for the dance act, he managed to ask him: "Please spare me fifteen minutes."

Sampath looked at him in pained surprise. He was wearing a silk shirt with gold studs, and on his wrist gleamed a platinum watch, bound with a gold strap. He wore a pair of spectacles nowadays. "Every sign of prosperity is there," Srinivas remarked to himself. "All except your old personality, which is fast vanishing." He went everywhere now by car, and that habit had given him a new rotundity. Srinivas felt like saying: "I do hope you will not acquire the appearance of Mr. Somu in due course. Pull yourself together in time."

"Anything urgent?"

"Absolutely," Srinivas said.

"I will free myself after seeing the dance test. It won't take ten minutes. Come along, have a look at it." Srinivas excused himself and stayed behind in the garden. Presently Sampath came down. "This dance idea is very good, you know. It is going to make the picture top-class, the most artistic production in India. We may even send it abroad. Of course, you are not annoyed about these changes, are you?"

"Not at all; why should I worry about it?"

"We are only taking liberties with the details, you know, but we are keeping to your original in the main treatment."

"Oh, yes, yes," Srinivas said, feeling that this was the familiar eyewash every film-maker applied to every writer. "It's not about that that I wish to trouble you now. It's about another matter." He mentioned it gently, apologetically. At first Sampath pooh-poohed the entire story. But later said, with his old mischievous look coming back to his eyes: "Some people say that every sane man needs two wives—a perfect one for the house and a perfect one outside for social life . . . I have the one. Why not the other? I have confidence that I will keep both of them happy and if necessary in separate houses. Is a man's heart so narrow that it cannot accommodate more than one? I have married according to Vedic rites: let me have one according to the civil marriage law. . . ."

"Is it no use discussing it?"

"I'm afraid not, Mr. Editor. . . . You will forgive me. I love her, though you may not believe it."

"How can you ever forget that you are a father of five?"

"As I have told you, man's heart is not a narrow corner."

"Think of your wife."

"Oh, these women will make a scene. She will be all right. She must get used to it." He remained for a moment brooding, but soon set himself right, saying airily: "It's her nature to fuss about things sometimes. But she always changes for the better. I've been meaning to tell you about it, Mr. Editor, but somehow———"

"I can't say that I'm very happy to hear this news, Sampath. I do hope you will think it over deeply," said Srinivas, feeling a little uncomfortable at having to sound so pontifical. He got up. "You have to take into consideration the future of all your five children."

"Oh," Sampath remained brooding. "Well, I'm going to

have different establishments. I'm doing nothing illegal, to feel apologetic. After all, our religion permits us to marry many wives."

"Yes, no law forbids you to have more than one head, so why not try and grow as many as you can?" asked Srinivas. "Let me be frank: I'm convinced that you are merely succumbing to a little piece of georgette, powder and curves. You have no right to cause any unhappiness to your wife and children."

"Well, sir," Sampath said with mock humility. "Here goes my solemn declaration that my wife and children shall lack nothing in life, either in affection or comfort. Will this satisfy you? If I buy Shanti a car my wife shall have another; if I give her a house I will give the other also a house; it will really be a little expense duplicating everything this way, but I won't mind it. Later on, when they see how much it is costing me, I'm sure they will bury the hatchet and become friends again. . . ."

Chapter Nine

I T WAS the great day of shooting the dance act. They were determined to complete the act in about twelve hours of continuous shooting, starting at six in the evening. The studio was stirring into tremendous activity.

On the floor of Stage A a gorgeous Kailas was standing—the background of ice peaks was painted by the art department. All the previous night and throughout the day Ravi had sat up there and painted it; foliage, cut and propped up, stood around. Shiva, with his matted hair and a cobra around his neck, sat there in the shade of a tree in meditation. De Mello, script in hand, was roving about giving instructions. The sound-van outside was all ready to record. Assistants stood around, fingering switches and pushing up screens and running to and fro. The make-up assistants constantly ran forward and patted the cheeks of the artists. De Mello stepped on the trolley, put his eye to the camera and cried: "Light—four—seven—baby—seventeen." As Shiva sat there in the full glare of several lights, Parvathi came up to him from a side wing. Sampath grew excited at the sight of her. Sohan Lal, Somu and Sampath sat up in their canvas chairs and viewed her critically. Sampath cried: "Shanti, move on a little more gradually," and she adjusted her steps. He ordered a make-up assistant: "Push away that lock of hair on her forehead, so that it doesn't dangle right in the center." He tilted his head to one side and surveyed her as the assistant went up to carry out the instruction. Somu murmured: "Yes, you are right. If

the hair is too artificially made up it spoils the effect."
Sampath went to the camera and applied his eye to the
view-finder. He stood there, looking for a long time at
Shanti, and murmured: "I think you had better remove
the foliage behind her." He took his eye from the finder
so as to enable De Mello to view her. He stood there for
a long time and said: "It's O.K. now," making some adjustment with the camera. He went up the stage to readjust
the branch of a tree. "Yes, we shall have a final rehearsal
now," said Sampath, "Ready!" he cried. Lights were
wheeled about. He looked at them with bored indifference.
As they were getting into position he went over and spoke
a few words to Shanti, while she remained standing at her
post. "Do you want a chair?" he asked her, and carried a
chair for her. "How long am I to keep like this?" she asked
complainingly, and he said: "This is the final rehearsal.
We will take it; just one more rehearsal." She made a wry
face and sat down. Beads of perspiration stood on her
pink painted face. Sampath beckoned to an assistant and
had her face dabbed as she sat motionless like a piece of
lumber.

"Can I have an iced drink?"

"Oh, no!" He threw up his arms in alarm. "No ice for
you till this is over—not for the entire season."

She looked agonized on hearing it and made a wry face
again and grumbled: "You never give me anything I
want—never." Into their banter came the voice of Lord
Shiva, who had been asked to sit rigid in a corner and who
had been left neglected by everyone. "I want to go out
for a moment," he said. His face was steaming with
perspiration; his matted locks and beard were fierce, no
doubt, but his eyes were bloodshot with fatigue. He tried

to move in his seat. "Don't move," Sampath commanded him. "You have another rehearsal; it's going to be difficult to focus your place again."

"My legs are cramped, and I can't sit any more."

"Don't talk back," commanded Sampath. All the others looked at each other in consternation. "I'm not only talking back, but I'm going out—out of this." Shiva got up. Somu felt that he must smooth out the situation, and so said: "Don't get excited, please; let no one get excited. We must all pull together." Shiva's eyes (real ones, and not the third one on the forehead) blazed with anger as he said: "I've borne this with patience: five or six days of continuous rehearsals. Do you want to kill us with rehearsals? And yet you are not satisfied."

"Be calm, my dear fellow," said Somu, patting his back, and De Mello on the other side tried to pacify him.

"Leave me alone!" cried Shiva in rage. "All this sequence has already been shot, and yet you want to retake it—why?"

"We're not prepared to explain," said Sampath. "You had better read again your contract, particularly with reference to retakes and rehearsals. Our agreement is clear on that point. If you talk any further about it, it will go against you, remember."

Shiva was not to be cowed so easily. He said, almost grinding his teeth: "Yes, but an ordinary retake is different: now you have included two songs and a full-scale dance act. It's not in our agreement."

Sohan Lal tried to pacify the fighters now in his own way. "We must not quarrel over such small matters. Of course, you take a lot of trouble, we all appreciate it. Every film is a co-operative effort." Shiva, who tried to follow this conversation in order to find any useful suggestion, was more enraged when he found on analysis that there was nothing in it. He lost his head completely. He came toward the camera and said: "If you pay me another five thousand rupees I'm prepared to go through this act, re-hearsals and all, otherwise no."

"Why should you ask for extra pay, mister? You must not," said Sohan Lal.

"Why not? I'm laboring for it!" cried Shiva passionately. "And I am entitled to it."

"It is unthinkable!" cried Sampath and Somu in one voice.

"Not unthinkable in her case, I suppose?" Shiva cried, pointing at Parvathi, sitting on her chair and fanning her-self. "Aren't you giving her five thousand extra? Do you think I don't know all that?" He came toward the pro-ducers menacingly. Somu shrank back a little; Sampath stepped forward, rolling up his sleeve. "What are you up to?" The other checked himself. Sampath asked in a tone of finality: "Are you going through this or not?"

"I have said my say. Are you going to revise my con-tract?"

"I don't want conditions. We may give you more or we may not. Leave all that to our discretion. At the moment I won't have you talk of any such things on the set. Are you going to your place or not?"

"I'm not."

"Very well, get out of here," he thundered.

"Give me my salary; I will go," said Shiva, descending from Kailas defiantly.

"That'll be settled in a court of law. You have violated a contract, and you will have to face the consequences."

"What injustice is this!" cried Shiva, completely losing his head.

Sampath told De Mello: "De Mello, take him out of the studio. I don't want any further indiscipline in this studio," and De Mello assigned a couple of assistants to lead Shiva out. Sampath subsided in his chair, exhausted by the effort. There remained a strained silence as everybody waited, and top-light boys looked down from their platforms, and assistants stood hushed at their posts. Somu was the first to break the uncomfortable silence. He said timidly: "Well, Mr. Sampath, what shall we do now?"

"Leave that to me," Sampath said grandly. "We need not be at the mercy of these mercenaries. I will do Shiva myself. I've been an actor once."

He looked up at the make-up artist and asked: "You can make me up for Shiva?" The artist looked at him critically and said: "Yes, sir."

"But the dance, sir?" Somu said.

"We've bothered our heads with it for four days. I always felt that we might do it ourselves, save all trouble instead of trying to teach it to these fools. What do you say, Dance Master?"

"Yes, sir, they do not easily learn."

Sohan Lal said: "We must always be ready to do many things." And then he spoke for a long while with Sampath in his western Indian dialect, and Sampath smiled and said something in reply. Sohan Lal was perhaps recounting a reminiscence of a similar nature. Sampath went over to Shanti and said: "So sorry. Further delay. Forgive us, dear. I'll be ready in a moment. You can relax for half an hour in your room, while they make me up."

Some time later when Srinivas came into the studio he was surprised at being greeted by the familiar voice: "Hello, Editor, don't be shocked!" But it came from within a heavy beard and matted locks. "Sampath! What is the matter?" He wore a tiger's skin at his loins.

"Well, people do not realize that no one is indispensable in this world," he said and explained the position. Sampath's versatility took his breath away.

"We are determined to finish this scene today, even if it is going to mean twenty-four hours of continuous shooting."

"You have to wear a cobra around your neck."

"Yes, yes, I know; we've got that tame one, I tried it: it is not bad, though it feels unearthly cold at the first touch."

"Play back! Play back!" Sampath shouted presently. "Sound!" He went over and gave instructions to De Mello, who stood at the camera, and then went to Shiva's seat on Kailas. A song blared forth from the loud-speaker —a song with a sentimental lilt, and drums producing a kind of hot-air rhythm. The music department fully realizing the need of the hour had produced a brand-new tune by adapting a couple of tunes born in Hollywood from a South American theme. Srinivas despaired on hearing it. It produced anything but the holy-of-holies feeling that he had hoped would be the essence of the scene. As he saw Somu and Lal tapping their feet instinctively to the music he was filled with a desperation which he could not easily place or classify. Other feet picked up the rhythm, and presently he saw Sampath slowly stirring in his meditation. He rose to his feet. He twisted and wriggled his body and assumed the pose of a dance-carving one saw on temple walls. He moved step by step and approached the chair, which marked Parvathi's place.

"Cut!" rang out De Mello's voice. "This will be the

first cut," he explained. Shiva relaxed his rigid pose. "Call Parvathi!" he ordered.

People went out and returned, followed by Parvathi, with her anklets jingling and very modern ear-drops swinging on her ear-lobes and a crown scintillating on her brow. She stood there in her place. Once again the cry "Music!" and "All lights" and "Final rehearsals"; and lights shot up all around, and Srinivas noted how cunningly they had managed to make her clothes unnecessary by the No. 10 light, which shot up a beam of illumination from behind her at ground level. "What ingenuity!" he commented to himself. Her body stood out as if X-rayed, her necklace and diadem glittered and shone and seemed to be the only apparel she wore. Everyone, the principals in canvas chairs, went over to the camera to look through the view-finder and shake their heads with academic approval. There was suddenly a small discussion on the same academic level.

"Will the censors pass this?"

"Censors! What have they to object to? It's only artistic. At that rate they should stop all dances and Bharata Natya; while professors and ministers are clamoring everywhere that we should revive our classical art—" another said.

"Lights off!" rang the voice, and switches pit-patted.

"We will have a final rehearsal and take the first shot afterward."

"Music!"

Music—the South American tune—started once again. Shiva got up from his trance and executed his slow rhythmic steps, but Parvathi stood still, and when they questioned her about it pleaded: "No rehearsals are neces-

233

sary for me. Don't tire me, please." Shiva opened his eyes for a moment to say: "Yes, don't tire her out."

"Yes, yes, it is better that you don't tire her out," repeated three more voices, catching the contagion. Everybody seemed to be saying the same thing and feeling the same way. And then they sounded a buzzer and stopped the music. Shiva returned to his place and sat under the tree once again in meditation. He said: "De Mello, get ready to shoot. Call in the extras, Parvathi's companions. Fetch the cobra."

Lights were once again wheeled about, with their little wheels creaking, porters moved hither and thither, assistants took out their long entry-books and made notes, make-up assistants dashed backward and forward: the cameraman and his assistants disposed themselves around the camera like sentries on duty. Someone went up with a tape and measured, someone else held up an exposure guide over Parvathi's nose—elaborate rites of a very curious tribe, with their own high priests and medicine men. "This is really an anthropological specimen," Srinivas thought. His reflections were interrupted by the entry of Ravi at this stage. He came in bearing a portfolio in his hand and was waiting for an opportunity to catch the eye of the art director, who was busy on the set, making some final readjustment to the heavenly background. Seeing Srinivas, Ravi edged up to him and whispered: "I have to get his approval for a design and send it up for block-making immediately."

"He seems reluctant to get down from yonder heaven," whispered Srinivas, but found no response. Ravi's eye was caught by the figure of Parvathi, and he looked hypnotized. Srinivas wanted to jerk him back to his normal

234

state and asked: "What is that thing in your file?" Ravi answered absently: "Design and lettering."

"Is it urgent?"

"Yes—yes," replied Ravi, without looking at him, with his eye still on Parvathi, who was now fanning herself. He stood transfixed. "That is Sampath," he whispered. "See the cobra around his neck!" A live cobra was coiled about his throat, where he formerly wore his scarf, and it was making imperceptible gliding movements. Srinivas felt that he must say something to draw away Ravi's attention, searched about for a remark, and could only say: "What a dangerous thing!"

"It has no fang, unfortunately!" remarked Ravi. Srinivas felt that he had made a blunder, and hastened to repair it with some other remark, but all to no purpose. Ravi stood as if transfixed, with his eyes on Parvathi and answering in monosyllables. Srinivas: "Shall we go to the canteen for something? I feel rather parched."

"No. I've got to get that fellow's approval."

"Ready!" went up a cry. A whistle rang out. The extras lined up behind Parvathi and Shiva. "Silence!" rang out another cry. "Lights! All lights." The lights flashed out, X-raying the dancer once again. "Music!" Music started. "Start! Silence." The camera was switched on. Each man was at his post. The music squeezed all sense out of people and only made them want to gyrate with arms around one another. Shiva went forward, step by step; Parvathi advanced, step by step: he was still in a trance with his eyes shut, but his arms were open to receive her. Shanti's brassière could be seen straining under her thin clothes. She bent back to fit herself into the other's arms. The melody worked up a terrific tempo. All lights poured down their brilliance. Scores of people stood outside the scene, watching it with open-mouthed wonder.

It was going to be the most expert shot taken. The light-boys looked down from their platforms as if privileged to witness the amours of gods. If the camera ran on for another minute the shot would be over. They wanted to cut this shot first where Shiva's arms went round the diaphanous lady's hips. But it was cut even a few seconds earlier in an unexpected manner. A piercing cry, indistinguishable, unworded, like an animal's, was suddenly heard, and before they could see where it originated, Ravi was seen whizzing past the others like a bullet, knocking down the people in his way. He was next seen on the set, rushing between Shiva's extended arms and Parvathi, and knocking Shiva aside with such violence that he fell amidst his foliage in Kailas in a most ungodly manner. Next minute they saw Parvathi struggling in the arms of Ravi, who was trying to kiss her on her lips and carry her off. . . .

They soon realized that this scene was not in the script. Cries rang out: "Cut." "Power." "Shut down." "Stop." And several people tried to rush into the scene. Ravi attempted to carry off his prize, though she was scratching his face and biting his hands. In the mess someone tripped upon the cables and all the lights went out. Ravi seemed to be seized with a superhuman power. Nobody could get at him. In the confusion someone cried: "Oh! Camera, take care!" "Lights, lights, fools!" Somebody screamed: "The cobra is free; the cobra is creeping here, oh!" People ran helter-skelter in the dark. While they were all searching and running into each other they could hear Ravi's voice lustily ringing out in another part of the studio. And all ran in his direction.

He was presently heard saying: "She has slipped away again. Bring her, do you hear me?" His voice rose and filled the whole place in the dark. "I'm not to be cheated again. She is——" He uttered aloud a piece of ribaldry. "And if anyone goes near her I will murder him." And he let out a whoop of joy and cried: "Ah, here she is." And somebody else cried: "Oh, he has got me," amidst other noises. There was the noise of a struggle in the dark. "Leave me, leave me—oh, save me," some "extra" girl screamed. And the crowd rushed in her direction. In the meantime one or two candles were brought in, and by their flickering light, people moved about in the direction of Ravi's voice. But the moment they came there, Ravi's voice was heard in another part of the building challenging them. In this pale light Srinivas could be seen trying to follow Ravi and persuade him— persuade him to do what? Srinivas wondered in the middle of it all. He was blindly running along with the rest of them, catching the mood of the mob. It was evident that for most people now this was an exciting diversion, though the two who looked maddened and panicky were Sampath and Somu. Sampath had still Shiva's matted locks on his crown, and the tiger's skin girt his loins, but he looked despondent; even in that feeble light of a single candle his eyes looked careworn and anxious as he paused to say: "Editor, what is this! What devil has seized him! We are ruined. Do something. Stop him—" Ravi like a shadow was seen racing up a flight of steps. "Oh, he is going into the storage. Stop him, stop him." Somu's portly figure was hurrying toward the stairs. He was seen going up a few steps, when Ravi turned swiftly on his heel with a war-cry and tried to fling himself on him; and Somu, startled beyond description, stood arrested for the fraction of a second, and turned and ran down again at full speed. This was the first time anyone had seen Somu running; and people forgot their main pursuit for a moment in watching this spectacle. Sohan Lal came up from somewhere, moving along with the general stream of the crowd and cried into Srinivas's face: "I should not have given that advance on the picture. Now what is to happen to my money?" Somu was crying: "Sampath! Sampath!" pointlessly in the dark. Srinivas felt so dumbfounded by everything that he merely stopped where he was, leaning for rest on one of the creeper-covered shed walls. "Can't you get some more candles?" someone shouted. "They are all required near the fuse-box."

"Which fool is responsible for this?" Sampath cried somewhere. "Carrying open lamps!" He ordered all the candles to be put out. And utter darkness enveloped them again.

De Mello was the only person who seemed to plan the campaign with any intelligence. He conducted himself as though such things were a part of the ordinary Hollywood training. "There is no need to lose our heads over this," he was heard saying again and again. "It is only a mishap." With a handful of picked men from the works section, armed with sticks, he surrounded the block and led the procession up the staircase. He proceeded stealthily, flashing his torch. "Not enough torches to go round. That is our chief handicap." He tiptoed into the top room, as if going into a tiger cage when the tiger was not looking. There was for a moment no sound after he went in. People down below held their breaths and waited with anxious faces. Presently the door opened and De Mello appeared on the landing and declared: "He is not here."

"Not there! What do you mean, not there, Mr. De Mello?"

De Mello shouted something back and added: "God knows, vanished probably through the window. He has made a frightful mess. Come up, please."

They hesitated, trying to pluck up courage to go. Sampath moved a step or two, when a man came down. "Shanti has swooned. She has a cut on her forehead—bleeding." Sampath exclaimed: "Ah! Ah! Get a doctor," and vanished from the spot. Meanwhile Somu gripped Srinivas's hand and cried: "Please come up and see, sir."

"Yes, yes, it is better you come up and see also," added Sohan Lal, taking his other arm. Srinivas allowed himself to be steered. There was no need to question the relevancy of any action. This was not the moment for it.

This block contained the laboratory, storage, editing and allied departments, full of shelves, tables, wheels, troughs—all kinds of apparatus resembling an alchemist's workshop.

The torch flashed and went out as they examined their surroundings. Somu cried in despair: "Can't someone get a torch which doesn't go out?" The floor was strewn with broken bottles, chemicals and salt and trailing lengths of film. "Be careful! Broken glass," De Mello warned. Somu snatched a flashlight, stooped to the floor, picked up a film and held it up. They saw a close-up of Shanti, and farther along Shiva on Kailas, with dirt and scratches on both of them. "Who left the negatives about so carelessly?" Somu thundered, glaring from his kneeling position on the floor. No one answered. All questions at this moment were destined to die without an answer.

"Well, sir, no one is particularly responsible for this; it's usual to keep the cut negatives in these racks. Nothing unusual," said De Mello. Somu grunted and said: "Our loss must be heavy." He felt like saying a few other things, but somehow feared that he might hurt De Mello. He was too cautious even now. He suppressed many pungent remarks that rose to his lips, and merely said: "Won't someone get a light?" In answer to this they heard a thundering command go forth. "Here! Get Shanti and all her lights!"

Somu looked about panic-stricken and cried: "He is here, get the light quick!"

"Get Shanti lights!" echoed the command. De Mello flashed his torch and saw Ravi crouching under a table, his eyes sparkling in the torch light. De Mello acted quickly, too quickly even for Ravi. He just stooped, thrust his hand in and pulled Ravi out. Somu shivered and tried to run. He became hysterical and chattered incoherently. Ravi struggled in De Mello's grip and mumbled: "You are hurting. Love me, darling. Love me, darling," he said in a sing-song. "Darling, love me. Love is lust. Lust is portrait in oils, Editor. And all his color of rain. What color is lust?" In reply to all this, De Mello's left fist shot out, hit him under the chin and knocked him down flat.

The lights were ablaze once again at 5 a.m. The police arrived in a van soon after.

The major part of the next four days Srinivas spent in running between the Market Road Police Station and his home.

Ravi's household was in a turmoil. His father was mad with rage, his mother wrung her hands helplessly, and even the little brothers and sisters looked stunned.

After his outburst Ravi became docile and uncommunicative. He didn't seem to recognize anyone. When Srinivas addressed him through the bars, Ravi would not even turn in his direction. His look had no fixed point. He kept muttering something to himself under his breath. No one could follow the sense of it. It sounded like the language of another planet.

Srinivas became familiar with the comings and goings of the police station. He saw a policeman pushing in a jutka-driver for some traffic offense; he saw an urchin brought in and sent away with a couple of slaps on his face; he saw a terrified villager brought in for questioning and pushed away somewhere out of sight. All the while a sergeant sat at a table, implacably writing on brown forms, except when a bulky inspector came in swinging a short cane, when he stood up respectfully and saluted. Ravi sat hunched up in a corner seeing nothing, hearing nothing, but occupied with his own repetitions. Srinivas carried him food every day in a brass vessel. He had the lock-up opened, went in, sat beside Ravi and persuaded him to eat the food. Ravi seemed to have forgotten the art of eating. Srinivas attempted to feed him with a spoon, but even that was difficult. He kept a morsel on his tongue and swallowed only when he was persistently told to do so. It was an odd spectacle—Srinivas sitting there in that dark corner beyond the bars, coaxing Ravi to eat, as the Market Road babble continued outside. Sampath came on the evening of the fourth day and stood watching the scene through the bars. He had a few scratches on his face and he limped slightly: otherwise there was no sign of the recent events. He still wore his smart silk shirt and gold studs. He stood watching silently till Srinivas finished the feeding and came out. Sampath said with a sigh: "It was an evil hour that brought me and Ravi together. I never knew that a fellow could go so mad. Won't you come out? Let us sit in the car and talk." Srinivas followed him to the car outside. Sampath opened the door and sat down in the driver's seat with Srinivas beside him. It was five in the evening, and traffic rolled past them. The babble of the market place kept a continuous background to their talk as Sampath said: "I couldn't see you for three or four days, Mr. Editor. There has been so much to do, mainly checking up the damage! Why should a thing like this happen to us?" Srinivas remained silent, feeling that an answer was beyond him. Sampath said with the air of a martyr: "I've only been trying to do him a good turn and yet . . . You know our losses?"

"Must be heavy," Srinivas said casually, determined to discourage martyrdom at all costs.

"Damage to the settings, chemicals, lights, films exposed, and so on; we shall have to retake several shots. It is amazing how much havoc one man could do within an hour. It will be days before we set the studio right again. More than all this—Shanti. She is so much shaken that she will be unfit for work for many weeks. She swore she would never come near the studio again. I couldn't mention the word 'studio' without her getting hysterical. This would have been our greatest blow, but thank God, since yesterday she has grown calmer! I know I can manage her. She needs complete rest before she can return to work. But I'm sure she will be all right, and we will complete the film yet. Not a hundred Ravis can stop us from doing our work. Well, you will see us all up and doing once again. I'm sorry, though, to see that boy there, but I always felt he was not quite sound."

"I wanted to see you about him, too. Will you withdraw your complaint? He should be in a hospital, not in prison," pleaded Srinivas.

"But—but——" Sampath hesitated.

"He will not come near you or the studio. I will guarantee you that."

"Somu has lost his head completely. He is dead set on pursuing the matter."

"You had better explain to him how silly it will be and that he will gain nothing by it. Please withdraw your complaint. You will not be troubled by him. I will see to it. You can do it on behalf of the studio. I promise I will ask nothing else of you in life." He pleaded so earnestly that Sampath got down without a word, approached the sergeant, spoke to him and left with him a letter for the inspector. "It is done, sir," he said, getting back into his seat in the car. "I only came to say good-bye. We are going to Mempi hills tomorrow."

"Why Mempi hills, of all places?"

"It has a fine rest-house and it is a quiet place. I'm sure a couple of weeks' stay there will immensely benefit Shanti." His car moved off. Srinivas watched him go. A vast sigh of despair escaped his lips—at the irrepressible inevitable success that seemed to loom ahead of Sampath. "God alone can rescue him," he muttered to himself as he saw the car turn into Ellaman Street.

The inspector came down an hour later. He said: "Well, you can take your friend home. I am glad they have withdrawn the complaint. What can we do with mentally defective people? It is like dealing with drunkards. We

243

keep them in custody for three or four days and then send them off. If kept longer they prove a bother to themselves and to us."

Srinivas walked into the cell and persuaded Ravi to leave with him. The inspector followed them to the door. He said: "I used to read your *Banner* with great interest. What has happened to it?" This was a piece of encouragement from a most unexpected quarter. Srinivas stood arrested like a man recovering a lost memory. Traffic was passing, policemen were walking in and out with their boot-nails clanking on the hard stone floor. "Why, what's the matter?" asked the inspector, turning the little stick in his hand. "No, nothing," Srinivas replied. All the jumble of his recent months came in a torrent: Sampath, the press, film, rotary, Linotype—each struggling to be expressed and jostling the other out. Srinivas stood looking at the point of light in the inspector's belt-buckle, which caught a ray of light from the shop opposite. Ravi, his hair ruffled, his dress dirty and loose, stood beside him mutely. Srinivas felt that he himself had stood mute too long, and some answer from him was overdue. But he found himself tongue-tied. He felt he had been involved in a chaos of human relationships and activities. He kept saying to himself: "I am searching for something, trying to make a meaning out of things." The inspector kept looking at him, half amused and half puzzled. The groan of a man in custody was feebly heard. . . . The implications of *The Banner* and all that it stood for flashed across Srinivas's mind for a brief second. He said desperately, imploringly: "If I had a press I could start it tomorrow."

The inspector said: "What has happened to the press

you were doing it in?" Once again he felt it impossible to speak; he struggled for expression. He overcame the struggle with a deliberate effort and said: "Sampath, Sampath—you know he is no longer a printer."

"No, he is no longer a printer; I know."

"I can't get anyone else to print my work," said Srinivas, and felt like a baby talking complainingly. It sounded to him silly and childish to be talking thus at the police-station gate.

"If you will come here any time tomorrow evening I will take you to the Empire Press, who will print for you. He is a good printer and will oblige me. We must revive your weekly. It used to be interesting," said the inspector.

Srinivas gripped his hand in an access of inexpressible gratitude. "Please . . ." he implored. "I'll be here tomorrow at eleven positively."

He drew his arm through Ravi's and led him along through the crowded Market Road; a bus hooted, country carts tumbled by, villagers passed along with loads on their heads. But Srinivas felt that he had got back his enchantment in life. He chattered happily as he walked along: "Ravi, something to keep me sane—absolutely—without *The Banner*. . . . Well, you will be well enough again, and then you can draw dozens of pictures for our paper. It will be your own paper," he said and looked at the dull, uncomprehending eyes of Ravi, who walked beside him like a lamb, his lips muttering some unknown chant under his breath. They walked on a few paces thus, silently, on the edge of the road, avoiding and pushing their way through the groups of people going in the opposite direction. Srinivas slackened his pace and whispered: "Don't you worry any more about Sampath or anyone else. . . .

245

They all belong to a previous life." He looked up at the
other as he said it. A feeble ray of understanding seemed
to glow in Ravi's eyes: that was enough for Srinivas. His
heart was filled with joy and he forgot all else in the relish
of this moment.

Chapter Ten

SRINIVAS HAD nowadays little time to bother about the outside world, being fully engaged on the revived *Banner*. It now emerged from an office in Market Road itself—coming off the Empire Press, which, though small in itself, seemed to Srinivas a vast organization; it had at least half a dozen type-boards, a twin cylinder machine turned off the forms, and one did not have to wait for four pages to be printed to get the types ready for the next four. In contrast with the Truth Printing Works, this appeared to be a revolutionary step forward. A small room was partitioned off with a red movable screen, and that separated the printer from the editor. The printer was a taciturn, dull man, who took no interest in the matter he printed, who would show no accommodation in financial matters, but who was thoroughly punctual and precise in doing his work.

Srinivas found himself facing, for the first time, financial problems as a reality. He couldn't restart *The Banner* without paying an advance and buying the paper for it. There was no longer Sampath between him and financial shocks. He spent long worrying hours speculating how he should manage it. He solved the problem by writing a letter to his brother, asking for the amount out of his share in the ancestral property. He hated himself for writing thus, but it was the only way out. He avoided deliberately any highfalutin references to his work, any abstract principles involved in it, but tried to appear sordid. He wrote: "You know the old fable of a man who mounted a tiger—I'm in the same position. *The Banner* has to be kept fluttering in the air if I'm to survive. I may tell you that it has built itself up nicely, and there is not much groundwork to be done for it now. I've still all the old subscribers' rolls, and I'm also taking in a few pages of advertisements; and so don't you worry at all about its finances. But I require some temporary accommodation. If you can lend me a couple of thousands or, if it is impossible, give me two thousand out of my share in our property, I shall be grateful for the timely help." His brother accepted it as a legitimate demand and sent him the amount with only the admonition: "Please be a little more practical-minded in the management of your affairs. I would strongly advise you to have an accountant to look after your accounts and tell you from time to time how you stand. Don't grudge this expense." He added a note of warning: "You will understand that ancestral property is after all a sacred trust, and not loose money meant for the fanciful expenditure of the individual; it really belongs to our children and their children." "Children and their children"; it produced a lovely picture on the mind like the vista of an endless colonnade. But the first part of the sentence made him indignant. "He blesses with his hand, and kicks with his feet," he moaned. "Shall I send back this amount?"

His wife advised him: "He has merely said that you must be careful with the money. Why should that make you angry?"

Srinivas cooled down and said: "All right then, I will take it now, but return it at the earliest possible moment." He wrote to his brother to this effect, while acknowledging the amount, and it had the unexpected result of bringing from him a warm letter appreciating the resolution and repeating the advice to provide himself with an accountant. He accepted the reasonableness of this suggestion and acted upon it immediately. The Empire Press man lent him his own accountant for a couple of hours each day, for a small consideration.

Srinivas turned his back on Kabir Lane without a sigh He rummaged his garret, filled a couple of baskets with all the papers there, and descended the steps for the last time. The building was now held on lease by Sunrise Pictures, and no life stirred there. The door of the registered offices and of the director of productions remained locked up. He felt he could no longer stand a meeting with Somu, Sohan Lal or De Mello. They seemed to him figures out of a nightmare. He merely sent the key to the studio with a messenger. Out of all the welter of paper he was carrying away he took care not to miss the little sketch of Ravi's in the cardboard file.

"Nonsense—an adult occupation" was one of the outstanding editorials he wrote after *The Banner*'s rebirth. He analyzed and wrote down much of his studio experience in it. Adulthood was just a mask that people wore, the mask made up of a thick jowl and double chin and diamond ear-rings, or a green sporting shirt, but within it a man kept up the nonsense of his infancy, worse now for being without the innocence and the pure joy. Only the values of commerce gave this state a gloss of importance and urgency.

This brought Somu into his office one day. His fingers sparkled with diamonds as he clutched his cane. Srinivas sent up a silent prayer at the sight of him. "Oh, God, save me from these people and give me the strength to face them now." Somu's incapacity to speak out was once again evident. He sat clearing his throat and trying to smile. Srinivas forbore to ask him about the studio or their picture. "Oh, God, don't involve me again with these people," he prayed. Somu asked: "How is it, you don't come near the studio?"

Srinivas felt it was unnecessary to give any answer. Somu persisted, and Srinivas merely said: "I have no business there."

"Ah! Ah! How can you say so? How can we run a studio without the help of story-writers like you, sir?"

Srinivas had no answer to give. He felt a deep hurt within him; seeing those fat cheeks and diamonds and the memory of Ravi in the cell, mumbling incoherently, he felt like crying out: "You are all people who try to murder souls."

Somu said: "Your journal, your journal. We see you have said something about us." This seemed to be interesting. Srinivas asked: "What exactly have I said?"

Somu tapped the table nervously and said: "I didn't read it fully."

"How much of it really did you read then?"

"H'm. . . . In fact, I meant to read it later, but De Mello took it away and told me about it. He said that there was something about the studio," said Somu.

"In that case you may read it now," said Srinivas, taking out a copy of the issue and handing it to him. Somu looked at it for a few moments, turned its pages curiously, and rolled it up. "Why are you folding it up?" asked Srinivas.

"I will read it at home," replied Somu apologetically.

"No. I want you to read it at once," said Srinivas. A look

of panic came into Somu's eyes. "All of it?" he asked, looking at the rolled-up copy in his hand.

"Yes, it is only twelve pages."

"Oh, sir, please excuse me," begged Somu. Srinivas became adamant. He enjoyed very much bullying Somu. It seemed to him that he was getting a bit of his own back after all. He wanted to cry "Ah, how should I have felt when you fellows worried me to death and had everything your own way?" He enjoyed Somu's discomfiture, and again and again insisted upon his going through the journal on the spot. He wondered why Somu did not brush him aside and ask him to mind his business. But he didn't. He meekly said: "I came only to spend a few minutes with you and find out about the articles."

"Yes, but how can you talk about it unless you read it? Go on, at least read the article you wish to discuss." Somu looked at him appealingly for a moment, took out his glasses and poised them over his nose, spread out the issue and tilted it toward the window light. Looking at him thus, Srinivas felt that this must be counted as a major conquest in his career. He attended to the papers on his table, and a clearing of the throat from the other drew his attention: he looked up and saw Somu anxiously looking at him, wondering if he would be permitted to put down the paper now. He started taking off his glasses when Srinivas looked at him fixedly and said: "Yes?"

"I've finished reading it."

Srinivas wondered for a moment whether he could command him to go through the next article, but he refrained: it might prove to be the last straw: Somu might, after all, assert his independence and refuse. Srinivas felt, seeing the agonized face of the other as he was put through this trial, that all his wrongs of recent months were sufficiently

253

avenged, and he felt his humanity returning. He became almost tender as he asked: "Well, sir, what about it now?"

"De Mello said there was something about our production in it," said Somu. "That's why I came here."

"Now you find nothing in it?" asked Srinivas.

"Nothing about our production. I don't know what made De Mello say so." He appeared indignant at the trick played upon him.

Srinivas said quietly: "De Mello is right. If you take the copy home and read it carefully, you will understand, and then you can come and talk it over with me."

He looked puzzled. "Why should you attack our film, sir?" he asked angrily. "After all, you wrote the story. It is not right, sir, that you should be unkind to us." He clutched his walking-stick and got up to go.

Srinivas said: "You must read the paper regularly if you are to understand my point of view. It is not unkindness. Why don't you take out a subscription for a year? It is only ten rupees."

"I have no time to read, sir, that is the trouble."

"Just as you find the time to eat and sleep you must find the time to read a paper like *The Banner*. It's meant for people like you." Somu took out ten rupees and placed it on the table. Srinivas wrote out a receipt and gave it him. Somu folded it and put it in his purse and started to go, but said, stopping half-way: "After all, we spend lakhs of rupees on our pictures, and you must be careful not to prejudice the public against us and damage us."

Srinivas kept Ravi in his own home. He had more or less the task of running both the households on his own means. Ravi's little sister came in several times a day with a petition for a rupee or two, and Srinivas ungrudgingly parted with them and advised his wife to do so in his absence. Ravi's father had given up talking not only to Ravi but also to Srinivas. He let out a sort of growl whenever he sensed Srinivas passing in front of his house. He was reported (by Srinivas's wife) to be continually saying: "He ruined my son by putting notions into his head. Now he wants to ruin the rest of the family." This naturally roused her indignation, and she asked: "Why should we ever bother about these people when they are so ungrateful!" Srinivas merely told her: "Don't waste your energy listening to what he or anybody says. Just give them any help you can."

"For how long?" she asked.

Srinivas scratched his head. There seemed to be really no means of saying how long.

"And what are you going to do about him?" she asked, indicating the corner of the hall where Ravi sat mumbling his chant. Srinivas kept him with him because he had a feeling that Ravi's own home might hinder rather than help a possible recovery. He fed him, looked after his personal needs and kept him there. "He must be protected from his family," he explained. All this discussion had to be carried on in subdued voices in the kitchen while dining, since the front half of their house was occupied by one or the other of Ravi's relations. His little brothers and sisters came round and sat there in front of him. Sometimes they laughed at him and sometimes they ran away in fear. Unremittingly he kept repeating his sentences, though no one could follow anything that he was saying. Often his mother came up and sat in front of him, coaxed him to eat this or that, some special preparation that she made at home with her meager resources. Srinivas's wife, after her initial protests, was often moved by this spectacle and sat down with her and tried to comfort her.

The old lady was beginning to think that the matter with Ravi was that he was possessed. She recounted a dozen instances similar to his, where exorcising restored a man to his normal state.

So one evening, returning home from his office, Srinivas found strange activities going on. Ravi had become the center of the picture. In front of him were set out trays of saffron and flowers, huge twigs of margosa leaves, and a camphor flare. A wild-looking man with huge beads around his neck, clad in red silk, his forehead dabbed with vermilion, officiated at the ceremony. He looked very much like Shiva in makeup. The air choked with incense burning in a holder. He had a couple of assistants sitting behind him, one bearing a cymbal and the other a little rattling drum which produced a peculiarly shrill noise. The chief man had a thin cane of a whip-like thinness at his feet, and he had smeared it with saffron and vermilion. Ravi's mother sat near this group with a reverent look in her eyes, and Srinivas saw his own wife running about, ministering to their wants ungrudgingly. Little Ramu and the other youngsters of the neighboring house stood peeping in at the doorway. They looked slightly scared and thought it safer to keep their distance so. Srinivas stood at the threshold, arrested by this scene. Ramu had wanted to bound toward him and tell him in advance, but he was unwilling to forfeit his place in the doorway, and so kept calling in a suppressed voice:

"Father, Father." But before he could say anything more Srinivas had come upon the scene. An exclamation of surprise escaped his lips. His wife came to him in great haste and drew him away into the kitchen. She closed the middle door and cautioned him: "Don't say any inauspicious word now."

"Whose idea is this?" he asked sourly.

"That lady has been wanting to do it. You must not say anything against it. Where can she go, poor lady? Her husband might not allow it or he might swear at them all the time."

"Ah! You know now why I wanted Ravi to be kept here, do you understand?" he said with mild glee. She accepted his triumph without a protest. "Yes, yes, with that old man there, how can they?" And this pacified Srinivas. He realized at once that he had become mildly vengeful: the other day it was Somu on whom he had tried to take it out, and today his wife. "At this rate I fear I may do a lot of people to death in due course," he told himself. He looked at his wife. He found her eyes dancing with interest. She was fully part of the affair and seemed to feel specially gratified at being the hostess of this exotic function. He muttered under his breath: "The whole thing is too silly for words." He recollected the tribal worship done before the camera at the studio on the inauguration day. "This is no worse. At least this is more innocent and uncommercial," he reflected. His wife said: "It is also a good thing, you know. He knows all about the ghost that haunts this house that people talk about. He says it has got into Ravi. He will drive it out, and we can live here with a free mind afterward." Seeing that she had not made much of an impression, she asked: "Isn't it wonderful?" He replied: "He probably got the story out of some gossipmonger."

"I don't know why you are so cynical," she said and left him and went away to the front room. He followed her, feeling that he might as well watch the scene. Ravi's mother looked up at him from time to time with grateful eyes. The magician was reciting something monotonously in a stentorian voice, and his pauses were punctuated rhythmically by the cymbals and the rattle-drum. Her eyes were shut, and Ravi sat oblivious of his surroundings: a few margosa leaves were scattered on him. The chants and rhythmic beats went on and on and produced a kind of hypnosis in everyone assembled there, and Srinivas saw Ravi gradually shaking his head and swaying. He found the atmosphere oppressive and unbearable—the gong and the drum-beat, the pungent, piercing smell of the incense, its smoke hanging in the air, and the camphor-flare illumination. Srinivas suddenly said to himself: "I might be in the twentieth century B.C. for all it matters, or 4000 B.C." In that half-dim hall a sweep of history passed in front of his eyes. His scenario-writing habit suddenly asserted itself. His little home, the hall and all the folk there, Anderson Lane and, in fact, Malgudi itself dimmed and dissolved on the screen. There was a blankness for a while, and then there faded in an uninhabited country; the Mempi jungle extended everywhere. The present Market Road was an avenue of wild trees, a narrow foot-path winding its way through the long grass. Presently appeared on this path Sri Rama, the hero of Ramayana. He was a perfect man, this incarnation of Vishnu. Over his shoulder was slung his famous bow which none could even lift. He was followed by his devoted brother Laxman and

Hanuman, the monkey-god. Rama was on his way to Lanka (Ceylon) to battle with evil there, in the shape of Ravana who abducted Sita. The enemy was a perfection of evil with all its apparent strength and invincibility. Rama had to redeem righteousness. He was on his way to a holy war, which would wipe out wrong and establish on earth truth, beauty and goodness. He rested on a sandy stretch in a grove, and looked about for a little water for making a paste for his forehead-marking. There was no water. He pulled an arrow from his quiver and scratched a line on the sand, and water instantly appeared. Thus was born the river Sarayu.

The river flowed on. On its banks sprang up the thatched roofs of a hamlet—a pastoral community who grazed their cattle in the jungles and brought them back home before nightfall and securely shut themselves and their animals in from prowling tigers and jackals. The jungle, with its sky-touching trees, gradually receded further and further, and cornfields appeared in its place. The waving tufts of rice, standing to a man's height, swayed in the air and stretched away as far as the eye could see.

When the Buddha came this way, preaching his gospel of compassion, centuries later, he passed along the main street of a prosperous village. Men, women and children gathered around him. He saw a woman weeping. She had recently lost her child and seemed disconsolate. He told her he would give her consolation if she could bring him a handful of mustard from any house where death was unknown. She went from door to door and turned away from every one of them. Amongst all those hundreds of houses she could not find one where death was a stranger. She understood the lesson. . . . A little crumbling masonry and a couple of stone pillars, beyond Lawley Extension, now marked the spot where the Buddha had held his congregation. . . .

The great Shankara appeared during the next millennium.He saw on the river-bank a cobra spreading its hood and shielding a spawning frog from the rigor of the mid-day sun. He remarked: "Here the extremes meet. The cobra, which is the natural enemy of the frog, gives it succor. This is where I must build my temple." He installed the goddess there and preached his gospel of *Vedanta:* the identity and oneness of God and His creatures.

And then the Christian missionary with his Bible. In his wake the merchant and the soldier—people who paved the way for Edward Shilling and his Engladia Bank.

Dynasties rose and fell. Palaces and mansions appeared and disappeared. The entire country went down under the fire and sword of the invader, and was washed clean when Sarayu overflowed its bounds. But it always had its rebirth and growth. And throughout the centuries, Srinivas felt, this group was always there: Ravi with his madness, his well-wishers with their panaceas and their apparatus of cure. Half the madness was his own doing, his lack of self-knowledge, his treachery to his own instincts as an artist, which had made him a battle-ground. Sooner or later he shook off his madness and realized his true identity—though not in one birth, at least in a series of them. "What did it amount to?" Srinivas asked himself as the historical picture faded out. "Who am I to bother about Ravi's madness or sanity? What madness to think I am his keeper?" This notion seemed to him so ridiculous that he let out a laugh.

The others in the small room looked at him startled. His

wife came near him and peered into his face anxiously and asked: "Why did you laugh?"

"Did I?" he asked. "I recollected some joke, that's all. Don't bother about me."

Now they had stopped their recitations and drum-beats. Ravi, with half-shut eyes, was swaying. The exorcist picked up his cane and thwacked it sharply over Ravi's back and asked at the same time: "Now will you go or not?" Ravi smarted a little under the blow, rolled his eyes, and the thwacking was renewed with vigor. The question was addressed to the evil spirit possessing him. Ravi winced under the repeated blows. Srinivas felt an impulse to cry out: "Stop it! It is absurd and cruel." But he found himself incapable of any effort. The recent vision had given him a view in which it seemed to him all the same whether they thwacked Ravi with a cane or whether they left him alone, whether he was mad or sane—all that seemed unimportant and not worth bothering about. The whole of eternity stretched ahead of one; there was plenty of time to shake off all follies. Madness or sanity, suffering or happiness seemed all the same. . . . It didn't make the slightest difference in the long run—in the rush of eternity nothing mattered. It was no more important or remembered than an attack of malaria in the lifetime of a centenarian. Whether one was mad or sane or right or wrong didn't make the slightest difference: it was like bothering about a leaf floating on a rushing torrent— whether it was floating on its right side or wrong side.

He got up abruptly and left the room. He went into the street and stood there uncertainly, looking up and down. There was a momentary haziness in his mind as to what period he was existing in—existence seeming so persistent and inescapable. Later Ravi's mother came out to say: "Shall I take Ravi to the temple at Sailam? It is a day's journey from here. The exorcist says that if Ravi is kept there at its portals for a week, he will be quite well. There are hundreds of people living there."

"By all means," said Srinivas, and added with conviction: "He is bound to get well again. Even madness passes. Only existence asserts itself."

"Your wife has promised to look after Ravi's father's needs." It was with difficulty that he could repress the remark: "It's all the same whether he is looked after or not. What if he perishes?"

"What can we do? We have to trouble you. He is so unreasonable and difficult to manage. We are sorry to put the burden on you, but for the sake of that boy——"

"We don't mind the trouble in the least. We will look after the old gentleman."

Later Srinivas's wife told him: "I've given them twenty rupees of housekeeping money. You must replace the amount. Poor folks!"

"Of course, of course. I will replace it and more. Go ahead and do what you like." His wife felt baffled by his elated manner.

Srinivas engaged a carriage to take Ravi and his mother to the railway station next evening. The old lady had rolled up a couple of carpets and pillows and tied them with a hemp rope. She had stuffed a few items of clothing into a tin trunk. She had a basket in which she carried a pot of water and a few plantains. The old gentleman was in an utter mental confusion. If he could have got up and moved about he would have prevented the trip. He kept on shouting at them, "Why should she go? With whose permission is she leaving the town and traveling? What brazenness has come over our women!" The old lady finished an early dinner. The numerous children gathered around and pestered her for this and that, and all of them set up a howl, demanding to be taken along to the railway. She carried with them the two youngest; she had oiled and parted their hair, washed their faces, and thrust them into new clothes. They were bubbling over with joy. The other children threw murderous looks at them and shouted imprecations. The old man shouted above it all: "Why should she go, leaving these children to cry? Is there no one to whom she will listen?" He cried: "Mr. Editor, oh, Mr. Editor!" He had spurned Srinivas all these days, but turned to him now out of desperation. He called so insistently that Srinivas could not help responding. He went up to the doorway and stood there and asked: "What is it, sir?"

"Oh, you are there! Come nearer! Come and sit down here. Take a seat; you are a learned man. . . ."

"I'm quite comfortable here, what is it?" Srinivas asked.

"Please tell her to stop. She is going away. She is disobeying me."

"She will be back in ten or fifteen days, don't worry."

"You need not tell me that. She must not go."

"She is not going for her pleasure. She is going——"

"Yes, I know. For that brigand's sake. Why should she go? He is not our son. No man who has been in prison can be our son. Why should she trouble about him? If she is my wife let her give him up. What has she to do with him?"

"Don't lose your head, sir. Be calm."

263

"Who are you to tell me about my head? You have ruined that rascal son of mine by dragging him into your associations, and you are ruining my wife and family. You are out to blight our family."

"Don't mind what he says," said the lady, wringing her hands in despair. But her face was bright with the anticipation of a journey.

"Not at all," Srinivas said. "He will get his food all right."

"Food! I will fling it out, if anyone brings the food cooked in another's house," raved the old man. Srinivas looked at the lined face of Ravi's aged mother. "How much must she have stood from him for forty years," he reflected and admired her fortitude.

The jutka arrived at the door. The lady picked up her baggage and the two children and went to her husband to bid him good-bye. The old man averted his face, put out his arms without a word, and touched the two children. Tears rolled down his cheeks. Srinivas went over to Ravi's corner in his house and told him: "Come along, let us go to the station." Ravi looked up at him. That was some improvement. After the thwacking he was showing responses to stimuli. Srinivas helped him up and led him to the jutka and assisted him in. His mother and the children followed. She took an elaborate farewell of Srinivas's wife, who followed her down the street and, for inexplicable reasons, started crying when the jutka began to move. "Any farewell or parting will bring tears, I suppose," Srinivas reflected as he sat beside the driver and urged him to run fast enough to catch the 8:20 train toward Trichy.

Chapter Eleven

I T WAS late in the evening. Srinivas sat in his office jotting down details of the vision he had had at the exorcist's performance in his house, and attempted to communicate it to his readers. He jotted down the heading "The Leaf on the Torrent." He didn't like it. He noted down an alternative title "The Cosmic Stage: the willy-nilly actor on the Cosmic Stage." He thought it over. It didn't satisfy either. He didn't like to use the word "cosmic" if he could help it. The intensity of the experience seemed to be gradually disintegrating now in commonplace expression. He sat brooding, when the printer's office boy came up and said: "There is a gentleman to see you, sir; asks if you can see him." Srinivas looked sadly for a moment at the scribbling on his pad and its incomplete characters, wondering how he was going to finalize it for the press next day. The office boy stood before him, awaiting his reply, and suggested: "Shall I ask him to go away, sir?"

"Bring him in," said Srinivas, picking up his pen and desperately hoping to jot down something in the short interval that lay before him.

The door opened and there stood Sampath before him. "Sampath!" Srinivas cried. "Sampath! Why couldn't you come straight in?"

"Oh, I didn't like to disturb you. This is Thursday, and I know what you should do today." He came over and sat in the chair. There was a subdued quality about him. He still wore his silk shirt; but he had an intimidated look in his eyes. "Well, how are you?" asked Srinivas.

Sampath leaned over and whispered: "I'm still a monogamist. Don't worry."

"Ah, that's very good."

"Things have happened as you wished."

"How did you like the Mempi hills?"

"Oh, full of tigers and all sorts of beasts, howling all night, and I had a most harrowing time keeping Shanti quiet. She was hysterical throughout and wanted to get away from there the moment we reached the place. Have you been there?"

"No; some time I hope to."

"I hope you will have a better companion and a more reasonable companion to go with; otherwise it is not worth the labor. Do you know how one goes? The train puts you down at Koppal—that's the last railway link. From there you go twenty miles in a bus and then up in bullock carts; and then you allow yourself to be carried by porters in a sort of basket slung on bamboo poles; and then you reach the place, practically on foot. And when you have arrived there, what do you expect to see?"

"Someone to welcome you?" asked Srinivas.

"Not a chance, sir. . . . A bleak forest bungalow full of horrible, wide verandas, sir. God knows what fellow ever thought of putting up a building there, and how he managed to gather the materials and men to build, for, do you know, we could not get a single person to bring up a glass of milk or a banana for us. We had carried a hamper and that saved us from starvation. The jungle life comes on you when there is still light, say, at about five o'clock. The birds make a tremendous uproar, the huge trees seem to close in on you, and the jackals start their wails. Ah, those jackals: every time they cried, this lady

268

let out a shriek and trembled all over. She tried to shut herself in, but there was only one room, and that was full of glass shutters, evidently built by someone who wished to watch the arrivals and departures in the jungle at night. She gave me hell that night. I have never been so much bothered by anyone before. We could see in the dark jungle eyes shining. She was a miserable sight, I tell you. She became roaring mad. If you had seen her you would have thought Ravi was sanity itself!"

Srinivas tried to receive this narrative as casually as possible. He felt that there was no need for him to put any question. So much was coming out spontaneously.

"Every time a tiger roared she had fits, she was sick; it became disgusting to stay with her in the same room. So I went over and stayed in the veranda, not minding the risk. I preferred it to her company."

Srinivas could not help remarking: "I cannot imagine how she could've become suddenly so unacceptable."

"Well, I didn't much mind her physical condition. It was her temperament that disgusted me. She was quarrelsome, nagging. In all my years of married life I have never been nagged so much before. She demanded to be taken back to the town that very night and wouldn't leave me in peace! Imagine! It was at that moment that I decided to stick to your advice. Next afternoon I arranged for her descent. At Koppal I put her into the train and bade her good-bye. She went toward Madras, and I came away here, and I thank God for the relief." He smiled weakly and looked at Srinivas. Srinivas sat biting a corner of his lips, his eyes were on the caption on his pad. "Cosmic . . ." A corner of his mind seized it and struggled with it. "Cosmic! Cosmic what . . . What other title, I must find it before tomorow, this time . . ." He looked up. Sampath watched his face to study his reaction to the story. Srinivas observed that Sampath's face did not register the satisfaction and relief that his words expressed. He looked downcast. He knew that Sampath was only waiting for a remark from him. He revolved the whole episode in his mind and declared: "Sampath, what you say seems too good to be true."

Sampath covered his eyes with his palm and shook with laughter. He muttered: "My editor knows me too well; nothing short of absolute truth will pass with him."

"Won't you tell me exactly what happened?" Srinivas asked. He added: "Don't, if you don't like to talk about it."

"I wouldn't be here if I didn't want to talk about it, sir, the only thing left for me now." He paused, looked about; the press was running inside. "The press seems to be working; I can tell from its sound it is a good one. Is it Simkins' double cylinder?"

"Perhaps it is. How do you know?"

"By mere sound. I am a printer, when all is said and done. Do you agree?"

"Undoubtedly."

"This is purely a temporary arrangement, I hope. When my plant is ready I cannot allow *The Banner* to come from any other press. It's my responsibility, sir." Srinivas muttered something noncommittally and asked: "How near are you to your rotary?" Sampath stretched himself out across the table and whispered: "Come out, let us sit down somewhere and talk. I don't like to speak about anything in a fellow-printer's establishment." Srinivas threw a desperate look at the paper on his table. He put it away resolutely. He got up. When they came out Srinivas hesitated on the last step, looked up and down and asked: "Where is the car you used to ride in?"

"I suppose carburetor trouble, like me," Sampath said, tapping his heart.

"Shall we walk?" Srinivas asked.

"It's good exercise, isn't it?" Sampath said.

They walked along in silence down the Market Road. Traffic flowed past them. Dusk was about them. A few lights twinkled here and there. They walked on in silence.

Srinivas said: "When did you come? You have not told me that."

"There is a great deal more I haven't told you," he said. Conversation once again became difficult; Srinivas allowed the silence to envelop them completely. He felt mystified by Sampath's talk and actions. When they had gone a couple of furlongs he asked Sampath: "Where shall we go?"

"Anywhere you like; where we can talk quietly."

"Shall we go to Anand Bhavan restaurant, to that special room upstairs?" asked Srinivas, recollecting their first meeting-place. Sampath said: "Yes, a good idea," paused for a second and then said: "No, sir, not now. I wouldn't like to go there now; say somewhere else; why not to the river?" Srinivas gasped with surprise. "I didn't know you cared for the river," he said. "One has got to like all sorts of things now," Sampath said, and ran across to a wayside shop to buy a packet of cigarettes.

At the river he stood on the sand and looked about as if searching for a seat in a theater hall. Clumps of people were sitting on the sands. "I don't like to be seen by anyone," he said. Beyond the other bank, half a mile off, they saw the glare of the studio lights. He blinked at them for a moment and said: "They seem to be very busy there." Srinivas led him along, and they sat down in a quiet nook, where there was no one. Darkness had gathered about them. The river flowed on into the night. Sampath remained silent for a moment, drawing circles on the sand. Srinivas left him alone and listened to the murmur of the river and the distant, muffled roar of the town. Sampath said: "I told you a lie, and you found it out. How I wish it had happened as I said! Then it would have left me without regrets. Could you guess what percentage of it was true?"

"Yes, up to your reaching the bungalow on the hill-top," said Srinivas.

"Well, sir, you can grant me even a little more. That bungalow was as I said, and her terror was real as she saw the flashing eyes of panthers on the other side of the glass at night; but oh, how sweet she was! I could see her trembling with fright, but she said not a word. She sat up all night trying to brave it. Few women there are in the world who could have helped screaming, under those conditions. You know she was not in the best condition of nerves, but all the same, what self-possession she showed! She sat speaking of some books she had read in her younger days." He paused to take out a cigarette and lit it. He blew the smoke into the dark sky. "She stood it for three or four days, and then suggested that we might return. I was also glad to get back. As you might know, we should have gone up to a registrar before leaving for Mempi, but she always made some excuse or other and put it off. Finally we decided that we were to go through the formality on coming back here. That was our understanding. We got down from the hills, and we were to catch our train at Koppal at five a.m. next day. It is the most unearthly station you can imagine, with jungles on all sides and a disused railway compartment serving as the station-master's office. We stayed cooped up in that little office all night. The station-master allowed us to stay up there. We sat on a couple of stools and tried to talk through the night. The bus had put us down at Koppal at six in the evening and we had nearly twelve hours before us for the train. We ate our food and then sat up, intending to talk all night till the arrival of the train. But really there was so little to talk about. Having done nothing but that for five days continuously, I think both of us had exhausted all available subjects. And a passing thought occurred to me that we might have to spend the rest of our lives in silence after we were married. This problem was unexpectedly simplified for me. I must have fallen asleep on my stool. When the train arrived and I woke up, her chair was empty. The train halts there only for four minutes or so, and we had to hurry up.

"The station-master said: 'She left by the eleven down. I gave her a ticket for Madras.'

" 'When?'

" 'At twenty-three hours.'

"I gnashed my teeth. 'What time is that in earthly language?'

" 'Eleven at night.'

" 'What nonsense!' I raved at him.

" 'But the lady gave me to understand that you were going to different places,' he said.

"I shook my fists in his face and said: 'Don't you see that a husband and wife have got to go together?'

" 'Not always, not necessarily,' he said, and went on to attend to his business. The train halted there for only four minutes.

"One had to hurry up. 'Can I go to Madras?' I asked.

" 'No train toward Madras till . . .'

"I was appalled at the prospect of spending half a day more there. I felt like knocking down the station-master. 'You should not have allowed her to go.'

" 'We cannot refuse tickets to bona-fide passengers.' He quoted a railway act.

" 'Oh! Great one, what shall I do now?' I asked. I must have looked ridiculous.

" 'Only a minute more, sir, please make up your mind. I cannot delay the train for anybody's sake.'

"I discovered meanwhile a note she had left. It was scrawled on a brown railway sheet. 'I am sick of this kind of life and marriage frightens me. I want to go and look after my son, who is growing up with strangers. Please leave me alone, and don't look for me. I want to change my ways of living. You will not find me. If I find you pursuing me, I will shave off my head and fling away my jewelry and wear a white sari. You and people like you will run away at the sight of me. I am, after all, a widow and can shave my head and disfigure myself, if I like. If it is the only way out I will do it. I had different ideas of a film life.' Well, sir, that was her letter. . . ."

Sampath pulled out his kerchief and dabbed his eyes and blew his nose. "I went to Madras, Trichy, Coimbatore, Mangalore, Bombay and a dozen other places, and tired myself out searching for her. . . . It has all turned out to be a great mess."

"What is to happen to the film?" Srinivas asked.

274

"It must be dropped. We've been abandoned by both Shiva and Parvathi. And only Kama, the God of Love, is left in the studio."

"And he, too, will have to remain invisible for the rest of the story," Srinivas added.

"I shall have to become invisible, too. Otherwise, Sohan Lal and Somu have enough reason to put me in prison," Sampath said. He remained in thought for a moment and added, almost with a sigh: "Well, I may probably try and save myself if I can interest them in a new story." Now Srinivas suddenly saw that this might prove to be the nucleus of a whole series of fresh troubles. He roused himself and said: "I think it is time to get up. Tomorrow is press day."

They walked back in silence. At Market Square, Srinivas realized that they must part. He wanted to ask where Sampath's family was, what he had done with them, what he was going to do with himself, and so on. But he checked himself. It seemed to him a great, unnecessary strain, sifting grain from chaff in all that he might say. He might probably have his family about him. He might have abandoned them; he might, after all, still have Shanti with him and be planning further adventures, or he might disappear or still dangle a new carrot for Somu and Co. to pursue. But whatever it was, he felt that he was once again in danger of getting involved with him if he asked him too many questions. He saw Sampath hesitating in the square. Bare humanity made him say: "Will you come home with me and dine?"

"Thanks. I'm going to the railway station. I'll manage there." Srinivas forbore to ask "Why the railway station?" He told himself: "He may meet someone, or go away somewhere or have a dozen other reasons, but I've nothing to do with any of them." So he merely said: "All right then. Good-bye," and passed on resolutely. While turning down Anderson Lane he looked back for a second and saw far off the glow of a cigarette end in the square where he had left Sampath; it was like a ruby set in the night. He raised his hand, flourished a final farewell, and set his face homeward.